KESTREL'S MIDNIGHT SONG

Best wishes!

R Parker

12-22-2010

J. R. PARKER

FLAMING PEN PRESS

Endorsements for *Kestrel's Midnight Song*

"Because of his youth and the genre, people will no doubt compare J.R. Parker to Christopher Paolini. I don't claim to be a prophet, but I think Parker very well could be better. *Kestrel's Midnight Song* is a wonderful first novel. . . . Parker's language is quite stunning without being wordy. Marauders, stolen children, haunting mystery, and ever-present danger make this a book worth reading."

—Wayne Thomas Batson, bestselling author of *The Door Within Trilogy, Isle of Swords, Isle of Fire*, and *Curse of the Spider King*

"*Kestrel's Midnight Song* is a solid addition to the fantasy genre. Jacob Parker writes an imaginative tale, filled with adventure, mystery, and unique characters. The storylines intertwine and keep the reader turning the pages, desperate to see how it will all work out. I can't wait to read the sequel."

—Jill Williamson, award winning author of *By Darkness Hid*

"J.R. Parker's debut into the literary world couldn't have been better. Though still in his teens, his craftsmanship is on par with Rowling's and his world-building skills are up there with Tolkien's. I lived and breathed with the characters, and every surprising plot turn threw me for a loop. The motley crew populating *Kestrel's Midnight Song* are a charming bunch; unique and captivating. After the last page fell, I immediately began to miss them all—even the villains. I'll be waiting anxiously for Parker to spin his next breathtaking tale."

—Christian Miles, age 17

"*Kestrel's Midnight Song* is a phenomenal book. Beginning with mystery and suspense, J.R. Parker doesn't let up until the final page. He hooked me from the first paragraph and had me ripping through pages to discover the ending. Unique characters, very intriguing mysteries, beautiful writing, and an ending that blew me away—I couldn't put this book down. J.R. Parker is a much welcome addition to the fantasy genre."

—Nathan R. Petrie, age 16

"When it comes to youth fantasy, this is about as good as it gets. I kept having to remind myself how young Parker is and that this is his debut. This is an amazingly well-written story . . . Look for what's coming next from Jacob Parker. No doubt there will be many more where this one came from."

—Stephen Taylor

"In *Kestrel's Midnight Song* J. R. Parker introduces us to a wonderful and imaginative world of fantasy. Action packed and full of rich characters this page turner kept me enthralled and feverishly reading through to the last word. Parker is wonderfully descriptive; I actually found myself gasping aloud at the twists and turns each character encountered on their way. I could hardly wait to see where his unique journey was going to take me next and now I am anxiously awaiting the sequel."

—Christina Morrison

To Mom and Dad
For allowing my creativity to grow

Prologue

O nly a sliver of the moon peeked through the clouds of the night sky, as if the celestial orb couldn't bear to watch what transpired below. No owls hooted, no crickets chirped, and no monsters stirred in the shadows—only an eerie silence.

Wheezing and gasping, Isaac Ganthorn stumbled over another mountain crag. His staccato breaths and flying steps intruded on the night's stillness like an impudent funeral guest, making him feel like the only living being on Earth. But he knew he wasn't alone.

He shot a glance behind him, down the mountain slope. He readjusted his grasp on the infant hidden beneath the flap of his cloak. How he wished his black Marauder's cloak could melt him into the darkness. But such a desire was futile. Nothing could hide him. Not from the thing that hunted him.

His legs plunged into deepening water with a splash—a lake. He stopped, cursing himself. How could he have not seen it? Cold water seeped into his boots and bit at his ankles. A flash of lightning cracked up the night sky behind him. For that split second, he stared down at his rippling reflection in the lake. Fear, the emotion that always masked his victims' faces, now gripped his own face. That long nose, those two narrow streaks of silvery hair—this was him. *He* was the victim now.

So this is what fear feels like. The realization jolted his heart. He turned and ran, curving his path around the lake. He hadn't made it three strides out of the water before a tree root snared his foot. He flew forward and hit the ground rolling until, with a final thud, he sprawled onto the dew-soaked ground. The infant bounced out of his grasp. It let out a short cry with each bump, but its blanket cocoon held tight.

"Hush," Isaac pleaded, clawing his way toward it with another glance behind him. The urge to leave the child, to be rid of the burden, filled him. No one would see him abandon it. But the thought dissipated as quickly as it had formed. He couldn't. The Marauder King's instructions had been clear. The consequences of disobedience would be too terrible.

A second strike of lightning flushed out the darkness, illuminating the black silhouette of that hideous creature now sitting at the top of a tree in his path. The flood of light revealed its curved, murderous beak and outstretched wings as it gathered itself to swoop down on him.

"No!" He curled up, his heart pounding out its final beats. In seconds he would endure the same fate the rest of his team had suffered that night. His skin tingled in anticipation of the pain. With each second that passed he drew himself into a tighter ball, for every second brought him closer to his gruesome demise. Sweat trickled down his forehead. Bile built up in his throat. His heart hammered. Minutes passed. If he ran, if he moved at all, the creature would kill him.

Thunder blasted into his ears. He jumped and just barely bit back a scream. *It's just thunder.* He breathed. *Just thunder.*

He eased his head upward, away from his chest. Another flash illuminated the tree. Empty. Nothing but a thick, twisted branch.

Pull yourself together, Isaac!

Breathing heavily, he gathered up the infant and rose again, breaking into a run. *Deliver it and this will all be over.*

At the top of the next hill, he caught a whiff of sulfur. The mists of a nearby hot spring wafted over him. He stopped and took a deep breath, then another. He'd made it. A laugh rattled out his throat. He had made it! That thing couldn't follow him into a hot spring; all the captains said so. Safety. He wanted to remain in that cloud of steam forever, his only occupation to soak up its warmth. But the light of the watchtower knifed the darkness ahead, and though his instincts screamed otherwise, he knew the protection extended there as well. As he left the clouds of steam, cold air chilled his damp skin.

He crept over the hill and around the watchtower, into the village that lay nestled in an obscure crevice between two mountains, just as the Marauder King had described it. He felt his way along the houses and huts. No light illuminated their window frames at this hour.

Except for one.

A solitary lighted window slid into view like a lighthouse promising an end to his voyage. A black curtain hung from it, confirming this house as the one he sought.

With silent steps he approached the door and placed the baby on the doorstep. For a moment his eyes met those of the child; they stared up at him with curiosity.

Such a terrible fate.

He shook the thought from his mind. He couldn't afford sympathy.

Still, he felt drawn to the child's eyes. So innocent and so deep, as if he could fall right in and— he snapped his head away and stole into the forest. Although he blinked rapidly as he ran, he could not clear those eyes from his vision.

⊙⅛⊙

Grixxler swung the door open, unleashing a flood of light. His wide shadow complete with an outline of his balding dome stretched out on the ground before him. He stepped past the threshold and

9

glanced toward the line of trees just in time to see the darkness swallow a human figure. His gaze swept across the empty, silent village before falling to the bundle at his feet. He frowned, leaned over, and placed a finger to the baby's neck. His touch met a warm pulse. He cursed. "Confounded Marauders. I should have never—"

He clutched the bundle with one hand, turned inside, and closed the door.

For a moment, he held the loaf-sized infant an arm's length away, scowling. He sighed. If he'd known the boy would be so young, he would have never agreed to this.

He walked across the bookshelf-lined room, wiping the dew off his boots on the arrangement of bright rugs along the way, until he reached the slate tabletop. Then he cleared a pile of chicken bones aside and lay the baby in their place.

The corner of a scrap of paper tucked in the blanket caught his eye. He pulled it loose and unfolded it. "Ganthorn," he muttered. The rushed, scrawled handwriting made that obvious.

The note read: *I have succeeded. This is the child. It is called Micah.*

Grixxler looked the baby boy over with a wry grin. "Well, Micah, it looks like I have myself a new shepherd boy." He stuffed the parchment into a nearby lantern and watched the crackling flame consume it. The touch of warm light grew into a bright flood that filled the room. When it mellowed, the flame left behind a shrunken, charcoaled fragment that shortly disintegrated into ash. Grixxler knew that, with that scrap of paper gone, Micah's only chance at discovering his former life had just gone up in smoke.

CHAPTER 1

Years Later
and Miles Away

beautiful sky shone down on the inn—a single shade of blue broken only by a pink morning sun.

From his hiding place in the bushes, Captain Lewell smiled and rubbed his hands together. It was a perfect day for an explosion. It would be a fire to remember, total obliteration. His fingers twitched with impatience. He wanted to light that exploding powder now, before the Marauder King changed his mind.

The Inn stood on the corner of Heather Bay, looking out upon the vast Kepled Sea like a lonely maiden awaiting her sailor's return. There was no other building in sight. In the foliage around the inn the budding green life of early spring hadn't yet overcome the browns of winter.

Lewell slipped from the bushes and crept toward the inn, careful not to disrupt the clusters of foraging seagulls. He wove through the boatyard, where the half-finished hull of a ship lay like a set of whale ribs among scraps of rotting lumber and rusting tools.

On the water immediately past the beach sat a maze of wooden docking. On one side floated an array of ships of various shapes, sizes, and states of disrepair. On the other side lay a line of twelve identical virgin ships. His fingers twitched again at the sight of them.

He eased up to the side of the inn. Running his hands along the weather-beaten boards as he tiptoed up to the pot-sized window, he peered inside to find a long, narrow kitchen, with a cobblestone floor and wooden walls. Narrow tables lined either side and iron pots and pans hung from the walls. A square wooden hatch interrupted the cobblestone floor, leading undoubtedly to the cellar.

Excellent.

The young innkeeper, Robbyn, lay sleeping on the floor beside the stove. She looked just as the Marauder King had described her, with long, wavy copper hair splayed over the cobblestone. Her head rested on her arm and her mouth hung slightly open.

This was going to be too easy.

He grimaced. She was younger than he had expected. She hadn't experienced much of life yet. He shook his head and rebuked himself. Killing the young came with the job. It would be more than worth it in the end.

She stirred, and her eyelids fluttered. Flashes of river-pool green eyes shone through her lashes. He ducked away from the window.

∾

Robbyn bustled into the dining hall balancing two trays, one of eggs and bread and the other of filled coffee mugs. The bumps of the cobblestone beneath her feet gave way to the wooden boards like those that covered the inn's walls. An unlit river-stone fireplace protruded from the far wall. Log rafters lined the ceiling. The door stood propped open, offering a view of the ocean and allowing the sun to shed some light on the room.

She paused to survey the guests. Most of them had slumped against the eight tables in various forms of pre-coffee stupor. She smiled. *Time to liven up the place.* "Nobody wants any coffee, do they?"

The seamen who occupied the nearest three tables, met this with roars of mock disapproval.

"Aww, Robbyn!"

"What do you think?" she said with another smile.

Other people lifted their heads off the table, eyeing the coffee. Most just laughed.

"I didn't think so." Robbyn chuckled and rounded the room, leaving coffee, eggs, and bread before each guest. She had to make two rounds for the sailors occupying the nearest three tables. "The captain must be starving you men!"

"You have no idea." The hook-nosed sailor glanced sideways at his captain and disappeared behind his cup.

"You ever been to sea, Miss?" Another sailor's chapped hands hovered over the steam curling from his mug.

"Only once." Robbyn looked up from the coffee she was pouring and grinned. "I prefer dry land." She moved on to the next table. A steady chatter arose in her wake, and she left the room a livelier place than when she had entered it. *That's more like it.*

When she returned with a needle, some thread, and a ripped curtain, chatter filled the room. She paused again to survey everyone, this time more carefully. She picked out each face—the sailors, the traveling tradesmen, women, and children. But none looked even remotely like the blonde, thinly bearded man she'd glimpsed as she'd awakened. She ran her hand through her hair. *Probably nothing. Just some leftover fragment of a dream.*

The name "Kestrel" popped up in several conversations in the space of a few seconds, pulling her from her thoughts. She plopped into one of the seats near the sailors, where she figured she would hear the most recent news on Kestrel, and threaded the needle into the curtain.

"My cousin's going to his hanging." The young man wore an impish grin.

The captain laughed. "Yeah, him and all of Gable."

"I wouldn't bother going if I were yeh." An old man with eyebrows that drooped like melting candle wax crossed his legs and leaned back at the end of the table.

All heads turned to him.

"And why might that be?" someone asked.

"'Cause there ain't gonna be no hanging."

"Right," the captain rolled his eyes, "because the winged sunshine sheep are going to break down the castle and carry him away to their kingdom in the clouds."

Everyone nearby laughed.

The old man's brow lowered as he stared the captain down. His voice came out low. "With that fool at the throne, a flock of *normal* sheep could break down the castle."

The captain leapt to his feet. His end of the bench shot backward, causing its other occupants to nearly lose their balance. "What did you say about our King?"

The old man stood and leaned across the table, his set face inches from the captain's. "I said he's a fool. The Marauders are gonna walk into the castle and break their Head Captain right out. I'll bet James Kestrel's pretty bloodthirsty after seven years in prison. Mayhap he'll kill off a few from the crowd that came to see *him* hang."

The captain leaned back, threw his head toward the ceiling, and let out a laugh so loud it should have stopped all other conversation, but the chatter continued. When he brought his face back down, all humor had drained from his face. "You're the fool! Break into the tallest tower in the strongest castle in the world? Guards 'round the clock. No visitors! There's a reason no one's ever escaped."

"And what better first time than now? We're talking about the *Marauders*."

"Yeah, Marauders! Raiding villages is one thing. A castle is quite another. Besides, no one's seen them for fourteen years!"

"Seven!"

"Fourteen!"

"Seven!"

Robbyn rubbed her temple. Perhaps if she settled the smaller argument they'd quiet down on the larger one. "You're both right."

The captain and the old man stopped arguing and turned to Robbyn. "They've been gone for fourteen years. But they came out of hiding for one raid seven years ago. So you're both right."

At first, no one at the table said anything. The captain turned to the old man. "It doesn't matter. More likely than not, they're lounging in paradise anyway. Them and their treasure. Some faraway tropical island, I'll bet."

The old man scoffed. "Have yeh fallen asleep for the last twenty years?" He nodded, staring the captain down. "That'll 'splain it. You just missed all the cities they've destroyed, an' all the armies they defeated."

The captain started to speak, but his first word trailed off into a grunt. The old man leaned closer and lowered his voice. "They are more than raiders and pirates now. If treasure's what they be after, they would 'ave taken their gold and sailed to paradise years ago."

The captain's face grew redder. "You seem to know an awful lot about them. I'll bet you've donned the black cloak yourself."

"Yeh angry gull! I don't have to be one to see what they're after. They had the Caelum Flute of all things! If they wanted treasure and paradise they would've traded it for more than they could ever want. But they kept it. They tapped its secrets."

"More fairy tales." The captain smiled at the people seated around his table. "When will the lunacy end?"

The old man ignored him and lowered his voice again. "They want power, and once they break Kestrel free and he shows 'em where he buried the flute, the rest o' the world'll be helpless to their will."

"Seven years! Kestrel's been locked away seven years! And now the Marauders are going to free him?"

"Fine, then!" The old man dug into his vest. "Let's see if yeh got the gold to back your stupidity. Five gold coins!"

Robbyn prepared to object to gambling inside the inn when darkness covered the room, leaving only the candlelight from the corner tables. The chatter died as people swiveled in their chairs. Robbyn glanced toward the door. A humongous, bear-like mass eclipsed the light shining through the doorway. With a booted step over the threshold it ducked and entered the inn.

The light rippled back and the gigantic man stretched to his full height, his head inches from the wooden beams of the ceiling. He had wild, dark brown hair that grew down into a tangled beard and hung as a bushy bundle down his back. His rolled up sleeves revealed matted fur along his bulging arms.

"Hello, Drift." Robbyn sprang from her chair. She willed the people behind her to quit staring and get back to their conversations, but the room maintained its silence. "How can I help you?" She offered him her most inviting smile.

His wild, stark blue eyes, nearly lost beneath his overgrown hedge-like eyebrows, squinted about the silent room as if searching for a threat, before settling on her. "Could you spare me a room, Robbyn?" His deep rumble of a voice sent a tremor through the hall.

"Always." She swung her open hand to lead inside. "Have a seat. Would you like me to take your cloak?"

He started to pull off his enormous, dark gray cloak, which could have been cut from a sail with a dull knife. The clothing beneath consisted of various scraps of dark cloth sewn together. The crooked stitch suggested that he'd fashioned it himself. He shook his head, and pulled his cloak back on. "No, but thanks." With a courteous nod of his bushy head he found a seat in the corner.

"Would you like anything to eat?"

He nodded. "I would like that."

As if on cue, the rest of the room trickled back into chatter.

Robbyn stepped toward the kitchen, eying the old man from the argument. If he had gold to gamble with, then he had gold to pay for his room. She would approach him after she served Drift's breakfast.

"Robbyn?"

She turned to the voice and a frowning man rose from his seat, clasping a hat in his hands.

"Can I talk to the owner of this inn?"

She paused. No doubt he would complain about Drift's presence. But that mattered little. She opened her mouth to respond. What should she say? *He's dead! He's dead!* She yearned to set her secret free. How easy it would be. She need only say two words. "He—"

"Ryefield goes south for the winter." A nearby guest spoke through a mouthful of eggs.

"Oh."

Robbyn smiled. "I'm afraid you're stuck with me for now."

"You?"

Robbyn closed her eyes. *Here it comes.*

"But you're not even a full grown woman. Why, you're just a girl. You're—alone?"

"This inn's never empty." She opened her eyes again. "That's what I love about it." Her answer did little to fix the guest's dumbfounded face.

"Hey, could yeh top me off over here?" The old man raised his cup.

"Excuse me." Nodding apology to the dumbfounded guest, she flashed the elder man a smile. "One moment." She flitted into the kitchen, retrieved the coffee pot, glided back into the hall, and refilled the man's mug.

As she poured, his gaze wandered to the white stripping wrapped around her left forearm. "Say, Robbyn, yeh ever say what's under that bandage you always wear? Can't have hurt yourself, can yeh? Yeh've worn it for too long."

Her smile wavered like a candle flame struck by a breath of air. All at once she wished she were still trying to come up with a way to tiptoe around Ryefield's death with the other guest. She stopped pouring. The pot began to tremble, so she set it down. Her right hand instinctively closed around her left forearm, around the bandage that hid her darkest secret. Her throat felt dry. With a glance at the attentive, curious eyes, she forced herself to smile. "A—map."

All those watching leaned in collectively.

"A map?" The old man raised one eyebrow. "Of what?"

She paused for effect, still smiling. "That's between me and James Kestrel." She winked.

The immediate area, especially the sailors, exploded in hearty roars of laughter.

Spinning on her heel, she walked out of the room, leaving it buzzing in her wake. But once she entered the kitchen, her smile faded. Dizziness confused her steps. She staggered against the wall, sank to the stone floor, and burst into tears. She covered her face and let the sobs shudder out. For minutes she sat there, hoping nobody would enter the kitchen and find her in such a state. Then, with the tears still flowing, she unraveled her bandage with slow, shaking fingers.

The strip of cloth fell away, unveiling the black ink design etched into her skin, an "S" bearing a horizontal rod with a bucket at each end. "I need to tell someone," she whispered. She pictured herself entering the dining hall, walking up to a guest, and spilling her entire predicament. *Um, sir—I'm in a bit of trouble. The Marauders killed my parents and enslaved me when I was little. Then they sold me to Ryefield. But he's dead now and he didn't have any heirs. So, according to Gable law, this inn and myself fall into the possession of the next person to claim us—Please don't claim me.*

She would have laughed if it hadn't been so sad, but she had to do something soon. Any week now the boat builders would come through looking for work, and Ryefield would be expected to be back from his yearly trip. *Run away!* The thought pushed its way into her mind for the hundredth time. But she couldn't bring herself to leave the inn. Where would she go? What would she do? But then again, how long could she keep her secret?

Robbyn sighed, sniffed, and rose to her feet. "Have faith." She prayed a silent prayer, blinked herself back into composure, and took a deep breath before replacing the bandage over the slave mark. As she prepared to head back out into the dining hall, a commotion erupted from it.

"Oy!"

"Grab him!"

Pounding feet, wood screeching against wood, and grunts. Then three inn-shaking crashes. She burst through the door. Drift held the old man by the collar up in the air. The old man's white face trembled between the rafters. His legs swung freely beneath him. The sailors surrounded the two, posed as if ready for a fight. A trail of toppled tables and chairs littered the floor.

"Pay the good innkeeper." Drift growled through bared teeth, glaring up at the man. He shook him slightly, causing his head to bump against one of the rafters.

The old man dug a shaking hand into his pocket and pulled out a collection of coins that jingled to the floor. Drift lowered him to the ground and unclenched his massive hand. The man scampered out the door like a freed rabbit.

"Ungrateful whelp!" One of the sailors shook his fist after the old man.

The captain turned to Robbyn. "You should have made him pay up front, lass."

"I know. He claimed his family would arrive today with the money."

Drift bent over and grasped at the coins on the floor. It took several attempts to pry the coins off the floor with his thick fingers. "He left you a tip." He grunted as he offered his calloused fist. She cupped her hands and received the money.

"Well," she hoped her eyes hadn't become red and puffy from her tears, "it's a good thing I have such watchful men around. Thank you."

"We'll take care of this mess," the captain said. The sailors didn't take long in propping up the chairs and tables. Then the captain turned again to Robbyn. "And now we must be off. Our stay has been, as always, nothing short of the best." He proffered a sack of coins and dropped it into Robbyn's hands.

She smiled. "Bless your voyage."

The sailors filed out.

"Robbyn, can you show me to my room?" Drift's rumbling voice stopped several nearby conversations in mid-sentence.

"Oh." Guilt for crying in the kitchen when she should have been preparing his room washed over her. "No. I'm sorry. I'll clean up a room for you now."

"No, that's fine. I'll be in my ship." He cast an accusing eye around the room before cracking his knotted knuckles. "Let me know if another one breaks for it."

She glanced at the other guests, several of them staring at Drift out of the corner of their eye. "I don't think it's going to be a problem, Drift."

He grunted, turned, and left the inn. In his wake, a blanket of shadow swallowed the room and then disappeared.

She stood at the doorway as he walked up the dock to his ship, a tiny vessel with a sail that would have provided little more than enough fabric for his cloak. Oversized oars hung out either side. Drift planted one booted foot in the boat, causing it to veer slightly. As it steadied, he placed the other foot in and carefully balanced his way down into the cabin, which looked too small to fit him.

☙❧

As she hummed a cheerful tune a traveling bard had once played at the inn, Robbyn wiped dry the last earthen dish. Through the kitchen window she witnessed the golden orb of the sun sink into the sea, escorted by the downy pink bedding of a cloud cluster. Just as the top of the orb submerged, something flashed in and out of view—something black.

Her song died mid-note. The dish in her hand slipped, plunged, and shattered. She froze, her eyes trained on the window. Then, slowly, she leaned against the washbasin and peered through the window. Inwardly, she pleaded for a crow or a blackbird to hop into view. Even a grayish sea gull would suffice. But nothing appeared.

It's happening all over again. Her heart banged against her ribcage. Fear clogged her mind and blurred her thoughts. She glanced down and found her arms frozen in time, still holding an imaginary dish. She plied them loose and lifted the cast iron rod used to stoke the fire. It took both quivering hands to hold it upright. She tiptoed across the room and leaned against the wall beside the doorway, listening to her heart race. With one last shaky breath and with faltering steps, she crept into the dining hall.

Long forgotten memories poured through her mind, burning like flame poured over reopened scar tissue—memories so vivid they obstructed her view of the empty dining hall. Her parents, the Marauders, the village in flames—all spun through her mind.

The trailing edge of a black cloak disappeared at the top of the steps along the far wall. Or maybe another projected memory? Suddenly, Robbyn realized she could be imagining it all. Was she losing her mind?

She turned the corner and ran headlong into a man's chest. She bounced back, took in the black-cloaked man looming over her with a couple dozen men behind him, and all of her uncertainties died. The shine of his golden tooth distracted her attention only momentarily from the cold indifference of his eyes—like looking into the eyes of a mountain lion. Atop his dark head sat a crooked crown, copiously jeweled with multi-colored gems. The Marauder King.

"Robbyn," he said with a smile. But his eyes did not change.

Robbyn's heart fluttered. Hearing her name uttered so casually by those evil lips plunged her into a new depth of terror. Something snapped, and the full force of her anxious energy shot forth in the form of an upward swinging fire rod. With a resounding clang, the iron made contact.

The swing missed the King's head but sent his crown sailing across the room. It bounced off the far wall and rolled before the legion of waiting Marauders, depositing a single red ruby on the floor before their transfixed eyes.

"I—" Robbyn started, as though she'd just spilled a goblet of wine over a guest. A surge of panic rose within her. What now? Run as fast as she could? Or would that serve only to elevate the wrath she had just incurred? At the same time, the urge to strike him again burned within her and she brought the iron rod back again for a second blow. At the top of her swing she locked up, helpless to her own indecision.

The King's bracelets and rings jangled as his hands flew to his mess of thin black hair.

"You—insolent—you." He wrenched the bar from her grasp and threw it to the ground. Then he grabbed her bandaged arm. She yanked back but the King only strengthened his grip until she dropped to her knees in pain. With a flick of the wrist, he laid her arm bare, revealing her slave's mark, now in the center of a red, hand-shaped imprint. Even though only Marauders occupied the room, she felt naked.

The King gazed down at her as if he had just uncovered a stash of stolen goods. "Tsk, tsk, tsk." He turned to his men. "Tie her."

Three Marauders swept forward, grabbed Robbyn by her arms, and dragged her over to a chair beside the fireplace. The strength of their grasps quelled any notion she had to struggle free. Two pinned her against the chair while the third set to binding her to it.

"Captain Lewell?" The king turned to his crew.

A man stepped forward, and once he separated himself from the others, she recognized his face as the one she had seen that morning.

"All guests are being held upstairs, Your Highness."

"We are ready then. Let us raid."

The Marauders moved forward as a black wave even before the

King had finished his sentence. Those near the fallen crown parted for it, giving it a wide berth.

"Kill those upstairs quickly. As for this *girl*—" spit flew in Robbyn's direction as he said *girl*. "Let her burn."

"As you wish, your highness."

Robbyn lost what little breath the tight constraints allowed her.

Lewell crossed the room and ascended the stairs.

She shook her head, and tried to say, "No," but couldn't. They were going to die. *Her* guests had only seconds, maybe minutes, to live. She tried to wriggle free from the rope, but it cut deeper into her numbing limbs.

Lewell disappeared. Robbyn turned to the King even as the Marauders spread mounds of straw, obstructing the walls of the inn.

The king meandered over to his crown. He snatched up both the crown and loose ruby. A smile graced his face as soon as he rested the crown on his head.

"Why are you killing everyone?" Robbyn's eyes stung with collecting tears. "Why not enslave them?"

The King turned on her. The lines in his face deepened and his tone reddened as his scowl devolved into something hideous. He pointed a quivering finger at her. "Be quiet, slave!"

She jerked back, causing her chair to tip onto its back legs and then clunk down onto all fours.

The King paced away and a dumping of straw hid him from view.

Taking a deep breath, she exhaled in an attempt to still her pumping heart and fend off her tears. Minutes passed. The Marauders formed a line into the cellar and carried out all the food supplies. When even the sounds of their raiding died away, she listened for any sign of her guests. A scream, a sob, anything—nothing but silence answered her. She was alone.

A *boom* hit her ears amidst the sounds of cracking wood, banging iron, and shattering glass. It was the kind of *boom* that only exploding powder made. Whoops and hollers from outside followed.

Flames licked the kitchen door frame and crawled along the floor. Smoke rolled into the dining room, followed by the spreading fire.

She rummaged through her mind for some way to escape. Maybe somehow the guests were still alive. Maybe she could free herself then free the guests. She could figure the rest out when the time came. She looked around for something to cut the ropes. The tables didn't have any sharp edges. She needed a knife from the kitchen, where the fire was strongest. She threw her weight forward. The chair hopped a smidgeon. She'd never make it anyway.

The crackling roar of the flames grew steadily in volume. The smell of smoke invaded her nostrils. Sweat slid down her face.

She threw glances everywhere, desperate for some semblance of inspiration. She looked up, but the twisting grains of the ceiling offered no means of escape. She continued to study those lines leading to nowhere even as an ever-thickening layer of smoke obscured them.

The hall grew brighter as the fire wasted through the straw toward her.

She pushed back the helplessness and gritted her teeth. It wasn't her time and it wasn't her guests' time. She clung to that fragment of optimism even as the cloud of smoke thickened and tears flowed out of her eyes. Her coughs came out in pained gasps.

Everything around her, even the flames, faded through a veil of gray. The heat surrounded her, trapped her, and pressed in on her from all sides.

Her stinging gaze drifted down to the fire. She was coughing more than breathing now, and each breath hauled in another batch of bitter smoke. She shut her eyes tight, but she still saw fire. Finally, she surrendered to her fate, prayed to God, and passed out.

CHAPTER 2

THE SHEPHERD

Micah had to be dreaming. He *had* to be. Any second now this nightmare would dissipate and he would wake up drenched in sweat and tangled in covers. Just like all those other times. But it certainly looked and felt real. The breath clouds spurting from his mouth, the snow-covered mountainside, the storm clouds rolling in from the east—it all felt and looked painfully real. He shook his head. No, it was too horrible.

"Ariel!" He scoured the mountainside again. Reilly, Jordan, Rachael, Gabrielle, Logan, and Hannah. Six heads maintained their gaze at Micah, their chins grinding away at their cud. But no Ariel. His eyes must be playing tricks on him again. White sheep blended into snowy backgrounds, especially sheep as white as his. In a few moments, Ariel's small outline would pop out of the pervading white. But with every second that his searching turned up empty, his heart pounded faster.

Then he spotted a small set of tracks leading off into the distance. He tore after them, crook in hand, feet crunching through the thin crust of stale snow, cloak snapping behind him. He looked up the meandering trail and faltered, for the hoofprints disappeared at the edge of a cliff. The sight hit him like a well-aimed bludgeon.

"Ariel!" Micah's panicked pitch echoed off an adjacent mountain-side. Heart hammering, he skidded to the edge and read the terrible tale so plainly written in the snow. Ariel's hoof prints stretched to the cliff's edge and disappeared over it.

His knees melted and hit the ground. This couldn't be happening. He winced at the sight of the scrabbling marks in the snow that testi-fied to Ariel's struggle to stay up. The horrible scene played through in his mind. His crook fell from his limp fingers and skittered away over the snow, off the cliff.

How could he have been so careless?

Reluctantly, he peered over the edge. His vision spun at the sheer distance to the ground below. In that sickening whirlpool of white, he found only some disrupted snow and hoof prints leading off.

"She survived." He breathed, his hope restored to a glimmer.

As if to kill this meager ember, a cold wind swept over him, bear-ing the first traces of snow. Micah gazed up. The storm clouds loomed upon them. He glanced back up the slope. A flock of snow gulls bur-rowed for cover. His six sheep followed his every movement with their gazes.

Then he spotted Grixxler leaning on his cane beneath a fir tree. He merely stood, staring at Micah, stroking his graying beard. "I dare you to do it," his posture seemed to say. "Go ahead; defy me."

Micah hesitated. Grixxler would not approve of him abandoning his flock to chase after Ariel. It went against the advice he'd relentlessly pounded into all his shepherds' heads. Then again—

He peered over the edge of the cliff. The thickening snow nearly obscured the place Ariel had landed. An image of Ariel freezing to death in the midst of a blizzard flashed through his mind. He couldn't let that happen. He felt disgusted with himself for even considering it.

"You stay here," he called to his flock. They gave no sign of reas-surance, not even a flinch. They chewed away at their cud. Their silence highlighted the soft pat of falling snow.

Would they survive the storm? Could they find their own shelter? Maybe he could rush them to his cabin and come back for Ariel. But would he beat the storm? He glanced up at the dark clouds. Not a chance. He had to get down, get Ariel, get back up, and find some temporary shelter. Maybe he would be able to make it to Grixxler's stable.

He eased himself over the side of the icy rock face. There he paused, glancing once again toward Grixxler. How would he respond?

Grixxler reacted no differently than the sheep; he stared, not moving from under the fir tree. Micah wished he would do something—scream, chase after him, spit in his direction—anything to give him some idea of his master's feelings. But he knew he wouldn't, not until Micah completed the rescue. Unless he died.

Micah lowered his leg and found a foothold. As the view of his sheep disappeared, desperate bleats of abandonment followed him over. Each outcry of pain hit him like an icicle through his heart, adding to the guilt already eating at him. In an attempt to blank out their cries, he turned his attention skyward.

The dark clouds warned of the terrible snowfall to come. He winced. He had just left his flock alone in a pending blizzard. With a deep breath he began his descent, praying with each slippery step that he'd reach his lost lamb in time.

CHAPTER 3

The Giant

A single footstep on the deck plates above his head, summoned Drift from the numbness of technical thought. He seized the lantern from his desk and lumbered toward the door. The stench of a stranger filled his nostrils. He froze and clenched his fists, but kept his back to the door.

The intruder crept almost noiselessly over the deck of his ship.

Each step, though expertly placed, shifted the balance of the ship to an almost undetectable degree. He felt each vibration like a spider feels a wriggling fly caught in its web.

The intruder stopped. The boat steadied. Several seconds passed in complete stillness. Then the cabin door flew open, revealing a dagger-wielding Marauder barely visible against the darkness.

Drift sprang forward just as the cabin door hit the wall. He lifted himself by the rafters and crashed down hard, ramming his shoulder into the wall. *The Wooden Swan* pitched so violently it teetered on the edge of rolling. The Marauder tumbled down the slanted floor. Drift dashed the short distance to his foe. The rocking of the boat turned the floor into a series of shifting inclines, but he traversed it with ease.

The Marauder kicked off the wall. Drift reached down to grab him but the man rolled past. A sudden pain burst from his thigh—an invasion of metal in his flesh. He whirled around, clenched the Marauder's wrist, and twisted it. The Marauder buckled, raining kicks on Drift's shin even as he did so. He hefted the man off the ground, stepped out into the cool night air, and flung him. The Marauder sailed over an adjacent ship and shattered the water's surface.

Drift surveyed his surroundings. Black cloaks swarmed the beach as they loaded Ryefield's ships with supplies from the inn and patrolled the neighboring woods. A black hull and sail at the far end of the dock marked the presence of the Marauder's enormous vessel, *Lady Midnight*. A cluster of the mysterious bandits were loading some sort of contraption from the Marauder craft onto one of Ryefield's ships.

He grasped the hilt of the dagger still lodged in his thigh. He had found the Marauders—or they'd found him. Now was his chance. His whole leg stiffened as he gritted his teeth and yanked the dagger loose.

He'd lost focus, and now the Marauders had staged an invasion without the slightest sound to alert Drift to their presence. Had he any time to spare, he would have run into his cabin, crumpled his maps and charts, and thrown them into the sea. Instead, he unfurled the vessel's sail with a slice of the Marauder's dagger and cut the rope anchoring it to the dock. The wind pushed the still-bobbing ship seaward.

Fighting his every instinct to charge the inn with swinging fists, he climbed into the nearest of Ryefield's ships, ducked behind the railing, and waited. He would have to plan his moves carefully. If a couple dozen chased after his empty ship, then that would be a couple dozen less he would have to fight.

"Captain Lewell, there's a giant in that ship!"

"A wha—You're dripping wet!"

"He threw me into the water. Look, see that light out there? He's sailing away!"

Drift hunkered lower.

"Go."

"You three, deal with him."

Only three.

Footsteps banged up the dock, growing louder.

Drift whacked himself in the head. They were coming to *his* ship, the one *he* was hiding in. He rolled into the cabin and rose on his good leg behind the door. If they entered the cabin, the open door would hide him for a moment.

Footsteps hit the deck of the ship.

"I've got the wheel. You untie us from the dock."

"Aye. We'll raise the sails."

The sail snapped full with wind. The ship lurched and eased forward.

Drift squinted through the crack in the door and saw a fuzzy-haired Marauder securing the sail. He squeezed his eyes shut and suppressed a groan. *You're a fool, Drift.*

The ship gained momentum.

"We're gaining on him easily. I don't think he's using his oars."

"What? He's not using his—"

"He probably sent his ship out empty. The fool! Probably still back at the inn."

Laughter echoed into the cabin. "We should blow up his boat and be done with it. It would be easy enough with this puppy." Two metallic *dings* rang into the cabin, as if someone had slapped a black-smith's anvil.

Drift frowned. What were they talking about?

"Enough fooling around. Go fetch me a telescope."

He tensed.

"As you wish, Sir Crab-face." Footsteps drew closer.

Drift tightened his grip on his dagger and raised it to shoulder height. He slammed the door shut just as the footsteps reached the other side, crushing the Marauder between the door and the doorpost. Drift yanked the door open and the Marauder crumpled to the floor. He grabbed him by the collar, stepped onto the deck, and threw him into the water.

"There he is!" The wheel spun out of the Marauder's hands as Drift turned to face him. The man pointed.

Drift charged. He flung the dagger at the Marauder's foot. The Marauder leapt onto the other foot. The dagger buried itself in the wood and his charge hit the Marauder hard in the midsection. They landed several feet past the dagger.

Sching!

He rolled away to find the crab-faced leader standing above him, poised to plunge his dagger. Drift crossed his arms to block the dagger. But nothing happened. He uncrossed his arms to see the leader somehow now standing at the far end of the ship, and before he could fully realize what happened, a spinning dagger careened toward his head. He threw up his hand. The dagger ripped through the callus of his palm and glanced away.

Something solid hit him in the side of the jaw, knocking his head sideways. He pushed himself off the ground as another blow hit his head, this time from the other side. His vision blurred. Anger mounted in his chest.

He reached out, snagged two ankles, and jumped to his feet. Two Marauder heads hit the deck and he stood with an upside down Marauder in each hand.

Bang! An explosion peeled out over the ocean followed by what sounded like a roll of thunder. He glanced toward a foreign-looking contraption comprised of brass, iron, and wood in the middle of the deck. At first he thought that's what the explosion had come from, but then he realized it had come from behind. He whirled around to see smoke, lit by the flame that created it, pouring into the sky from the kitchen window of the inn.

"Robbyn." The word fell from his lips without any breath to lend it sound. She could be in there, struggling for her life, screaming for her life. Or worse, she could be— He swallowed. He had to get into that inn. He had to get into that inn *now*.

He swung the Marauder in one hand over his head and into the sea. He spun the man in his other upright, seized him by the collar, and slammed him against the wall of the cabin. He brought his face to within an inch of the Marauder's. Although he could hardly see his features in the darkness, he felt the Marauder's breath on his face. "What are you planning?"

The Marauder chuckled.

Beads of sweat began to roll down Drift's forehead. He didn't have time for this. What he imagined to be the sound of Robbyn screaming rattled through his mind. He roared in the Marauder's face, turned, and launched him away into the sky. Then he bolted to the wheel and turned the vessel to the northeast. He lashed the wheel in place with a loose stretch of rope just as the Marauder hit the water.

He ran straight toward the distant inn, threw himself over the railing, and plunged into the frigid sea. He swam toward shore, the icy water stiffening his joints. The salt caused the wounds in his hand and thigh to burn. Nevertheless, he kept his eyes on the growing inn.

The smoke spread until it rolled in billows out of every window. By the time he thundered up the beach, flames licked up every seam of the inn.

His rage built with his momentum. Any black cloak that stood in his way would be flattened. He stampeded through the boatyard.

"Seize him. Seize him!"

A Marauder emerged from the shadows and drew a dagger. Drift barreled into him with his outstretched forearm, flattening him. A guttural sound rose in his throat as more black cloaks emerged and converged on him. He busted his way through, scattering bodies and

ignoring the dagger stabs that rained on him. The guttural sound rose
into a roar.

He crashed through the smoking inn's door at the crest of his
momentum, breaking through the door frame as well as a substantial
chunk of the wall. The broken door fell away and flames rushed at
him. He covered his head and didn't break stride.

His legs crunched through what felt like a dining table. He toppled forward and landed with a crash that shook the floor beneath
him. He stood to find himself in a world separate from the dashing
and slicing Marauders. Here, only mountains of fire existed. He stood
in an area clear of flame, however scorching it felt. The clouds of
smoke gnawed at his watering eyes as he searched the fire for Robbyn,
but he could only see an all-encompassing flame.

"Robbyn!" he roared, choking on the smoke.

For a moment the wall of fire parted, revealing the fireplace at the
back side of the inn. And there she lay—a small, wilted form covered
in soot, her hair a much duller version of the flames that surrounded
her. With a rush of fury at the evil that could do such a thing to this
girl, he yanked the Marauder's dagger from his belt, rushed forward,
and sliced through her bonds. He killed the few small flames feed-
ing their way up Robbyn's clothing by wrapping her in his arms. She
coughed. But her eyes didn't open. Her features didn't change.

"You're alive."

He pressed her body to his chest and whirled about for his escape.
Which way had he come from? He could not see, for the ring of fire
roiled all around him.

With a rumble, a horse-sized chunk of the burning rafters broke
away and crashed at his feet. The building leaned, creaking and
moaning.

He steeled himself and thundered in the direction he happened
to be facing. He gritted his teeth, cradled Robbyn in his arms, and

led with his shoulder into a wall of pure inferno. Ignoring the searing pain, he pumped his legs harder. A series of dining tables splintered into kindling beneath him. Breaking free, he put on a burst of speed. The inn wall appeared in front of him a fraction of a second before he crashed through it in a cascade of burning rubble. He gulped in the cool air tainted by the taste of residual smoke.

"Catch him! Kill him!"

Drift didn't slow down. He simply lowered his shoulder, kept his legs churning, and shot past the Marauders before they could react.

He ran into the forest. His thigh, calf, and shoulder screamed with each step, but he bit his tongue and ignored the pain. The Marauders couldn't catch him now. The longer he ran, the faster he flew. Trees shot by in a blur on either side. The light of the fire faded into moonlight. The footsteps of the pursuing Marauders faded into silence, and though his head swam from loss of blood, Drift kept running.

CHAPTER 4

An Uninvited Visitor

Micah clung to the rock wall with numb hands. Whirling sheets of snow pounded him from all directions. Shards of ice cut at his raw skin. As he prepared to take another step downward, his foot slipped. His chin smashed into the rock wall, and he fell backward into the winds of the storm.

He hit the ground hard, pain shooting through his back. But he'd reached the bottom. He climbed to his feet and leaned into the wind, squinting through his ice-encrusted eyelids to no avail. He could barely make out the rock wall he'd just fallen from, let alone find a white lamb in a blizzard.

He pressed forward, one hard-fought step at a time. His lamb would have no chance at survival unless she found the cave. So he pushed toward what he guessed to be the right direction. He willed himself not to stop. A blind step forward was better than none at all. And as his feet sank into numbness, he found it easier to shuffle them forward. He clung to the cloak as the storm tried to rip it from him.

"Ariel!" he called. But his voice could not penetrate the storm. His legs grew stiffer and his trudging evolved into a staggering. He fell to his knees. Or had the snow mounted that high? He had to reach the cave. But where was it? He couldn't even find the rock wall anymore.

The storm poured snow on him even harder, as though sensing the coming demise of its victim. He tripped over something, his body pitched forward, and he fell into the bank of snow.

Once submerged, he swam around to stabilize himself. And for a brief moment, his hand found empty space. With the nimbleness of a turtle, he pulled himself in that direction, poked his head out of the snow, and gradually squished the rest of his body into the newfound refuge. The farther he crawled into the darkness, the bigger the cavity grew. The ground beneath his hands changed from snow to dirt to stone.

His stiff limbs rejoiced at the warmth, or at least the lessened cold. The howling of the wind faded behind him. This had to be the cave. When the ceiling allowed it, he stumbled to his feet and, clinging to the last fragments of hope that his sheep still lived, he plodded deeper inside. He hadn't gone far when his wandering hands fell upon a small bundle of familiar fuzz.

"A-Ariel," Micah stuttered, his voice reverberating off the walls.

Ariel bleated weakly. It was a call to her shepherd to make it all better.

Micah fell to his knees. "I'm so sorry," he whispered over and over again, his voice more distressed with each repetition. The spoken words rustled back at him off of the cave walls, lending reality to the terrible situation.

He tried to wrap his arms around his lamb, but his frozen joints proved too stiff to comply. But he strained against the invisible bonds until he cradled the small body. Despite her thick carpet of wool, Ariel felt cold.

He took Ariel and placed her underneath the folds of his shirt and cloak. Her wet nose burrowed around in his shirt until her bristly head popped out his collar. Her tiny heart beat against his. He wrapped his arms around the two of them to trap the warmth. He leaned against the wall and slumped to the ground.

Within minutes, his legs started shaking. He crossed them and sat on them. But the cold gnawed at his edges. "We'll make it, Ariel. Don't worry." He rocked back and forth to the distant wail of the storm.

They sat cuddled together through the night. Micah recited tales from the Story to keep her calm. Every now and then the blizzard raged to a fevered pitch, and the sounds of surging gales resonated into the cave amidst the cracking and falling of trees. But then they receded and he assured Ariel that the storm couldn't harm them.

Several hours after the storm died, strange sounds echoed into the cave. Micah widened his drooping eyes. He pushed his legs out from under himself, rolled onto his knees, and groped toward the entrance in the darkness with Ariel still in his arms. *Scrape, chink, clink.* Something shattered, and a beam of light fell to the ground in front of him.

"Micah?"

A pickaxe scrabbled through the hole and continued to grind an opening out of the ice covered hole.

Micah's heart sank. *Grixxler.* "I'm—here."

"Get out of there."

"Yes sir. Take the lamb first." He pulled Ariel out of his shirt and pushed her into the hole. Grixxler said nothing, but Micah felt someone grab her. He put his head forward and wriggled through until his head emerged in fresh air and sunlight once again. He found the air wafting over him surprisingly warm, and the sun shone brightly from a clear blue sky. The snow that, just hours ago, had blown with such violence, settled as a blanket over the landscape.

"How many times have I warned you?" Grixxler droned. "Never name your sheep—never assist another shepherd with their sheep—never trade, sell, or buy sheep." Grixxler loomed over him, staring at him with weary eyes. Two shepherds, Gorm and Fallob, stood beside Grixxler with a shovel and pickaxe in hand, glaring at Micah.

Micah grunted and pushed himself all the way out.

"And never, ever, *ever* risk the lives of yourself or your flock to rescue one sheep in danger."

Micah rolled onto his back, panting.

Grixxler trudged forward and stood over him, his gut hiding all but his narrowed eyes. He gazed over the cliffs. "You're the one with the good memory. Why don't you ever remember my four simple pieces of advice?"

Micah pushed himself off the ground and rose to his feet. *Here it comes.*

Grixxler grabbed Ariel and held her up. She bleated in protest. "What's its name?"

Micah swallowed. "Ariel, Sir."

"When did I give it to you?"

He stared at the ground. "You—didn't. I bought her from another shepherd."

Grixxler opened his mouth to talk, but Micah cut in. "She was sick. He was going to let her die!"

Grixxler whacked him on the side of the head. Micah pressed a hand to his head to stop the pain.

"Hundreds, boy! Out of hundreds of shepherds, you're the only one that can't seem to follow my simple pieces of advice."

Micah hung his head. Nothing could be gained by pointing out that he hadn't broken any rules.

"You're lucky I happened to be watching. Your sheep might have died."

Micah bit his lip, holding back his retort. *Happened to be watching.* How many times had Grixxler used those exact words? He always *happened to be watching.*

Grixxler snapped his fingers in front of Micah's face. "Wake up."

Micah jerked his head back and forced his eyes wider. He couldn't help the sleepy shape of his eyes any more than Grixxler could help his permanent sneer or his graying beard.

With a frown, Grixxler stepped forward, grabbed a fistful of Micah's hair, and yanked.

Micah winced as the hand caught several tangles.

"You need a haircut. If you wait much longer you'll become one of your sheep."

Gorm and Fallob snickered.

As the man released his hold, Micah smoothed his hair back down. It did feel remarkably similar to wool. "My flock'll be due for a sheering soon. I'll do it then."

Grixxler sighed and pulled a shepherd's crook from behind his back—Micah's crook.

"Thank you, Master." Micah accepted the crook but when he pulled back it remained rooted to the spot by Grixxler's grip.

"This is an awfully nice crook. Where'd you get it?"

"It was a gift."

"Recently?"

"No." Micah's mind wandered to that day years ago, the blessed day Grixxler gave him his sheep. He could still feel the warm spring breeze wafting over him as he wandered the streets of the mountain village of Sampter. The hammering of a blacksmith rang through the air. He could feel the crumpled scrap of paper clutched in his hand, bearing Grixxler's wandering, scratchy letters—the address where his sheep waited. The local carpenter, covered in sawdust, had waved to him from the corner.

"No what?"

"I got it." The crate of six lambs floated into his vision. The sight of those fuzzy white loaves, with their oversized heads and blinking eyes, always brought him a tingle of warm nostalgia. What a happy memory. And then an old man had noticed his dance of celebration—

"Where?" Grixxler's voice interrupted his daydream once again.

Micah blinked and opened his eyes; he was back on the snowy mountainside. "I got it the day I got my sheep. An old man—he was retired from shepherding—he gave it to me. He gave me this cloak I'm wearing, too."

Grixxler squinted into Micah's eyes for a few seconds, and then his mouth curled into a knowing smile. "You stole it, didn't you?"

"No! I'm telling the truth!"

"Don't lie to me, boy. You didn't have a crook or cloak on the wagon ride home that day."

Micah suppressed a sigh of frustration. He could see it so vividly in his mind. The crook had lain in his lap, the curved end hooked over the wagon rail. In fact, he had told Grixxler all about the crook and cloak, how the old shepherd had made him promise to take care of them, and how the wool of the cloak came from a rare breed of East Plain Sunshine Sheep.

Plus, the crook had accompanied him all over the Heather Mountains, over every hill and across every treacherously narrow pass. Grixxler had seen it hundreds of times. He just didn't care to remember—another example of his will to assume the worst of Micah.

Grixxler leaned in. "I don't care if you steal, as long as it's not from me, but don't you lie to me again. Understand? Just because you remember everything doesn't mean I'm gonna believe everything you say."

Micah looked down, and gave a small nod. Grixxler relinquished his grip of the crook. Micah pulled it to his side.

A silence followed.

"Thanks, Master," he said finally. "I'm sorry I was so careless with Ariel—er—it, and I'm glad you were nearby when I went after *it*."

Grixxler paused at this, studying Micah as he stroked his beard, as if he found the concept of an apology foreign. He grunted and nodded at Ariel. "How's its health?"

"She seems to be fine." Micah ran his hands along her sides, feeling for injuries. Ariel bleated in protest. Save for a few small bruises she had survived the fall unharmed.

"Good. Your other sheep are in your cabin." Without another word, he limped back toward the village with Gorm and Fallob staring Micah down in Grixxler's wake.

Micah sighed and scooped up Ariel. It would be best to stay out of Grixxler's sight and wait a few minutes before he began his own journey home.

◊X◊

After Grixxler made his way along the winding road through the village, mounted the hill to his home, and stomped inside, it didn't surprise him at all to find a black hooded cloak hanging on his coat ring. He studied it briefly, leaned his cane against the wall, shed his bearskin coat, and draped it over his visitor's.

He snatched his cane up again. Even being without the waist-high knobby stick for a few seconds pained his leg. He hobbled over to the window and gazed out. Micah was still making his way toward his cabin with the lamb in his arms, far away from the activity of the shepherds and villagers below.

A light tread signaled the entrance of a visitor from the hallway behind him.

Grixxler maintained his stare out the window. "Have a seat, Captain Lewell."

The footsteps paused. The wooden chair scraped across the floor and creaked with the sound of new weight.

"The time has come." Lewell's voice sounded cocky and jovial, as though his sentence carried long anticipated celebration. Then he paused, his voice becoming much darker. "Which shepherd do you choose?"

Grixxler didn't immediately answer, though as he studied the villagers and shepherds going about their business in the valley below, he knew exactly which shepherd he would choose. He had known for years.

"Micah." He adjusted his focus, so that he saw Lewell's reflection on the windowpane.

Lewell scowled and leaned back. "Are you sure?"

Grixxler recalled the various observations that had informed this decision, some of them dating back to before the construction of Micah's cabin. Back when the boy had lived with him. He couldn't hold back a smile as he thought back to the morning he had walked out to the stable to find Micah asleep amongst his sheep, having snuck from his warm bed to stay the night there. "Yes—Yes, I'm very sure."

Lewell fidgeted in his chair. "You're certain Micah is the best shepherd for the job? You've observed all the shepherds very closely?"

With a growl, Grixxler turned from the window. "Do you think I'm trying to cross you?" He hobbled toward the table.

Lewell waved this notion away. "The four suggestions. Who most closely followed the suggestions?"

"The shepherds haven't reacted to your suggestions as you'd hoped. In fact, they've done the opposite of their purpose. The shepherds haven't become better for the task. They've used them as an excuse to be irresponsible and lazy."

"And Micah?"

"Despite consistently breaking every suggestion, he is by far the most responsible shepherd I own."

"But whose sheep have the whitest coats?"

"Micah's," Grixxler said with a thud of his cane.

Lewell folded his arms and leaned back in his chair. "You're asking us to rest our entire plan on the shoulders of a mere boy? A scrawny boy at that!"

Grixxler waved his hands in the air. "I honestly don't care about your 'plan.' Why don't you go and inspect the shepherds yourself?"

Lewell made a grumbling noise. "It's just—I find it a little strange that, of all the shepherds we could possibly send, *he* is the one. Don't you?"

Grixxler caught the reference. His mind wandered to that night years ago, the night Ganthorn had dumped the infant on his doorstep and disappeared. He turned toward the door. "I've never been one for superstitions," he said with an air of finality. "I've told him nothing about where he came from or how he got here." He pulled his bearskin from the coat hook, took the Marauder's cloak off, and hung the bearskin in its place. "Are we done here?" He held out the cloak.

"It would appear so." Lewell rose from his chair. He donned the black cover as Grixxler opened the door. Lewell paused halfway out. He nodded. "The boy it is, then?"

Grixxler shut the door.

CHAPTER 5

The Journey

The next morning, Micah woke just before dawn to find his sheep still asleep. He crawled out of his wool blanket and tiptoed around them to the door, slipping on his cloak and rabbit skin sandals along the way. He grabbed his crook, which leaned against the log walls of the small cabin. He stopped in mid-stride, glancing at Ariel. She looked content and healthy. He eased out the door into the crisp morning air.

Immediately, he veered from the path to the village and headed up the mountain slope. He plodded through the undisturbed snow, making his way through the trees, and soon emerged into a clearing.

He didn't want to think about anything. Thoughts of his sheep, Grixxler, and the horrible events of the previous day could wait. For now, he needed to get away. He needed to clear his mind.

Snow gulls littered his path, celebrating with a symphony of cries the survival of another storm. He wove his way through several of the hot springs so abundant in the Heather Mountains. With another deep breath, he strode by them, taking advantage of the thin snow around their edges that made for easier walking. Their swirling mists bathed him in a moist, fleeting warmth.

He faced north. The sun hid behind a mountain across the canyon.

A faint breeze animated the bushes. The ground narrowed into a game trail and hugged the steep mountainside so that he had a perilous drop to one side and an almost vertical cliff face on the other. He placed each foot with care, for ice layered the path.

The trail broke open to a wide rock platform wedged into the mountainside. As he turned the corner, the sun erupted from behind the mountain, immersing him and the mountainside in a golden blanket of warmth.

Everywhere the sun touched, the snow melted. Far below, miles of fir trees gave way to rolling green hills. Beyond that the sandy beaches bordered the waves of Heather Bay and the Greater Kepled Sea reached to the horizon. It was a dizzying sight to behold.

He edged close to the fringe and gazed out across the sea, admiring the wonder of the depiction before him. No matter how hard he looked, he could not see past the great expanse of the ocean. It disappeared into nothingness, as though the edge of the world hung right at the edge of his sight.

His breath rose in clouds that dissolved in the sunlight. As entrancing as the view was, he had the care of his sheep to look forward to. He whirled to race back and ran headlong into something solid. He bounced to the ground.

From his seat on the cold stone he looked at Grixxler and the silver telescope. "Master?"

Grixxler didn't even bother to remove his eye from the scope.

Micah rose, careful to avoid the projected path of the telescope. *Something must be wrong.* He gazed in the direction the scope pointed, but saw nothing except the endless waves of the sea.

The air shifted into a faint, whistling breeze, tossing Micah's hair about.

Grixxler lowered his telescope but kept staring at Heather Bay. "Micah," he said in the dark, rich manner people sometimes use to inform each other of a death in the family. "I have a task for you."

All peace that this hike had brought to Micah's mind shriveled. "What kind of task?"

"A journey. A long and very important journey—I want you to take your sheep to the Gable Kingdom Castle—for them to be sheared and their wool to be used for King Darius' wardrobe. He has required it."

The Gable Kingdom? That's quite a journey. But it didn't make sense. "Couldn't the wool be delivered in bags?"

Grixxler broke his seaward gaze and turned to Micah. "The King's Royal Wool Spinner claims the wool is better when freshly sheared."

Micah frowned.

"She is slightly insane." Grixxler's quick and short response reflected the tightening of his temper.

"But why me? There are plenty of more experienced shepherds." A knot grew in his stomach.

"Because, boy, this is a very treacherous journey, and you have the best chance of making it."

"Me?"

"Yes," Grixxler growled. "You're the best shepherd I've got. Sad, isn't it?"

"I—"

"Get over yourself." Grixxler lowered his gaze straight into Micah's eyes and clenched both of his shoulders. His breath smelled of roasted duck. "It's an important quest."

Feelings of terror and suspicion coursed through Micah simultaneously.

Grixxler abruptly turned to leave, hobbling at a brisk pace.

Micah chased after him. "But when do I leave?"

"Today," Grixxler said. "Get your stuff together and meet me at the orchards. And be quick."

"But—"

"Deal with it."

Micah slowed to a stop and let Grixxler disappear around the bend. His mind could not grasp how everything had changed so suddenly. He turned once again to the view below; the shadow-infested forests, the hills that hid thieves waiting to pounce on lone travelers, and the dark waves of the ocean that had slaughtered many a crew in her rage. What did lie beyond the ocean's horizon? More than ever, he wished he knew.

He trudged back to his cabin and his sheep awoke, bleating for breakfast. He glanced around the bare walls of his cabin. He didn't have many possessions to bring. He took his ragged wool blanket, ripped a square from it, poured the last remaining handfuls of dried venison from his cupboard onto the square, and tied it into a bundle. Standing at the doorway, shepherd's crook in hand, he took a last surveying glance around his home. He wouldn't be seeing it for a while.

He then headed down the mountainside with his flock following. Grixxler met him in the woods to the south of the orchards, mounted upon his young red horse.

Micah's sheep nibbled the nearby brush, keeping a curious eye on the horse.

"The Land of Gable," Grixxler said, his gaze southward, "is not like anything you've ever experienced. Living your whole life in these secluded mountains, you don't know much about what you're heading into."

Micah didn't need to be told this. Grixxler's sentiments echoed the chorus playing in his head. But he decided it better not to say so.

"It's been described as the 'land of the birds,' and you'll see a lot of those. But the Green Isles have also been called the 'land of legends and secrets.'" Grixxler returned his gaze downward. His tone darkened. "And if I were you, I'd hope you don't run into any of the things that wander Gable in secret."

Grixxler dismounted and pulled a rolled up parchment from the saddle bag. "It's a map. Make your way directly south." He stared into Micah's eyes. "I have more pieces of advice. And this time, you'd *better* obey them. If you don't, you and your sheep will die." He cleared his throat. "First, never go near the ocean. Second, start a fire at the mouth of your sheepfold before nightfall—every night." Grixxler's eyes widened. "And don't *ever* let that fire go out before dawn the next morning."

Micah swallowed. This journey grew worse by the moment.

"Third, and most importantly," Grixxler arched his eyebrows, "stay out of the Wilderness."

Micah nodded. He didn't see any reason to disobey those rules.

"Now, I have this canvas pack for you." He pulled the gray pack off his horse. It had been stitched to hang over the shoulder and perch at the hip. Grixxler untied and opened it. Inside lay two small, dark loaves of bread, a leather flask of water, a flint and steel, some dried cedar bark, and a small golden coin. Grixxler dropped the map inside, closed it, and handed it to Micah.

"Thank you." Micah placed the venison inside the pack and swung it over his shoulder.

"There's another thing." Grixxler said, placing a hand on Micah's shoulder.

Micah had to concentrate to keep from shrugging the hand away.

"There will be trials and there will be hitches, and you'll be tempted to turn around and come back." He scanned Micah's eyes. "Don't." With a hearty slap to Micah's back he climbed atop his horse. "You'd better reach the castle before the full moon after next week's." With that he trotted away, his words stinging fresh in Micah's mind.

In the ensuing silence, the snow-entrenched forest grew darker the longer he stared at it. He had never ventured farther south than the orchards. From the view earlier that morning, he knew he would be trekking through more mountains. But after that he had no idea.

Despite the uncertainty crawling through his mind, he clutched his crook, took a deep breath, and made the first of countless steps into a new world.

Only one thought he couldn't ignore—Grixxler hadn't mentioned a return trip.

CHAPTER 6

THE MARAUDERS'
SECRETS

R obbyn woke to a dark room with nothing but a crack of light
glowing at her feet. She groped forward, and her hand knocked
into a solid surface—a door. The door creaked outward.

What happened to the inn? The fire? The Marauders?

With a few tentative steps, she entered a torchlit hallway.
Intricately cut dark wood, inlaid with black and gold trim, covered
the walls. Various articles of furniture and chests, mismatching but
beautiful in their own right, lined both walls between each black and
gold door.

Her soft steps echoed down the hallway. She touched the sweep-
ing curve of a chair back but the hairs on the back of her neck
prickled and she cringed. She peered around the room for the source
of her unease. Not simply because she had no idea how she had gotten here, but because it all seemed familiar, and for some reason this
hall evoked fear. Her gaze settled upon a brocade settee. Where had
she seen it before? How had she come here?

With a sudden pang, she remembered. She shot glances in both
directions and everything fell into place exactly as she remembered it.
They had brought her aboard the *Lady Midnight*.

She whirled about and stopped cold at her reflection in a tall, oval mirror lined with pearls. Bruises covered her body. Her wide, fearful eyes stared back. Angry red cuts indented her ankles and wrists, and a dirty scrap of cloth garbed her. What happened to her clothing? Had the fire done that?

The features of her face—too round, too youthful. She tore her gaze from the mirror and glanced at her hands. The same cuts glared up at her, confirming the mirror to be no illusion. A burning sensation lanced through her left arm. She turned her wrist over and found the mark, an "S" holding a rod upon which hung two buckets. But this mark looked almost wet, fresh. She touched it and recoiled at the stinging pain.

The final cog fell into place in her mind. She was reliving a long forgotten memory—her escape attempt. She shuddered, for she knew how it ended.

Maybe someone—God—had given her a second chance. She turned around, plotting a way to escape, but stopped again. In front of her stood a heavy iron door much larger than the others. Three massive bolts locked it in place. Entranced despite her predicament, she took a step toward it. A deep rumble rose and fell on the other side. She placed a hand on the cold metal and felt the vibration, the life, on the other side. She moved her ear closer.

"It's breathing," she whispered. This conjured all kinds of visions of large and foul creatures. What could be lurking behind such a solid door? She peered into the shadows of her memory, but could recall nothing.

A grunt, abrasive and animal, interrupted the rumble of breath. She took a wary step back. The faint tap of her foot echoed off the hallway walls.

As though her foot had triggered a trap, a thunderous barking ripped out from behind the iron door. She backpedaled into the mirror and tipped it over with a crash.

As she sat amongst the pearls and shards, the creature pounded furiously against the door. The bolts rattled with each assault. Vicious howls and snarls peeled out amidst the attacks.

"She's down here!" a voice shouted from one end of the hall, followed by a stampede of footsteps.

She scrambled to her feet. This was exactly how it had happened.

"Don't run!" she tried to scream, but the terrified little girl in her had taken over. She was running for the other end of the hall, taking Robbyn helplessly along for the ride. She couldn't even close her eyes to keep from witnessing the Marauder appear in front of her and wrap her wriggling body in his arms.

"I'll teach you to run away!"

ⓔⓧⓞ

Robbyn coughed and sat upright. Her eyes sprang open and then shut as the stinging, smoky pain set in. Breathing deep draughts of air, she put her shaking arms out to support herself. Raindrops pelted the roof as she ran a hand through her tangled hair. She opened her eyes in increments, her vision drifting into focus. A mass of brown fur evolved into the face of Drift, gazing down at her. Even his bushy eyebrows couldn't hide the concern in his eyes.

"Are you all right?"

She realized then that she lay in a hammock, covered in blankets, in a wooden, windowless room—the barracks of one of Ryefield's ships.

"What happened?" she asked, but a raspy pain consumed her throat. It felt as though she had swallowed lumps of burning sand. She hacked and wheezed as the taste of smoke invaded her mouth.

Drift handed her a leather canteen. "Drink this."

She gulped down as much of the water as she could. "You saved me, didn't you?" she whispered.

He grunted.

"I-is—" She bit her lip.

Drift put a hand up. "Save your voice."

"Is there—anyone else?"

Drift looked away. "I'm sorry, Robbyn."

She stopped breathing. The pattering rain filled the silent room. The guests—all dead.

"Are you hungry?"

She shook her head. The prospect of food didn't interest her in the least.

"I'll let you have a moment." Drift turned to the steps.

"No, stay." She reached for him from underneath her blankets. She felt childish for doing so, but she didn't want to be alone right then.

Drift stopped.

"I—" She pressed a hand to her temple and closed her eyes. "I'm sorry—I just—I'm—" She took a deep breath.

Her rescuer didn't move. Soot covered his clothing. Bruises and bandages covered his face. This was her hero. He had fended off who knew how many Marauders and entered a burning building to save her.

"Thank you for rescuing me." She wanted to hug him and had she been standing she would have tried.

Drift shrugged and nodded.

"Where are we?"

"We're north of the inn—or what's left of it." He paused. "I sent one of Ryefield's ships up here before I got you. We're inside it."

"I recognized it. I clean these every now and again." She pulled away her covers and sat up. As she moved, the pain of her various burns flared up. She still wore her apron, which now had several holes burned through it. As she reached back to untie it, the bandages on her arms caught her eye. She held her arms up to inspect them in the candlelight and gasped. The ugly black mark on her left arm glared up at her, naked.

Her throat dried up. Her darkest secret had been spilled, just like that. It seemed wrong that it could happen so suddenly, so carelessly, as if a cave in the heart of a mountain could be brought to light by the opening of a curtain.

"Where's Ryefield?"

Robbyn kept staring at the mark. "R-Ryefield?"

"Isn't that where you want to go?"

"I'd—I'm—" Robbyn looked up. Tears collected in her eyes, but she blinked them back. "S-stop pretending like you don't see it!" Her hollow voice betrayed her imminent tears.

Drift took a step back and widened his eyes. "See what? That blotch of ink?"

Robbyn glanced down again. "It's a slave's mark. It means I'm a slave."

"Says who?"

"Says everyone."

Drift grumbled something under his breath and dismissed the issue with a wave of his hand. "I never pay attention to everyone's opinion."

"It's not as simple as that. Ryefield. He's—" She bit her lip and forced the words out before she could change her mind. "He's dead. Ryefield's dead. My family's dead. And now, under Gable law, I will be enslaved by the next person to claim me."

At first Drift stared at her until, after a few moments, she averted her gaze. "No. No one will enslave you, Robbyn." He pounded his fist into his hand. The *thud* that resulted could have killed a fair-sized wolf hog. "I'd like to see them try."

"You mean—?"

He lowered himself to one knee and bowed his head. "From now on I am your humble bodyguard."

She smiled until she beamed. If she hadn't been clutching the netting of the hammock she might have floated to the ceiling. "Thank you."

"Now, where to, m'lady?"

"I-I have no idea."

"Think about it. I'll check on them Marauders."

He turned toward the stairs, but as his weight shifted to his right foot he winced and sank about a foot onto his buckled knee.

"What's wrong? Are you hurt?"

His face cleared. "I'm fine. Sore from yesterday is all." He ascended the steps without any further sign of pain.

Robbyn wrapped a blanket around herself. Where should she go? To some faraway village to start a new life? It needed to be somewhere the Marauders could never find her. But somewhere with people—somehow. She'd thought the inn would be safe. She never imagined the Marauders would invade the inn and murder her guests. But now? Now she knew that no one lived outside their reign of terror. The old man from the day before had been right; the Marauders hadn't sailed to paradise. They'd been hiding, waiting. But waiting for what?

❦

Robbyn mounted the top step with her blanket still draped over her shoulders. An iron wood stove sat in the corner and a narrow table with seven chairs sat in the center of the room. Three circular windows and two wooden doors hung along the walls to her right and left. Outside, two of the three windows revealed only dense foliage. The third offered a view of the ocean.

The familiar room had a musty feel and smell. Cobwebs marked the corners and crevices, and broken coats of dust revealed Drift's traffic pattern, which seemed to be a steady pacing between the windows.

She opened the door on the left and ducked inside. It had no handle, just a short stretch of rope tacked on at both ends. She scrounged through two rolled up hammocks made from fishing nets, a few miscellaneous medical supplies that had already been broken into, a stack of more blankets, some rolled up maps, a sextant, a compass, and a telescope. Behind these she found a healthy stock of firewood, some peculiar, pointed cylinders made of iron before she finally found the crates and barrels filled with food and water. The Marauders had the ship well stocked. She opened the spigot of one of the barrels, releasing a trickle of water into her hands, which she splashed onto her face.

She walked to the window. Drift circled a mechanical contraption on the deck, scratching his beard and holding one of the peculiar, pointed cylinders in his hand. The device consisted of a combination of brass, wood, and iron parts. Lots of cryptic gears and levers connected at various angles, and a long iron tube pointed toward the ocean.

Opening the door, she stepped into the drizzle. "What's that?"

Drift grunted and shrugged. "They put one on every ship."

She stood shivering as Drift circled it. "What are you looking for?"

"I'm trying to figure out what they're up to."

Robbyn pointed. "Those holes look like that's where it's supposed to be bolted to the deck."

"Hmmm." Drift hefted the pointed iron cylinder that he had retrieved from the cupboard. A wooden peg with a length of string wrapped around it stuck out from the flat side. "This fits in here." He slid it down the iron tube. The peg and string popped out a small hole in the bottom.

"That string looks like a candle wick. Maybe it's meant to shed light on it, so it can be worked at night."

Drift pulled out a chunk of rock and a dagger she recognized as one of the Marauders'. "Stand back. This thing reeks of exploding powder."

She took three backward steps. "It should be safe. That's a long wick. Just put out the flame before it reaches the tube."

A couple of well-aimed strikes sprayed sparks from the rock onto the wick, but nothing happened.

"It might be too wet."

The third strike caught and an orange ember formed. Then, hissing like a viper, the ember shot up the string very much unlike the wick of a candle. A split second of silence followed before an air-shattering explosion pealed out like condensed thunder. A plume of fire billowed from the end of the tube, propelling the cylinder—now a fuzzy blur of gray—into the sky with incredible velocity. One second the cylinder exploded from the tube, the next it was a speck fading into the dreary sky. The force from the blast shot the entire contraption in the opposite direction. It slammed into Drift and, its momentum unbroken, crashed the giant halfway through the cabin wall.

Robbyn gasped and rushed to his side. He sat embedded in the splintered remains of the wall, the contraption pressed against him. His gaze remained fixed on the soaring projectile. "Drift, are you all right?"

He nodded toward the sea. She turned just in time to see a ball of fire erupt from the water's surface at the edge of sight. The explosion sent waves leaping into the sky and plummeting back into the sea. It ended as quickly as it had started. The drizzle dispersed the few traces of smoke that lingered.

She stood with her mouth agape and her eyes wide. An incessant, high-pitched buzzing filled her ears, drowning out the sound of the rain. If Drift were not sitting in an imploded wall with the device perched in his lap, she wouldn't have believed what she had just seen.

"Wow," she said, but her voice didn't carry over the buzzing in her ears.

Drift leaned forward and pushed the contraption away with some effort. It fell and hit the deck with a resounding clang. He paced the deck, brow furrowed.

"What was that?" Thoughts whirled through Robbyn's mind like swarming gnats. How had the Marauders acquired these weapons?

Who else knew about them? And, most importantly, what were the Marauders going to use them for? She shivered.

"This isn't good." Drift growled at the floorboards. His pace quickened and lengthened. He looked southward. "We're still safe. We're a long ways from the Marauder camp."

"The rumors are true; the days of the Marauders raiding the coastline for trinkets are over." A new thought struck her. "They could break into the Gable Kingdom Castle with these."

Drift stopped pacing. "They could *destroy* the castle with these." He abruptly reentered the cabin and opened the cupboard.

She followed.

He stabbed one of the barrels with the Marauder's dagger and held out his hand as a gray dust poured out. He sniffed it, and then dumped it into the pile collecting on the floor.

"More exploding powder," he said.

"They're planning something major."

Drift grunted.

The idle gossip at the inn the day before rose in her thoughts and then it struck her. "Could this be a plot to free James Kestrel?"

"The timing works."

"And w-we're the only ones who know about it." Her heart quickened. "Drift, we have to *follow the Marauders!* If they sail south we have to warn King Darius."

"You sure?"

She stopped. Drift was right. This plan was ridiculous. Follow the Marauders?

"It'd be dangerous," he said. "I'd rather take you far away, to where it's safe."

"But what if the Marauders attack the castle? Those people—"

"I'll follow you wherever," Drift said. "It's your decision."

She hesitated, then nodded as she made her decision. "We must follow the Marauders. We have to warn whoever they're planning to attack."

Drift nodded.

"Let's just hope people will believe the words of a slave and a giant, for Gable's sake." Robbyn watched the last of the stream of exploding powder trickle to the floor.

CHAPTER 7

THE MYSTERIOUS MARKS

Micah looked back at the mountains, their majestic peaks dipped in snow. It felt strange to see them from so far away . . . Now he was a grain of sand on someone else's mountain view.

The air around him felt warm—almost warm enough to take his cloak off—and the ground held no snow. Maple and oak trees dotted the rolling green hills that surrounded him. They expanded to the south and east as far as he could see. Someone could be crouching on the other side of any one of those foreign-looking hills, or all of them, waiting to surprise him. He could just see the horizon over the line of hills to the west, where the water met the sky.

He surveyed his sheep. Their blank stares reminded him that they felt just as clueless as he did, with the exception that their lives rested on his shoulders. His knees weakened just thinking about it.

He turned back to his nearly constructed sheepfold and added another branch to the circle. Would that hole be large enough for Ariel to squeeze through and escape? He crouched and pushed his arm between the boulder and the tree trunk.

Adding an extra branch wouldn't hurt. He did so, threw another log on the fire, and stood behind the fire at the only gap in the circle—the entrance. He cupped his hands around his mouth and called, "Logan!"

Logan meandered over from the flock, giving the fire as wide a berth as possible. Micah examined her for abrasions, bruises, and signs of sickness. He lifted all four feet and checked for gravel stuck in her hooves. Nothing there. He prayed for her and urged her into the sheepfold. Then he turned toward his flock again. "Reilly!"

When the last one, Jordan, lay safe inside, he turned and counted them as they drifted into slumber. How could they sleep so soundly, as if they'd never left their straw beds in the cabin?

Sitting cross-legged in the entrance, he faced the spot of the sun's last appearance. Though some glimmerings of twilight remained, most of the light that illuminated the grass around him shone from his fire. He took his pack off and laid it next to him inside the sheepfold. He rested the shepherd's crook in his lap, memories of the man who had given it to him flashing through his mind.

Hopefully, tonight, he wouldn't have any trouble with wild animals—or worse. He added another log from the stack beside him to the fire.

ℝx₠

Micah gripped his crook tighter.

Hooting owls, chirping crickets, and other, stranger noises echoed out from the darkness that surrounded him, seemingly just at the edge of the firelight. Any second now some ugly head would rear into the light. He felt sure of it. His eyes darted from patch of darkness to patch of darkness to his sheep behind him, anticipating where it would make its appearance. Or maybe a swarm would come all at once. His fire had grown large enough to roast a hog. Its heat pressed against his face, but he added another log. He imagined an owl large enough to swallow a horse bursting through the sheepfold wall, plucking Jordan off the ground, and popping her in its mouth—and he added two more logs.

He took a deep breath. "Have faith. Have faith." He sighed. *This is going to be a long journey. Father keep us safe.*

Hours crawled by. Even as he grew used to the noises—and they became less and less frequent—his restlessness didn't cease. He lay back and folded his hands behind his head. He could hear Grixxler's contemptuous voice as though he, too, were calling from the darkness, whispering snippets of his mysterious instructions. "Stay away from the ocean—start a fire—the Wilderness."

Was this really a journey to deliver wool to the Royal Wool Spinner? Micah browsed through the events of the past week for any clue for what might be really happening. The only strange occurrence had been Grixxler's sudden and awkward instructions that morning after Ariel's rescue. Maybe Grixxler intended this as some sort of punishment for his mistake with Ariel.

He sat up, added another chunk of wood to the fire, and rolled onto his other side, catching a glimpse of the moon as his gaze raked across the sky. The shining orb hung a few shavings short of full; it had already begun to wane. He forced all speculation from his mind and struggled into a light slumber.

☙✦❧

The sun rose and Micah croaked with relief. He stretched away the long night and, as he recollected his grim thoughts, they seemed silly now. The hill around him lay empty—no creatures except for a couple woodpeckers hammering for bugs and a formation of geese flying overhead. He had let the darkness and the weird noises get to him.

He ran into nothing, man, beast, or other, until three days later. A farmer allowed him and his sheep to sleep in his barn, which spared Micah having to build a sheepfold or keep a fire going, and he looked forward to a night of uninterrupted rest.

As he checked Ariel for injuries that evening, he noticed a faint discoloration on her back left hip. He looked closer and rubbed his hand back and forth across the patch of wool, but nothing changed. He rubbed harder, faster, and crumbs fell from Ariel's skin. He plucked some out of her wool and examined them in his palm. Hard, waxy little flakes. Ariel had spots on her hip from which the flakes had dislodged.

"What did you do?" He ran his hand over the area again, harder this time. He even used his fingernails in some areas until it all came off. Then he scrutinized her hip once again. He parted the wool fibers and found a small black line, then he shifted the fibers to make out its shape—a bird perched upon a cloud with wings spread wide. He stared at the mark for several seconds, his heart thumping. He had no idea what it meant, but it couldn't be good news.

He held Ariel to still her fidgeting and wiped his hand over the mark, as if to wipe it from existence. But it remained, staring boldly up at him.

Ariel attempted to wriggle free, and he let her go. She bolted behind a nearby pile of hay.

"Reilly," he called, rubbing his hands together to rid them of the flakes. When Reilly arrived, he inspected her left hip first. Now that he knew what to look for he could make out bits of discolored white in her wool and on her skin. He went to work scraping off the coating. The same emblem materialized, emerging line by line. *So it's not a birthmark then.* Of course not. He would have noticed a birthmark long before now. He removed his hands and let Reilly run free.

Dozens of questions buzzed through Micah's mind: Who did it? When? How? Why? Someone could have snuck into the sheepfold during any of his brief dozes at night. But wouldn't he have been awakened by their presence? Why would that person then have covered it up with this waxy stuff?

One by one, he inspected each of his sheep, and every one bore the same ink design and white coating.

He sat hard on a pile of hay. He felt as though an invisible current tugged him toward some unseen end. Only a few days ago he had roamed the mountain valleys in peace. How had he ended up here?

Grixxler had told him there would be hitches, and that he should keep going. Surely Grixxler hadn't meant something like this. It seemed so much more than a hitch. Then again, this could have been the very event he had in mind when he had said not to turn back. The more Micah considered the idea, the more likely it seemed.

"No," he said to the still barn. "I'll keep going." Having made a decision gave him some comfort, but not nearly enough to allow for sleep.

CHAPTER 8

The Indifferent City

"We should reach New Serragin today," Micah told his sheep, echoing the farmer's words. It would be the first city they passed through on their journey. Part of him wished he could somehow stay out of the city, but part of him couldn't wait to see it.

As they traversed the rolling knolls, he reflected on his conversation with the farmer.

"It's a big, wooden city. You can't miss it. Although I would if I could." The farmer had added the last bit almost to himself.

"Why? What's wrong with it?"

"Nothing, I guess. It's just the Serragonians immigrated from the neighboring land of Serragin, and Serragin and Gable aren't getting along. They haven't since this whole conflict over James Kestrel and the Caelum Flute." He paused. "Just try to stay in the sunlight and out of corners."

"Couldn't I just walk around it?"

"No. New Serragin is the only bridge across the river gorge for miles and miles."

That hadn't made sense to Micah, but he had let the conversation end there.

He opened his map for the first time. When he unrolled it and held it up to the midday sun, he found a surprise waiting for him. The word "Treacherous" had been scrawled across his route in large, charcoaled letters.

Was this Grixxler's twisted idea of a joke? Or a reminder to heed his ominous warnings? Or both? Then a darker thought occurred to him. What if whoever had inked his sheep had also written this message as some sort of threat?

He immediately swung around, scanning the trees and bushes around him, as if a band of thieves would pop out at any moment. When none did he rebuked himself and turned back to the map. He'd made no enemies, and the only items he possessed worth stealing were his gold coin and his sheep. If a thief wanted those, they would have taken them by now, wouldn't they?

He looked past the large, black letters, and forced himself to focus on the map. As far as he could tell New Serragin wasn't far away. He rolled up the map, stashed it in his pack, and continued up the slope.

At the crest, the city of New Serragin rose into sight. It consisted of an enormous, wooden platform that seemed to hover over a river gorge. Seven equally spaced bridges offered access onto the platform. A waterfall spanning the width of the gorge tumbled down at the city's edge, falling into a series of spinning waterwheels. The wooden buildings stood tall and narrow, lining geometrical streets.

He hesitated. The other side seemed a long way off, the way filled with a bustling mass of people the farmer had warned him about. He followed the length of the river gorge with his gaze, but it disappeared out of sight with no other bridges to be seen.

Without wasting another moment, he clambered down the slope and connected with one of the dirt paths that fanned out from each of the bridges, upon which sparse clusters of people traveled. As he passed over the bridge, the two guards on either side stood like perfect statues. Two chains attached to the bridge led up to a tower, where a third guard sat. In case of an attack, Micah suspected, this guard would pull a lever to raise the bridge.

He paused to admire this contraption; nothing like it existed in the Heather Mountains.

He stepped up onto the bridge and entered the city with wide eyes. The constant tapping of his sheep's hooves accompanied the tapping of his crook.

The people, with their wraparound clothing, passed him by, stepping up to vendors' stalls and disappearing into shops. The knobby structure of their faces and the exotic braiding of their hair caught his attention. He had never seen people like this before. He found it difficult to catch a glance at their eyes. Almost none of them returned his gaze and those who did offered only a brief, sideways glance. In those brief glances, though, he discerned their eyes to be various shades of yellow. And they didn't look on him with kindness.

He quickened his pace.

Shops lined either side of the street. Lines of drying clothing crossed overhead, connecting the many stories of windows above the shops. Pigeons, ranging from dark gray to nearly white, rested on every quiet spot available—a shop awning, a cart roof, or an empty clothesline. White bird droppings lay splattered everywhere.

Everyone kept busy with something. Children played, fast-talking shop owners shouted advertisements for their wares, and blanket traders and merchants operating from carts crowded the street. Shirtless carpenters carried lumber and tools through the crowds, and the crowds parted for them. People surrounded waterwheel-powered grinding stones, throwing in wheat and carting out flour.

He continued past a line of children scrubbing the bird droppings off the ground. He kept constant watch over his sheep and a wary eye on anyone who came near. But everyone behaved as though he didn't exist; they offered little more acknowledgement of him than the guards rooted at the entrance. His sheep pressed against his heels as they followed.

The crowds thickened and the chatter rose the nearer he drew to the heart of the city—so different from the quiet of the mountains. As the crowd thickened, he felt the world around him tighten, press in on him. The faces multiplied, surrounding him. A pressure grew in his lungs. He turned for an escape but the Serragonians hemmed him in, bumping and shoving him on their way by. Their chatter roared in his ears. The pressure in his lungs tightened into panic. The sea of people pressed in on him, drowning him. He needed out. He needed out now.

He spun and scrabbled and crawled. His vision spiraled. *Deep breaths, Micah.* He fought back his panic, filtering out the chatter until it faded to a hum. He lowered his shoulder and ran, bouncing his way out of the crowd and into a side street.

His turning, twisting path delved into shade. The farmer's warning flashed through his mind, but he ignored it. Anything would be better than that mob. As he flew into the danker part of the city, the crowds thinned. He didn't stop until everyone had disappeared behind him. And then he leaned against a rotting wall, sucking in deep breaths of air as his sheep caught up to him.

In the quiet, his breath returned to normal and his heart calmed. After a few minutes of standing still, he glanced behind him and exhaled. No reason to be spooked by the crowds. He just needed to get used to them. He counted his sheep, turned, and walked back toward the main street.

A scream dragged his feet to a halt. "Help! Please help me!"

Micah stiffened. The cry echoed away.

"Help! Help!" The scream grew louder with each repetition. "Help!"

He tore off toward the screams, in the opposite direction of the main bridge. He turned right, then left, then right again. Deeper and deeper into the maze. When he didn't hear anything, he stopped, wondering if he had responded too late.

A flurry of sobs broke out, and he pounded in that direction.

"One last chance, Bart! Tell me the truth, or die."

"I don't know! I don't know! Please don't!" pleaded a hollow voice.

Micah slid to a stop around the corner. Before him lay a dim, dead-end alley, damp to the point that portions of the buildings had nearly rotted through. Propped against the far wall sat a plump man, dirty and tear stained. His hand clutched his chest as he shook with sobs. A man crouched over him, wiping his dagger with his black cloak.

"Help!" the victim screamed.

The black clad man raised his dagger.

"Get away f-from him." Micah tightened his grip on his crook. The attacker turned around, his dagger still poised for the strike. In a flash, he leapt away from his chubby victim and tackled Micah. They tumbled to the ground. The next moment, Micah looked into a set of swollen, glazed eyes—as if he was gazing into the eyes of a corpse. The sharp edge of a dagger pressed against his throat.

His attacker pushed back his long dark hair with his free hand, revealing two narrow streaks of silver. "Meddling in Marauder affairs was a terrible mistake," he said in a low tone.

Moisture from the water-logged wood beneath him seeped through Micah's clothing and soaked his back. His crook still lay clenched in his hand, he realized, so he struck upward. The Marauder kicked it out of his hands with a laugh and raised his dagger to the sky.

For a split second, Micah saw his own frightened eyes in the reflection of the blade.

His sheep bleated.

He looked into the hideous eyes of the man about to murder him.

The Marauder returned his gaze and froze. Nobody moved. Nobody breathed. His expression melted into that of a frightened child. He turned his head, as if attempting to break the gaze, but his eyes remained locked on Micah's. "You." His voice came in a hoarse whisper. His shaking hand dropped the dagger like a venomous spider. Micah winced as it sank into the wood with a fleshy thud, inches from his head.

The Marauder slowly backed himself into the opposite wall, shaking his head back and forth, his expression filled with terror. "No, it's you!" He tensed and whipped his head every which way then tore off toward the alleyway opening. He nearly tripped over Micah's sheep as he rounded the corner and disappeared.

Micah lay still for several thunderous heartbeats, shaking as his mind raced over the sequence of events that had just taken place. It took the tentative bleat of one of his sheep to nudge him back into reality. He sat up, waited there for several more minutes, rose to his feet, picked up his crook, and wobbled to the victim's aid, giving the black, leather-handled dagger a wide berth.

The victim sat in a heap against the wall, mumbling incoherently, his head lolled to the side. His chest bore a burgundy stain.

He's been stabbed. He needs help. Micah cast a glance behind him at the still empty alley. He heaved the man to his feet and supported him as they staggered out of the dead end, leaning on his crook.

The victim did little to support himself. His booted feet skipped along the ground, forcing Micah to use all of his strength to keep him up. As he inched toward what he guessed to be the direction of the main bridge, he called out repeatedly. "This man needs help." A messenger whizzed by, unhindered by his pleas. "He's injured," he pleaded to a carpenter strolling by. "Somebody get a doctor!"

The population thickened as Micah dragged the man further into the city.

Struggling under the weight of the wounded man, he bellowed until his throat ran dry. But everyone ignored him. He might as well have been selling dumplings on the street.

A cluster of women cast him shifty glances, and he caught their sympathy in the instants in which their eyes met. But they made no move to help.

"Somebody help." His voice dwindled to a croak as he sagged beneath the weight. He leaned the victim against the wall as the strength left his legs. Bart—the Marauder had called the man Bart.

"Bart, wake up." He snapped his fingers in front of Bart's face to no avail; Bart remained unconscious. He tugged Bart's shirt off with some difficulty, uncovering the stab wound. "Stay close," he said to his sheep. Grimacing, he leaned in and inspected the stab wound. From what he could see, the knife had only hit flesh, or at least that's what he hoped. The Serragonians traveled by without pause, curving their path around Micah and Bart.

Micah grabbed the bottom edge of his cloak and pulled, wondering as he did so if that old man who had given it to him would appreciate his nice cloak being ripped apart for bandaging. He smiled. This was exactly the kind of thing the old man would encourage. In a way, he was continuing the old man's legacy, forwarding the act of kindness from one stranger to another. He glanced behind him and several sets of yellow eyes immediately looked away.

Then something bounced off his head and landed on the ground— a bundle of bandages. He looked up, and although the shutters of a third story window hung open, he saw no one. He untied the bandages, pressed an assortment of them onto the wound, and wrapped the strip of cloth from his cloak around Bart's torso to secure it. He had to pull Bart away from the wall with each round in order to feed the strip around his back.

The end result, though far from neat, appeared to staunch the blood. Micah squeezed between two nearby horses and soaked Bart's shirt in a freshly filled water trough until the blood stain dissolved, wrung out the water, laid it out to dry, and took a seat next to Bart.

The lack of Bart's shirt revealed more fully the roundness of his belly. The bulge rose and contracted in steady, peaceful rhythm.

"And now we wait." He patted his sheep as he watched the interweaving stream of Serragonians flow through the street. It seemed hard to believe that he'd been frightened by being in the midst of that. Being nearly stabbed by a Marauder tended to put things into perspective. His pulse quickened at the thought. The fear springing to those eyes flashed through his mind over and over. Why had he screamed? Why had he run? Micah leaned back.

A lady on the fourth story leaned out her window and yanked on a clothes line, sending a string of pigeons flying. The sun shone bright and Bart's shirt soon dried. Micah flipped it over, and his heart plummeted. For on Bart's shirt—though sliced in half by the Marauder's dagger—a bird perched on a cloud with wings spread wide.

He couldn't believe it. He had found him. He had found the man who had marked his sheep. He sprang to his feet and held his crook with both hands, focusing on the round face that had crept into his sheepfold. Who knew what he would attempt when he woke? Then another thought struck him. What if the Marauder had planted that mark on Bart's shirt? He recoiled as the thought evolved into a monster; what if the Marauders marked their future victims with this bird and cloud before stabbing them?

"No, it's you!" The Marauder's voice echoed through his mind. The Marauder had recognized Micah. Perhaps he had stole into his sheepfold and marked his sheep. But then why had the Marauder been so afraid?

Bart let out a groan, sat up, and slapped his belly. His sunken, narrow-set eyes blinked away his drowsiness.

Micah tensed. "Is your name Bart?"

"Oh, hello there. Yeah, I'm Bart." He scratched his neatly trimmed mop of brown hair. The same hollow voice that had begged for mercy not an hour ago sounded cheerful now.

Micah hesitated, unsure how to proceed. This man could be

pretending to be amiable, waiting for his opportunity to catch Micah off guard. "The Marauder who attacked you ran away."

Bart stared at him with the kind of stare a rabbit would sport if it had been given directions to the nearest well.

"Don't you remember? He was wearing black and he stabbed you with a dagger."

"I usually try to stay away from Marauders."

Micah frowned, checked his sheep out of the corner of his eye, and lowered his crook into a more defensive position. This didn't feel right. He pointed to the white bandaged wound around Bart's chest. "That's where he stabbed you." Bart's gaze followed Micah's finger downward.

"Oh." His face darkened. He looked up again, and his mouth slowly opened into a smile. His features lit up. "You saved my life from the Marauder!" He hobbled to his feet. Micah backed away with his crook raised, but Bart overtook him and grabbed him in a skin-filled hug. After several uncomfortable moments, he let go and pumped Micah's hand. "What is the name that my rescuer likes to be called?"

"Uh—I'm Micah."

"He hurt me before you got there." Bart pointed to his chest.

Micah didn't know what to say.

"I cried for help and he saved me," Bart said, now to himself, nodding.

Micah lowered his crook. Such a bizarre series of events. He hoped the rest of Gable didn't turn out to be this strange. "Do you want your shirt?"

"Yeah." Bart laughed. "Most places I go, they tell me to put a shirt on."

Micah handed Bart his now dry shirt, and Bart proceeded to wrestle with it for nearly a minute. Finally, his hair appeared through the collar, and then his beaming face. His arms followed. Despite

Bart's largeness, the shirt hung loose. The hole danced around his belly and chest as he wriggled around.

"Uh, Bart, what does that mark mean?" He pointed to Bart's chest.

Bart reached down and folded the flaps of the rip inward, showing the bird and cloud. He stared at Micah.

"He knew." Bart's eyes widened.

"He knew what?"

Bart leaned back. "He told me he knew what my mark meant. He knew what I was. And he stabbed me."

"But what does it mean?"

Bart didn't say anything for several seconds. Just as Micah prepared to repeat the question, Bart addressed his feet. "I don't want to say." He continued in a lower voice, almost a mumble. "He knew, and he stabbed me."

"You don't have to worry. I'm not going to—"

"Sheep!" Bart kneeled down and spread his arms to Micah's sheep, which had been standing a short distance away for the entire conversation.

To Micah's great surprise, they ran into Bart's outstretched arms, bleating with an excitement almost equal to Bart's. He'd never seen them behave in such a way toward a stranger, or anyone other than himself for that matter. Bart certainly could have gotten close enough to the sheep to have marked them. But as Bart patted each one on the head, it seemed hard to believe that he would do anything to harm them, or anyone else for that matter.

Micah gauged the sun. He still needed to navigate the swirling crowds of the city and gather enough materials for a sheepfold and a fire.

"Well I need to go now, Bart. I'm glad you're safe and—"

"Where are you going?" Bart looked up from the sheep, still smiling.

"I'm going to the Gable Kingdom Cas—"

"Me too!" Bart pushed himself off the ground and enveloped Micah in another hug. "We can travel together!"

"I—" Micah hesitated. Of course he must refuse. But what would be the best way to explain that? "I think maybe—"

"We're going to the castle together!" Bart gushed to a passing Serragonian.

The Serragonian walked past without even glancing at Bart.

Bart strode into the masses. The sheep glanced back and forth between Micah and Bart. Micah sighed, shrugged, and followed.

CHAPTER 9

LAND OF THE BIRDS

Samuel Kamloop strolled through the grove of leaf and pine trees. The latticework of the leafy canopy above projected a sun-speckled pattern on the path before him. The smooth dirt warmed his feet. He meandered along the rippling stream as the path opened to a lush meadow—his own little nest—tucked away from the rest of the world. He sat upon the weathered chair facing the stream.

With a sigh, Samuel inhaled a breath full of summer air, soaking up the songs of the birds that surrounded him—bluebirds, chickadees, robins, meadowlarks, mockingbirds, and any number of others. Their mingled calls comprised the sound of peace itself.

Ahhh, the land of the birds. He sighed, stretched his arms back, and folded them behind his head, closing his eyes. He listened to the symphony, singling out each cry and pairing it with the bird in his mind. He opened his eyes.

What are they saying? How strange that he would never think of birdsong as communication. Did they really sing simply for the pleasure of people? Or maybe they enjoyed singing as much as he enjoyed hearing them. He decided he liked that idea the best, but still—

He focused on the robin's call for a few moments, then whistled. The sound came out feeble and broken; he missed the notes and lacked any range—nothing close to the fine, simple beauty of the robin's call. And it warranted no reaction from any of the robins hopping about the meadow.

A crisp robin's call sounded from behind him, rising above the others. He twisted around to see Gloria smiling as she made her way up the path with a platter of pastries. Her short, dark hair waved in the breeze. She held her apron and skirt up with one hand, revealing her bare feet as she climbed up the incline.

"How did you do that?" Samuel asked as she sat down on the armrest. He grabbed a pastry from her platter. Golden and puffy with a hint of white cheese sauce melting out the ends.

"It takes practice." She took one and placed the platter on the other armrest. "Though I must admit, most people do better than that on their first try." She giggled.

Samuel laughed, and he listened to the songs as they ate their pastries.

"These are delicious, Honey." He stared at the robin a few feet away, moving his lips but making no noise, imagining the pure sound coming from his own lips. He spoke in a slow voice. "Do they ever say anything back?"

Gloria frowned and looked over at him a little uncertainly. "Not—that I've heard of."

"Hmmm." He glanced at the robin, "What if it's possible? What if, with enough practice, I could converse with the birds?" He searched her eyes for some kind of support.

Gloria grinned. Her smile spread until she burst out laughing. A friendly laugh—it didn't sting too badly. But when Samuel didn't join her, her laughter trailed off. "You'd better get busy then."

"I'm going to start tomorrow."

"Then let's enjoy these last happy moments of our marriage." She giggled again as they watched the sunset.

୧ଠୠ

Samuel wandered from the meadow path onto a rutted strip of dirt with thatched roof houses and barns on either side, lit by moonlight. Chesterton.

Birdsong still rang in his ears as he trudged to his house and dumped his armful of papers, quills, and ink bottles before the door. He paused and took a deep breath before straightening again. As he reached for the door handle, he caught sight of his ink-stained hand. He turned both hands over before his eyes. More ink than skin.

He heard what sounded like a bird call. At first he paid it no heed, assuming it came from the chorus in his head. But then he realized he didn't recognize it. He concentrated his thoughts. He wasn't imagining it. No, the sounds were definitely real. His right hand twitched, eager for a quill. He scanned his surroundings. It didn't sound like an owl, but what other bird would be out this late? Whatever it was, it came from up the road. He took a couple steps in that direction then stopped. He knew why he didn't recognize it. It wasn't birdsong at all. It was the music wafting over from the Chesterton Inn.

The inn. He hadn't paid George a visit in ages. He glanced back toward his yet unopened house door. He wanted to slump into the warmth of his bed and fall asleep. But it really had been too long since he'd talked to George. He strolled back onto the road. Gloria would forgive him for a few more minutes.

The closer he got to the inn, the less the assortment of stringed instruments sounded like birdsong. As he walked in the open door of the two story building, the sounds of chatter and music, coupled with the smells of food and drink, made him wonder why he had waited so long to pay a visit. The smith's sons twanged away at their instruments from the far corner, animated as ever, and the round tables throughout the wooden room were nearly filled with patrons.

"Hey Sam, how yeh doing?" the owner called from the bar. He had wispy eyebrows and a pointed noggin that had just begun to reveal its bald spot, like a mountain peak poking through a ring of clouds.

"Hello George. What's new?"

"Well, everyone's astir about the dragons—on the edge of dyin' off. They say there're only a couple left now." George shrugged.

Samuel blinked and ground his knuckles into his eyes.

"Yeh look tired. What've yeh been up to? Haven't seen yeh in a few weeks now."

"I am tired. You see, I've got a new project."

"Oh?" George asked, keeping his eyes on the mug he was wiping.

"I've been studying birds and from what I've found there should be a way to talk to them. I've only been studying for a few months, but it looks promising."

George looked away, nodding. He glanced at Samuel then shifted his gaze to the mug. Samuel knew what that look meant. The music and chatter continued, but in the corner of the room occupied by George and Samuel, the atmosphere went stale.

"What is it?"

"Samuel," George said. "Sam, I think—I think you just need to do some honest work."

Samuel started.

"None of your projects have ever worked out and, well, they're just getting worse. Some of your ideas are reasonable—ah, now don't get defensive—it's just that, it's different now; you have a wife to take care of. Projects don't provide food in the winter."

Hot blood rushed to Samuel's face.

"I'm trying to help, Sam. It's just—talk with the birds?"

Samuel stood up, knocking over his stool, and stormed out of the inn. He should have just gone to bed. *So the villagers think I'm crazy?* Samuel laughed. He couldn't wait to see their faces the day he had accomplished something more amazing than they'd ever dreamed possible.

He snatched up his papers and ink, stomped over to a nearby tree stump, dipped his quill in the ink, and started writing.

ༀ

"That's good enough!" Gloria called, finding her husband, again, bent over his papers in his meadow chair. She stood on the path, just at the edge of the shade. She couldn't take much more of this. She tried being supportive, but—

"No." Samuel shook his head. "It isn't."

"Honey, I've never heard such beautiful bird calls. There's no room for improvement."

"But there is!" Samuel dropped his parchment, stood up, and turned to his wife. "See, look at those two robins. They're communicating; I know it! I can almost join in on the conversation."

The two robins at opposite ends of the meadow alternately foraged and twittered at random. Their behavior showed no connection. In fact, they didn't look as if they knew of each other's existence.

"We're going to run out of money. Your parents' inheritance is nearly gone. We won't survive another winter."

"My voice is just missing that subtle pitch. I can hear it now! It's just beyond my grasp. It's like—" Samuel looked around. "It's like when you look up at the night sky and see the stars. You reach your hand up," he stretched his arm for the sky yearningly, as if he could see the stars hovering at the tips of his fingers, "and you see your fingers close around those twinkling, white lights." He clenched his fist and brought it back down. "But when you open your hand—" he looked down, entranced by his open palm, "it's empty."

"You'll never be able to reach the stars, Samuel," Gloria said, more coldly than she'd intended. "No matter how hard you stretch."

All at once, Samuel's body went rigid. His eyes widened, his mouth fell open. Gloria gasped. She rushed forward, but stopped after only two steps when he spoke again. His voice came softly, as though hazed through the filter of several worlds. "Not with the naked mouth." He collapsed into his seat and scribbled madly at the parchment.

Gloria turned away to hide her pained expression.

"I need—a device—an instrument."

She cast one more backward glance. His pen danced and his voice faded into a mumble. Reluctantly, she turned and left.

ॐ

"Onward, men!" Haelus glanced backward from upon his horse. All eight horses galloped through the puddles and up the slope, scattering an array of bathing birds in their wake. The thieves' patched clothing billowed as they rode. They had hacked their beards short that morning with a few strokes of the rusted swords hanging at their belts, and they had more earrings than teeth among them—a fact made evident by their open, grinning mouths.

They arrived at a stone cave that looked as if it had sprung up from the grassy knolls of its own accord, like the back of a stone sea turtle floating in a sea of hills; no mountain or rocks existed anywhere near it. The sunlight revealed all but the last few feet of its shallow depths.

"Almost there!" Haelus shouted, raising a fist to the sky. A chorus of whoops and roars answered him.

He leaped to the ground from his trotting horse and rushed, stumbling, into the cave. Grohm and the rest of the thieves followed.

Inside the cave, they gathered around a small, shadowy chest at the very edge of the sunlight. The chest was made of dark wood, its corners lined with dusty brass. No one moved to touch it. It was enough, at least for the moment, just to stare at it.

"We've done it," Haelus cried. "We've found the Caelum Flute!" His voice echoed out the cave. The birds that had wandered back to their puddles fled once more.

"Perhaps we should open it," Grohm whispered, rubbing his spindly, wrinkled hands together. A murmur of agreement rose from the group.

Tentatively, Haelus reached down and produced a rusty key from the pocket next to his heart. He brandished it, then knelt down and jiggled the key into the lock until a satisfying click bounced off the cave walls, swimming in the bated silence. Everyone stirred.

"Good thing we didn't kill that old guy," Blither whispered. One of his front teeth hung half as long as the other, causing a lisp in his voice.

"Yeah." Sparns scratched a scab along his prickly chin line. "If we had, he would'a' never told us where the flute is."

"Or given us the key," Blither said.

Haelus eased the lid open. It creaked horribly, like a monster yawning away centuries of slumber. Inside, a blunt tube made of iron lay on a pile of white sand. Its nicked and blemished surface told a tale of long decades of use. Haelus lifted it above his head. A collective "ahhh" erupted from the group. He turned it over in his hands, his heart thumping. Thicker than a broom handle, and heavier than it looked, it had only two holes—one at each end.

"Maybe you should blow on it, Sir." Grohm's fingers twitched.

Haelus brought the flute to his lips, sand trickling to the stone floor as he did so. He inhaled a big draught of air, paused as long as he could, and let it loose. Only the sounds of whooshing air and the stutter of spittle came. He blew harder and harder, but still nothing came. His lungs deflated. Sand and spittle shot out the end. He blew until he had no air left, and then yanked it away from his mouth and sucked in great gasps.

"What kind of bird was that? I didn't recognize it." Blither stared out of the cave with a hand shading his brow. The birds still danced and hopped in the puddles, calling and frolicking, oblivious to the summons that had just sounded.

The band went silent. Their gap-filled grins leveled off.

"We've been riding for two days," Grohm said through gritted teeth.

"We went on a worthless trip," said another.

Everyone murmured in agreement.

Haelus choked on his breathing, but he couldn't respond until he caught his breath. Yet again his leadership had come under scrutiny. He realized now that the old man had fooled them. But it was much too late.

Grohm folded his arms. "You've led us astray too many times, Haelus."

"Yeah!" said another. "And the only treasure we've ever found was that old lady's box of earrings!" He pointed to the robin egg blue chandelier hanging from his ear. Several others nodded indignantly in agreement, their respective earrings of glossy pink pearls and heart-shaped rubies bobbing up and down as they did so.

Haelus shifted his gaze to each of his fellow thieves, searching for some sign of support. "M-maybe somebody got it before us and put a fake here."

"I'm tired of your excu—"

"Hey," Blither called over his shoulder from the end of the cave. "There's somebody out there."

The thieves turned. Haelus seized his last chance. "It was him!" he thundered with as much conviction as he could muster. "He must have stolen the flute and put a fake here! After him!" Only after the words had left his mouth did it occur to him to wonder if it was, in fact, a male that Blither had spotted.

Everyone charged except Grohm. They drew their swords and loosed roars worthy of a castle siege.

CHAPTER 10

FLÍGHT

Micah didn't know what to make of the mob of men charging toward them. He looked over his shoulder, half expecting to see a charge coming from the opposite direction. But the hills behind them lay empty. They could do nothing in the open expanse of grass, not with a flock of sheep. So they would have to wait and hope for the best. They stood there, the sheep bunched up around their knees.

"I think we are about to be attacked by crazy men." Bart rubbed his chin. As the thieves drew closer, and the wares on their ears came into focus, Bart added, "Or women."

The sheep started bleating and their cries grew louder the nearer the thieves got. Micah bade them be quiet. When the mob arrived their battle roar had faded to a low drone. They circled Micah, Bart, and the sheep, clutching their knees and gasping for air. When they regained some breath, they pointed their swords at Bart and Micah's faces.

"What do you want?" Micah drew his crook up beside him.

"Wait here—our leader's—coming."

So they waited, Micah's stomach in a knot.

A thin man arrived on horseback, followed by a more solidly built fellow with thinning orange hair. The bigger one looked around at the mob, opening and closing his mouth several times before saying, "Good work." He stood almost half a head taller than any of the others, more than a head taller than the skinny one. "I am Haelus. This is Grohm, my second in command."

"What do you want?" Micah asked again, one of the mob's blades inches from his nose.

"Give me the Caelum Flute."

"What?"

"You know what I'm talking about!"

"We're just taking these sheep to the Gable Kingdom."

"Liar! Give us your things."

Micah hesitated until a sword point prodded him in the back. He carefully removed his pack so as to not to stick himself on the surrounding swords and held it forward. One of the thieves lowered his sword, snatched the pack, and threw it to their leader. Haelus burrowed through the pack. He threw the last scrap of stale bread over his shoulder, and pocketed the coin, map, and half-filled water flask. Then he tossed the pack back.

"Alright, tell me where the flute is." His tone dropped, as if Micah and Bart had hidden it as part of a game and the time had come to be serious.

"We don't actually own a flute, you know," Bart said, his fists clenching and unclenching. "In fact, I don't even know how to play a flute very well. I tried once, but it screamed. It didn't like me." He widened his eyes and nodded his head.

Micah looked up the slope toward the thieves' horses grazing near the cave, forgotten.

"Last chance. Tell me where it's at or you'll both die, along with your sniveling sheep." He kicked Hannah. She bleated and squeezed her way into the center of the flock.

Micah looked around for a means of escape. These thieves were really going to kill them over some type of flute he'd never heard of before. Maybe if he could find a way to scatter the horses.

Haelus turned from them. "Fine then." He turned his back and walked away. "We'll hang them on that tree." He pointed to a stout oak—the only tree in sight apart from those occupying the woods bordering the grassland at the far end.

With a stinging prod in the back, Micah stumbled forward. He trained his eyes on the ground for something—anything—that could be used as a weapon.

And then he saw it. Not ten feet ahead, a palm-sized stone sat on the ground. As subtly as he could, he slowed his walk, waiting for the next prick of the sword as an excuse to fall down. Instead, he received a blow from the end of the sword handle. He didn't have to pretend; he stumbled to the ground. His rib cage hit the rock, sending a thud of pain up his side. He rolled over, groping for the stone, and shoved it into his pack. He hurried back to his feet.

"Hey," one thief said as soon as they reached the tree. "If we kill 'em, we won't know where the flute is."

"Yeah, we almost did that with the old guy," another said.

"Blither brings up a good point." Haelus looked at the second thief. "You too, Sparns." He glared at Micah. "I suggest they just tell us where the flute is."

As soon as Haelus directed his gaze away again, Micah glanced at each of his captors to make sure they weren't looking and delved his hand inside his pack, holding his crook against his side with his elbow. His fingers closed around the damp, smooth stone. It fit almost perfectly into his hand, a little oblong at one end, but it would work perfectly. If he could throw the stone into the cluster of horses—but they lay quite a distance away. *Can I throw that far?*

"Oy!" cried one of the thieves.

Micah froze. Guilt washed over him and his fingers stopped cold.

The thieves stopped just before they threw the length of rope with the hangman's noose over an overhanging branch.

"Look at his shirt."

Then Micah realized they weren't talking about him; everyone was staring at Bart's shirt.

"Hey," Haelus nodded toward the mark, his eyes wide, "if we kill you, is anybody gonna come lookin' for you? 'C-cause we don't want trouble." The thieves' swords hung limp, their gazes locked on the emblem on Bart's shirt.

A stiff wind materialized, misting over the scene like a tainted breath. The land felt somehow gloomier than it had only moments before, as if the breeze had brought with it some kind of invisible curse. The gray sky had darkened. The horses shifted around uneasily. One let out a whinny.

The puddles . . . What had happened to all the birds?

Everyone glanced around. But the wet hills lay empty.

"What's happening?" Grohm said.

As if in collaboration, the horses broke into a fit of whinnying, bucking around in circles toward the edge of the woods just as Micah's sheep erupted into a chorus of bleating, tightening their cluster around Bart and Micah's legs. One young stallion sped off in a mad gallop for the woods. Half of the thieves sprinted after the stray horse.

Micah bade his sheep be quiet but to no avail. Ariel stared up at him, the steady stream of her bleating mingling with all the other panicked noises. He knew that look—the same one she had given him in the cave, begging him for protection.

Bart moaned, wringing his hands.

Micah whirled around, searching for the source of so much commotion, his crook ready to strike at anything that moved.

The horses could have been dying for the noises they made when, all at once, they bolted after the young stallion, falling and tripping over each other in the stampede. The majority of the thieves ran as well, not toward the horses, but the nearest woods.

A shadow plummeted out of the sky. Before Micah could see it properly, the figure slammed into the ground, nothing but a red blur that resulted in a shower of dirt and sod. A tremor spread from the point of impact. Everyone froze. The wind died, and Micah's heart felt as if it had followed suit. Those who had tried to flee stopped and slowly turned around. Silence fell over everything.

For there stood before them a massive, winged beast, over twice the size of any of the thieves' horses. Its hind talons had submerged into the ground, and its front dragon claws rested out in front of it. A hybrid of feathers, fur, and scales covered its body. A proud, curved beak protruded from its dragon-shaped head. The creature's eyes flitted without pattern, suggesting a vicious attack at any given instant. It trapped Micah's gaze and held it.

Everyone watched in silence as the beast swung its massive head with sharp, sudden movements. It hunched down, tilted its head at the ground, and stabbed the dirt with its tongue, licking up something—the discarded piece of bread. It tilted its head and gave a call—a melody.

Micah relaxed. It could have been the tune of a shy bluebird.

Then the creature lifted its head and screeched into the sky. The noise pierced Micah's eardrums and shot goose bumps up his neck and down his arms.

A collective cringe swept over them.

"Half bird! Half dragon! Half bird! Half dragon!" Bart was squeezing the life out of his hands, his eyes as out of focus as those of the beast.

Micah felt like a mindless animal. He needed escape. Now. He had to leave. He had to find safety. But then he caught sight of Ariel, staring up at him, and regained his senses. He needed to protect his sheep.

"I can't believe it," Sparns whispered. His words wafted easily over the dead air. "It's the Aegre Bird."

The Aegre Bird spread its wings, revealing its enormous

wingspan, and images of the mark on his sheep and Bart's shirt came to Micah's mind. It leapt into the sky with one powerful sweep of its wings. The resulting tidal wave of air nearly bowled Micah over.

Before he could regain his balance, the monstrous beast slammed into the ground in front of him, causing an earthquake that knocked him the rest of the way over. As the bird snapped down to grab from the cluster of sheep, he whipped his crook up from where he lay on the ground, and hit the creature where its beak met its skull. The bird closed its eyes and shook its head.

"Run!" he roared, still lying on his back. The thieves tore for the cave. Taking advantage of the bird's momentary confusion, Micah stumbled to his feet. *We're dead.* With just a couple short steps, the Aegre Bird would overtake and kill them.

"Let's go!" he called to his sheep, urging them on with whacks of his crook a little less forceful than the one he had delivered to the Aegre Bird. Bart ran ahead, and the sheep followed. The group accelerated into a sprint.

We're dead.

The monstrous bird crouched and winged into the sky.

Micah nearly fell over with relief.

The bird soared over its prey, its long tail swerving back and forth like an enormous snake behind it.

Micah tossed a glance upward just as it tipped into a streaking dive for the sheep. "Bart! We aren't going to make it! Turn around!" He dashed to the front of the pack, and shooed the sheep backward. "Go for the oak tree!"

The Aegre Bird folded its wings, propelling straight toward them. "Hurry! Run!"

Spreading its wings, the Aegre Bird stretched out its talons.

Micah dove forward and plowed the last of his sheep under the oak tree just as the creature whipped past and climbed back into the sky. A second screech wrung the air.

It flew too fast. They'd never make it to the cave. "We'll just wait here." They huddled around the trunk, peering up through the protective branches to spot their stalker. But the branches had grown too thick to see anything. They could only sit and wait.

The thieves made it to the cave, and he could discern roughly the location of the Aegre Bird by following the thieves' skyward gazes.

"Oh no. Look at that!" Bart said. And Micah saw it.

The bird flew low, inches off the ground, and straight at them, with claws poised for slashing. He stood and faced the attack, clenching his crook in his hands.

With a final flap and a burst of speed, it careened into the tree. In a blur of confusion, Micah struck downward and felt his crook connect with something. The sharp talons whizzed by his head. A loud *crack* split the air. Something struck him in the chest and knocked him to the ground. He rose to his feet, gasping for air. Bart struggled to his feet, as well.

Micah turned around in search of the Aegre Bird and found the oak tree gone. Where the trunk had been, now nothing but a shattered stump stood. In the distance, the Aegre Bird dropped the tree from the sky. It turned end over end before crashing to the ground.

"Get going! Go!" Micah shooed his sheep away from the trunk. "Go for the cave!"

Now without any protection, he looked wildly around for their pursuer and spotted it circling high above them. He felt like a field mouse fleeing from a dogged hawk. *It's playing with us.* He started to chase after his sheep, but stopped as the noose lying on the ground caught his eye. He grabbed it, coiled it around his arm, and ran after his flock.

The group raced to the cave, with Bart in the lead, and reached its entrance before the Aegre Bird even began its dive. But the thieves collected near the entrance, barring the way in with swords drawn.

"What do yeh think yer doing? Find yer own shelter."

Micah considered shoving his way through but that would mean death as certainly as being slaughtered by the bird. He groaned.

High above, the Aegre Bird continued to circle a slow descent.

It didn't make any sense. What was it doing? Playing with them? Or— "Bart, stay right here! Go for the woods when I say!" Why hadn't he thought of this before? The cave made a perfect trap, a tomb in which the Aegre Bird was cornering them.

He prepared to sprint back toward the oak tree, but hesitated. He imagined the Aegre Bird's talons ripping through him, leaving his sheep without a protector. A tingle flashed through his torso. Maybe they could escape some other way. Possibly, they could—no, he had to draw its attention away from the cave to give them a chance to make it. He tore off toward the oak tree, out into the open, fighting off thoughts of the Aegre Bird's talons.

The Aegre Bird spilled into a dive, straight for him.

His lungs heaved as he slipped his way over and around the hills, leaping puddles and plodding through the mud.

The plummeting Aegre Bird shifted into a red blur.

Micah wouldn't make it to the tree. He had to make his stand out in the open. At the top of the hill, he stopped, lungs heaving. He stabbed his crook through a seam in his pack and strung the rope through the pack's shoulder strap. Then he stood at his full height, the length of rope with the noose in hand, staring up at the rapidly growing figure of the Aegre Bird.

He blinked as the creature hurtled toward him. He had to struggle to keep his eyes open, for in seconds it would hit him. He gathered as much air as his lungs would hold and let the loudest bellow he could muster rip through his vocal cords. "Now Bart!"

He threw his arms up against the Aegre Bird and braced himself for the collision.

Instead, the Aegre Bird snapped out its massive wings just before it struck him. It flapped rapidly, sending whirlwinds of air that hit Micah like boulders.

He rolled backward down the hill and splashed into a puddle. Mud filled his eyes, nose, and mouth. He pulled himself up and wiped a glob away from his eyes to find the Aegre Bird standing atop the hill, its head twisted toward his fleeing sheep.

No.

The Aegre Bird stretched its neck up to the sky and loosed another screech.

Micah clamped his hands over his ears, certain his ear drums had exploded.

The Aegre Bird crouched and spread its wings.

Scrambling to his feet, Micah grabbed the rope, and swung the noose after the bird just as it launched into the sky. He ducked as the swirling air from the bird's wake battered down on him. When the turbulence cleared, the rope whipped across the wet sod at his feet, wearing a channel into the earth, the noose somehow looped around the bird's talon. He grabbed the slack end of the rope and, while running alongside, wrapped it around his hands several times. As the incline of a hill came upon him and the slack came to an end, he planted his feet and yanked back hard.

But the bird streaked on unhindered, and Micah pitched forward. He hit the ground and kept going, sledding on the wet sod. He closed his eyes against the spray of muddy water. He dragged his feet and tried to find purchase on something, anything to slow the Aegre Bird down. Jolting along, he skidded in pursuit until, with a final bounce, the ground disappeared. The earth fell beneath him as the Aegre Bird winged into the sky.

For the first two seconds of flight, Micah flailed his arms in a desperate attempt to free himself. A tingling sensation engulfed his stomach and his legs dangled beneath him. He tightened his grip on the tangle of rope.

Bart and the sheep shrank into wiggling dots and then disappeared into the haze of his spiraling vision. A wave of nausea hit him. He gasped and looked away.

But he'd seen what he needed to; Bart and the sheep wouldn't make it to the safety of the forest before the Aegre Bird struck, not even close. In fact, the Aegre Bird was still playing with them.

Micah squinted up at Aegre Bird's whipping tail. Something flew into his face, blocking his vision. Then something hard cracked against the top of his skull—his pack, with the crook still attached and the stone still inside. He pulled himself forward and reached through the tangle of rope to grab the pack and pulled it away from his face.

The stone— If he could hit the bird with the stone, maybe he could—not kill it—but injure it, or at least alter its course enough to buy his sheep time to escape. He wriggled his right hand loose from the tangle. Immediately, he slid down the rope. Burning pain ripped at his palms. Images of the end of the rope sliding out of his hands, followed by his flailing drop through the sky, coursed through his mind. He wrestled and clawed at the rope, and managed to tangle his hands again, which stopped his slide.

The Aegre Bird leveled off with a final extension of its wings. Its gaze remained on the ground below.

Micah wondered how much rope he had left, but decided it was best not to look. He pulled himself forward and wrapped the rope around his left hand several times. Then he snaked his right hand free a second time.

Thwip! The rope cinched tight, treating his left hand to the burning pain again.

He reached into his pack and pulled out the stone. He had one stone, one throw. He pulled the stone to his hip and tensed the muscles in his arm.

The Aegre Bird veered into a sharp dive. The rope bit deeper into his hand. The world melted into a blur as the narrow figure of the Aegre Bird pulled him into a faster and faster dive with each flap of its wings. Above him, his sandals slapped the bottoms of his feet.

He bit his tongue, struggling to keep his eyes open. He ripped his arm forward, unleashing the stone in the direction of the Aegre Bird. Then he ducked his head to shield his eyes from the wind, and waited.

The Aegre Bird didn't waver from its dive. Nothing happened that would indicate that he'd hit the Aegre Bird, let alone affected its flight.

Somehow he'd have to inflict damage himself. He slid his right hand up the rope, grabbed, and tugged. Then he grabbed with his left hand. He grunted. He didn't have time for this. The Aegre Bird would be upon his sheep any second.

Below him, the Aegre Bird's wings burst outward and caught the wind like sails. It stretched its talons toward the cluster of sheep now yards away.

Micah shot forward, straight at the Aegre Bird. He hit its gyrating tail and held on tight. His momentum yanked him and the tail under the bird.

A sharp adjustment in flight. The Aegre Bird veered upward, its wing tips rocking back and forth. Micah's sheep whooshed by unharmed within an arm's length.

He clung to that whipping tail as the Aegre Bird reeled sideways and rolled into a spiral. His nausea flared up, threatening to explode.

The Aegre Bird struck the ground upside down in a tremendous shower of earth and sod. The crash ripped Micah from the tail. He flew forward until a sharp tug at his wrist stopped him and dumped him on the ground.

Blinking the dirt out of his eyes, he looked over in time to see

Bart and the sheep disappear into the woods. A jolt of elation surged through him, but he swallowed it and set to work untying the knots on his wrist.

The Aegre Bird stirred.

"Please, Father," Micah said as he clawed another stubborn knot loose. He shook off the rest of the rope, grabbed his pack and crook, and sprinted for the woods, casting glances over his shoulder all the while.

The bird twitched, rolled over, and climbed out of its furrow. It shook its head, dirt spraying in every direction. Its eyes latched onto Micah. It leapt back into flight, this time remaining low, streaking for him with nothing but a small buffer of air beneath it.

Micah pumped his legs harder. *Just past the next hill.*

The hollow reverberations of the bird's wings shattering the air grew louder with every second, but he didn't dare look back. He leaned forward.

A screech blasted past his ears, sounding from just behind him.

He dove into the brush and skidded between the trees. From his cover in the weeds, he gasped for air, dizzy with the notion that he'd actually survived. He'd done it. He had escaped the—

A slicing talon split the air over his head. The Aegre Bird hovered in mid-air with intermittent flaps of its massive wings, shredding through limbs, vegetation, and trunks.

He scrambled to his feet, slipped, and hit the ground chin first. He rolled over but the Aegre Bird lashed down and its talons ripped through the flesh of his shoulder.

He rolled again and kicked away from the Aegre Bird. Something grabbed him by the good shoulder and dragged him deeper into the brush. Bart pulled him to his feet, and they ran until they could barely see the Aegre Bird behind them. Micah collapsed amongst his sheep. He lay gasping for breath, waiting for his stomach to settle, his dizziness to disperse, and his heartbeat to calm. "I think—we're safe," he sputtered.

Bart nodded. "He needs to find dinner somewhere else."

A scream of fury rent the air. The Aegre Bird gave one last slash and propelled upward, curving back for the cave.

Micah counted the sheep but he knew they were all there.

"It looks like we don't have a map anymore," Bart said.

Micah surveyed the woods. Black, limbless trees—no sign of life anywhere. A milky fog carpeted their surroundings thickly enough to hide their feet. The vegetation that grew at the edge of the woods was nowhere to be seen here.

He thought back to the map, trying to spot the label that would say where they stood. But he couldn't see past those large, crude, black letters that spelled "TREACHEROUS" across his path. Grixxler had been right.

As if to confirm this thought, the Aegre Bird let out another, more distant scream.

"We're in the Marsh Woods." He scanned his mental image of the map further. They must be in the Wilderness. Or were they? While the words "Wilderness" and "Marsh Woods" read side by side, he couldn't tell if this meant the Marsh Woods were a part of the Wilderness, or if they just bordered each other.

Grixxler's stern warning rolled through his mind. He'd made it sound as if the Wilderness promised just as sure a death as the Aegre Bird.

Micah examined his foreboding surroundings. He couldn't imagine such a dismal place being anything but the Wilderness. Even so, they couldn't go back into the open with the Aegre Bird around. And they couldn't wait where they stood; they had to get as far from the thieves as possible. They'd have to continue south through the woods.

He gathered his crook and pack.

Bart pointed at Micah's left shoulder. "You've got a cut."

Micah glanced at his blood-drenched shoulder. He touched it and rubbed away the film of blood that collected on his fingertip.

He ripped off a chunk of wool from his cloak and pressed it into the blood spot. They didn't have any medical supplies that would help any further. It didn't hurt, though it did tingle a bit now that he thought about it.

"We have to leave now. If the Aegre Bird gets distracted, those thieves will be after us."

Bart frowned, but he didn't object, and the group headed southward into the forlorn, fog-ridden wood.

CHAPTER 11

THAT UNWORLDLY HOWL

Drift leaned against the back of his wooden chair, tossing his knife up in the air and catching the blade between his knotted fingers. He reared it back and hurled it at the wall of the wooden cabin. It sank with a thud, quivering as it sent a hum through the room. Drift grumbled something about Marauders.

Robbyn groaned from her perch upon the table. "Why aren't they moving?"

Drift rose lethargically to his feet, walked up to his now still knife, and tore it out of the wall. Blade-shaped holes covered the wall. Splinters of tattered wood littered the floor. "Maybe they're loading something, or unloading something."

"You're sure you can't tell what they're doing through the telescope?"

Drift shook his head. "At least we know they aren't in a hurry."

"They're on a schedule though." She sighed. "The longer we wait the more it feels like this plan is more complicated than we think."

For a while neither of them spoke. Then she realized she wasn't being a very good companion. "Well, I suppose there's no use complaining about it. I'm afraid it has taken little time in a boat to turn me into a salty old sailor." She smiled.

The corner of Drift's beard turned up into a grin.

"Do you travel often, Drift?"

Drift glanced down at his unusual garbs. "I live mostly from my boat, with some treks through the Wilderness here and there." He shrugged his massive shoulders.

"Your boat! *The Wooden Swan.* I forgot all about it. What happened to it?"

Drift looked down "I had to abandon her in the escape."

"I'm sorry."

"Nah." He waved the notion away. "She'll be fine." He leaned toward her. "Might sound crazy, but I think she knows these waters better than me." He averted his gaze to the window. "She'll find her way home. Always does."

"What brought you to the inn?"

"A few weeks ago I started tracking the Marauders."

Robbyn laughed. "You found them."

Again, the hint of a smile crept up beneath Drift's beard. He leaned back and wiggled the point of the dagger between his teeth. "You know, we *could* warn the king now."

She considered this. "People have predicted the Marauders will free James Kestrel at some point or another for years. And they've always been wrong. We've found the Marauders; we can't waste this opportunity. If they don't attack the castle we'll have lost them again."

Drift nodded and rose from his chair. He walked up to the hole in the wall.

Robbyn watched the seagulls dip and circle out in the fading evening sky in front of him.

"But if they go south—" Drift said.

"Then we have to assume they're headed for the castle. And we'll warn King Darius. Once he sees this weapon," she waved toward the iron object on the deck outside the hole in the wall, "he'll have to believe us."

Drift nodded slowly. "I'll check on the Marauders," he said with as much enthusiasm as a gravedigger, stashing his dagger in his belt. He grabbed the telescope and trudged out the cabin door.

Robbyn scooted off the table and stretched her arms. Darkness had nearly fallen. Soon Drift would be relying on moonlight. She walked over to the hole. The view looked identical to the one from the inn, and that's where she imagined herself as she watched the light give way.

Despite the gnawing fear of being discovered, the world had been blissfully simple during her days at the inn. With a start she realized that, although it had only been two days since the Marauders had burned the inn to the ground, it already seemed like a distant past—a whole separate chapter of her life.

As darkness blanketed the scene, she peered into it, reminded of one of the tales from the Story, about facing a dark valley. The visitors at the inn had loved to gossip about night time in Gable.

Robbyn hadn't left the inn at night since arriving there as a slave girl. What secrets did the darkness really hide? What dangers lay poised and ready for her to step out of the light? Shaking these thoughts away, she gazed up at the beautiful, shining stars and listened for the crickets' first chirps.

A curdling howl, as deep as anything she had ever heard, ripped through the night. A shock coursed over her, as though she'd been plunged in ice water. A shiver travelled up her spine. When it trailed off, she released the air frozen in her lungs.

The Beast.

She dove under the table, knocking the chair over. Her heart rate flared.

Heavy footsteps sounded from outside the cabin. She should have locked herself in the barracks; the table wouldn't keep the beast away.

The tingling silence that followed unsettled her as much as the howl itself. The heavy footsteps drew nearer. Maybe it was Drift. Or maybe the hole in the cabin wall would be too small for the beast to fit through.

Thuds hit the deck, and she exhaled. Those were Drift's boots.

Drift burst through the door and into the cabin. "Robbyn?"

Her breath came out in sharp, uneven gasps. "I'm down here."

"Nothing to fear." Drift pulled the chairs out and reached his hand under the table. "It's a long way off . . . yet."

She grabbed his callused hand and allowed him to help her to her feet. "W-what're they doing? Did they l-loose it?"

"Huh?"

She swallowed. "The Marauders. Did they let loose their beast?"

Drift tilted his head and frowned. He looked over his shoulder and mumbled something under his breath.

"What did you say?"

"Just wondering— You're sure the Marauders own it?"

"Yes. My dream—I mean my memory—I remember that howl. The Beast's cage was a floor above where they held the slaves. Sometimes it would howl all night long." She eyed the hole in the wall. "I hope it doesn't do that tonight."

"It doesn't matter. It can't harm you. Not tonight."

Robbyn gave him an inquiring look. "You know what it is, don't you? What can you tell me about it?"

He shook his head. "You don't want to know. It's bad. An' if the Marauders captured it, it's worse."

She tried to probe the shadows around Drift's face for clues. "Why would the Marauders release it now?"

Drift shrugged. "Maybe they're gonna pillage some villages."

Dread filled Robbyn's stomach, but then again— "I don't think so. That would be foolish; it would give away their location. But maybe—"

"What?"

"Maybe they're going to attack the castle from the ground as well."

A long silence ensued.

"As a distraction," she finished. "That would make sense."

Drift didn't respond, his face furrowed, and eventually she bade him a reluctant goodnight. As she descended the stairs, he pulled a chair in front of the hole, facing the seat toward the moonlight. He sat down, folded his arms, and bowed his head.

☙❧

The next morning, Robbyn climbed the stairs and stumbled into the cabin. Drift was staring out the window through the telescope at a horizon uncovering the first strands of light.

"Good morning, Drift." She grabbed some flatbread from the pantry.

As she nibbled on one of the corners, Drift tensed. "There's some movement."

Rushing to the hole, she squinted in the direction of Drift's telescope. The distant outline of a ship emerged from the edge of the trees. "It looks like they're headed south," she said.

Drift didn't take his eye from the telescope. "We need to prepare to set sail."

They rushed onto the deck to ready the boat. Robbyn stopped in her steps. This meant the Marauders were—without a doubt—going to attack the castle.

☙❧

Micah and Bart lay sprawled in the dazzling sunlight. A green meadow surrounded them and a clear, glistening stream trickled by. But the dreary edge of the Marsh Wood lay not far off. And Micah's sheep grazed throughout the meadow. The noises from the previous night floated through his head, and he shivered. He couldn't help but wonder what would have happened if they'd opted to spend the night inside the Marsh Wood itself. Or if the damp logs, now a pile of charred wood between him and Bart, had proven too wet to catch fire.

He squinted up at the sun. It looked to be not quite noon.

Bart sat up. Micah tried to follow but the aches in his body forced him back to the ground. A bulge had risen from his upper chest, where something had hit him during the skirmish with the bird. Blood still wet the patch of cloak clinging to his shoulder. He groaned. He should have washed it and bandaged it last night.

"Hello," Bart's voice said.

Micah started. He whipped his head in Bart's direction, but nobody new had entered the meadow.

Bart grinned at the blade of grass pinched between his thumb and forefinger. "You are a nice blade of grass. I can tell."

Micah frowned. "Are you all right, Bart?"

Bart nodded in Micah's direction without taking his eyes off the grass. "We're going to the Gable Kingdom Castle. Do you want to come?" He pocketed it and turned to Micah. "Well, we'd better go now." He rose to his feet and stretched his arms.

"Not today, Bart." Micah winced. "Today we'll just rest. I think we need it. I do, at least."

Bart looked northward, from where they'd come.

"I think we've lost them for now," Micah said. "The Aegre Bird should keep them penned in there. And I don't think they'll be too eager to follow us into the Marsh Woods."

Bart shrugged, plopped back down on the ground, and pulled out his grass blade to continue the conversation. "We can't go yet. We have to . . ."

With slow, painstaking movements, Micah pulled himself into a sitting position. His heart raced and his shoulder throbbed. He needed to clean it out soon—it might have already become infected. He pulled himself into a sitting position. "Hey, Bart, could you watch the sheep for awhile?"

"Yes, yes, yes. I'm good at watching sheep."

Micah scooted across the warm grass on his knees and right arm. The sound of trickling water made his throat burn. He reached the bank and sat. Too tired to remove his clothing, he slid down the bank on one hip and sank into the stream. It was deeper than he'd expected, almost up to his neck. The cold water stiffened his already treelike limbs.

At first, Micah thought the slow moving water would carry his rigid body downstream like a piece of driftwood. But he adjusted to the temperature and gained his mobility. He stripped his clothing off and wrung the mud out, scooping water into his wound intermittently. A trail of blood and murk swirled away downstream.

He hurled his clothing up onto the sun-soaked bank, ripped a hand-sized leaf from the edge of the water and pressed it into his shoulder. He closed his eyes and eased his head onto a tuft of grass. An image of the Aegre Bird flashed through his mind. The image came from when it had first spread its wings and resembled the design inked into Bart's shirt and Micah's sheep. Perhaps the symbol represented a band of Aegre Bird worshippers. But, no, that didn't make sense. Bart certainly hadn't worshipped it during their encounter.

When he climbed back up and over the hill, fully clothed, he found Bart sitting cross-legged before a bare patch of dirt. After counting the sheep's heads, he walked up behind his companion. Bart had a scrap of parchment on his knee. With his right hand, he drew patterns in the dirt with a twig, constantly checking back to the parchment for reference.

Micah looked over Bart's shoulder.

The parchment contained the alphabet. But Bart's symbols didn't look anything like the letters.

"Bart," he almost feared to break the man's concentration. "Do you know how to read?"

Bart stopped the twig halfway through a circle. Without looking up, he shook his head.

Micah sat beside him and crossed his legs in a similar fashion. "I think I can teach you."

Bart turned to look at him. His smile gradually widened and his eyes lit up. "Yes!" He leapt to his feet and danced in a clumsy fashion. "I'm gonna learn to write!" He swept Micah up in a tight hug. Micah's chest and shoulder protested. What had he gotten himself into?

Bart's dancing grew erratic as he teetered around on his legs.

"I mean I'll try," Micah said. But Bart didn't pause in his elation to heed Micah's words. He ran around to each of the sheep and told them the great news. Ariel hopped to her feet and pranced around with him.

Finally, Bart settled down beside Micah in his original spot, twig in hand, and pointed toward the dirt. Micah tried to remember how Grixxler had taught him to read, but it had been so long ago, and he'd been so young, that even his memory didn't recall.

"Well, it's—um—a bunch of letters. And you put them together to make words and—well, why don't we just start with the letters." He scanned his memory for an easy letter to start with. "This is an 'o'." Micah leaned forward and drew the letter "o" in the dirt with his finger. "It's easy. You just draw a circle."

Bart pulled the twig through the dirt, forming a lopsided "o," mouthing the letter's name as he did so. He leaned back and inspected his work, brimming with excitement.

"Good," Micah said.

Their lesson continued until Micah grew drowsy and drifted off to sleep. Bart's voice woke him later that evening. ". . . and these are the four drawbridges . . ."

Micah opened his eyes to a pink sky and raised his head. Bart still sat cross-legged on the same patch of dirt where he'd been earlier. Reilly stood beside him, chewing her cud and facing the opposite direction. A mound of mud sat before Bart. "And this, Reilly, girl, this is one of the water troughs. But the water in that one doesn't taste very good."

Micah rolled to his feet and walked over. As he drew closer, the mud pile came into focus—a sculpture of a castle.

"Look what I made." Bart threw a half-glance over his shoulder.

"Bart, that's—" Micah nearly fell over in amazement. "You made that?"

Bart nodded, beaming, for before him sat a clay model of a castle, roughly waist high. It had several towers, drawbridges, courtyards, and even clay people walking the grounds. Micah leaned closer. Dozens of tiny windows marked the towers, and even—Micah's eyes widened—every little stone of its construction was defined and perfectly symmetrical.

Micah surveyed the meadow for someone else that could have made the sculpture, but only his sheep occupied it.

"Made it all by myself." Bart ran his hands up and down his clay coated ankles.

"Is it the Gable Kingdom Castle?" Micah circled the masterpiece.

"Yep, there are four drawbridges, five courtyards, eight watchtowers, eleven fountains." He paused, and pointed to the third tallest tower. "That tower has one hundred and thirty-two rooms, and sixty-six windows. That's the king's throne—King Darius. That," Bart leaned over and pointed to the tallest tower, "is the dungeon. It has one hundred eighty-five cells, one thousand one hundred and sixteen steps, and a hundred and eighty-six windows." Micah leaned closer. Thin, tightly spaced bars blocked the windows of that tower. Four guards stood atop the dungeon, gazing outward in evenly spaced directions.

Bart pointed to the two sides of the castle without drawbridges. Where the castle ended, a cliff face continued downward, as though a part of the castle wall continued into the ocean, which Bart had delineated with very realistic looking waves of mud. "The castle is at the bottom of Gable. Past that there's only water, lots of water." He paused, and squinted around. Then he pointed to the edge of the Marsh Woods. "Probably all the way to that tree, even."

Micah continued to circle the sculpture, absorbing the details. "You've been to the castle often, Bart?" He half-laughed.

Bart nodded vigorously.

"So," Micah scratched his head. "Where's the King's Royal Wool Spinner?"

Bart frowned and crawled around the castle, peeking through the towers like an enormous sea monster. "She was there," he pointed to a window near the stables, "but she's gone now."

"Gone?"

"Yep, that means she left."

"But then who spins the wool?"

Bart shrugged and turned his attention to his blade of grass.

Micah decided not to pursue the subject further. Bart was probably mistaken. Yet the intricacy of the castle before him made a mistake seem unlikely.

Before the sun rose the next morning, he woke before Bart and the sheep and began work on a line for fishing. Keeping warm by the last glowing remnants of the fire, he unraveled a thread from his cloak, eating away the bottom edge until he had a good length. He braided it together for strength. As he worked, something wet and cold brushed his arm in the dim light. He jerked away, but before he could scramble backwards, Ariel's nose popped into his field of vision. She bleated softly, as if to let him know it was her. He lifted her into his lap, and allowed her to taste the thread, but he made sure she didn't chew on it.

As the sun broke over the horizon, he finished the line and started work on a hook. He used a sharp stone to shave and sharpen a curved twig, and before the sun had cleared the horizon he was ready to go fishing. Ariel followed him to the stream. He took every step with care, on the lookout for bait. When he reached the stream and hadn't found anything, he sank his arm into the water and fished out several brown caddis from beneath the river rocks.

He tied these to his hook and threw it out, keeping the other end of the line wrapped tight around his fist. The hook drifted downstream just below the surface. When it reached the end of the drift and his line stretched taut from the current, he pulled it back in, hand over hand, and threw it back out again, scanning the water for any fish. But the water, shaded from the sun by several hills, proved too dark to see into. The bait drifted through again without any fish. He hauled in and threw out again, willing the sun to rise over the hills and warm him.

As he repeated these steps, he tried to clear his mind, but what Bart had said about the wool spinner still bothered him. Something mysterious was going on, and that fact gnawed at him. He sighed and cast out for the eighth time.

Ariel nibbled on the nearby grass as the sun peeked over the hill-tops. The warmth wafted over him and he relaxed. As the sun inched higher, the water's depths became visible. Squinting through the rays, he spotted a fish treading water in the current just upstream. So he took a few steps in that direction and threw out again. The hook landed a few feet past the fish. His prey struck the hook ferociously, and he hauled it in.

Ariel backed away from the strange creature as it flopped and writhed its way up the bank. Micah carried it back to the sheepfold, eager to silence the hunger that the sight of a fish had flared up in his stomach.

At camp, Bart had awakened, along with the rest of the sheep. "Fish!"

Micah built the fire back up and cooked the fish at the end of a sharpened twig. Both he and Bart devoured it until hardly a scrap of meat adorned the skeleton. They stamped out the fire and walked upstream to allow the sheep and themselves to drink from a still pool.

The group continued their journey south, the sheep grazing on the brush at the edge of the Marsh Woods as they went.

Around noon, the silhouette of a human rose up out of the distant hills. As it drew nearer, a flock of white sheep materialized behind it.

"Hello," a boyish voice called. The silhouette waved.

Micah waved back out of courtesy, but a stranger wasn't exactly welcome. He didn't think he could stomach more trouble.

The shepherd walked down the last hill toward them, his two dozen sheep trailing behind. He was young—younger than Micah. His boyish face betrayed that fact, but his crook fit him perfectly. About a third of his sheep had been freshly sheared.

"Hello," he said again, his voice as boyish as his face. Micah relaxed at his apparent innocence.

"Hello." Bart grinned.

"I'm Sandy, where yah headed?"

"I'm Micah, and this is Bart. We're headed for the Gable Kingdom Castle."

Sandy let out a low whistle—strikingly perfect and song-like, leaving no doubt as to how he passed the long hours of shepherding. "I've never been there before. It's quite a long ways away."

"Where are you going?" Micah asked.

"Oh, I'm just grazing my sheep. These are the pastures I hang around. Tomorrow maybe I'll head west toward the ocean and try and sell wool to travelers on the path."

"Is Fidell nearby?"

"Oh yes, you're quite close. I live there. But just to warn you, don't try and sell any wool there, the other shepherds might get mad, and they like to talk with their fists." Sandy rubbed his neck and looked away.

"Thanks, but it shouldn't be a problem. We're being chased by a band of thieves, so watch out for them."

"Oh yeah, I know them. They hang around Fidell sometimes. It was just last week that they stole Old Man Charlie's eggs. They were going to kill him, but he lied to them and told them he knew where the Caelum Flute was." Sandy giggled.

Micah frowned. He asked the question he wished he'd asked long before then. "What exactly is the Caelum Flute?"

Sandy gasped. "You really don't know? I thought everyone knew." He paused for a few moments, as if to come to grips with this new fact. "It's an ancient flute that has the power to communicate with birds. That's what Old Man Charlie says, anyway."

Micah forced a smile. A magic flute? Maybe Sandy was even younger than he looked. "Thank you—very much, Sandy." As Micah prepared to say farewell, though, a thought struck him.

"Hey," he beckoned to him as he knelt beside Hannah, "do you know anything about this mark?" He parted the wool on her left leg, revealing the bird perched atop the cloud bit by bit.

Sandy scrutinized it for several seconds. He rubbed dirt from the mark away with his fingers. "Well, I've never seen that mark before. Did you steal this sheep?" His voice shook.

"What? What do you mean? Of course I didn't steal her!"

"Then how come you don't know whose mark that is?"

"*Whose* mark?"

"Well yeah." He wrung the crook with his fingers. "You really aren't from around here, are you?" He sighed. "Every sheep owner inks his mark into the hind left hip; at least, that's how they do it here. I'm not sure about everywhere else because I've never been past Serragin or into the Gable Kingdom."

Sandy dragged one of his own sheep over, one of the full-coated ones, and displayed her left leg. "See?"

A black circle had been inked there, with short lines extending from it. It came to roughly the same size as the design on Micah's sheep, though a bit more blurred. What most interested Micah about the emblem, however, was the fact that the wool that otherwise would have covered it had been shaved

"It's a sun, don't you see? And it has seventeen lines around it.

I'm the only shepherd with sheep marked with a sun with seventeen lines."

Micah rubbed his chin. It still didn't make sense that these tattoos had appeared on his sheep with some kind of white wax to hide them.

"But seriously," Sandy continued, "don't go around asking people what mark that is. That's quite stupid. They'll know—I mean think—you stole that sheep from some sleeping shepherd."

"But you don't know whose mark it is?" Micah asked.

"No, but that guy over there has it on his shirt, except it has a hole in it. Maybe you should ask him."

"I've already asked."

"Oh, I—" Sandy trailed off. "Is he stupid or something?"

Bart was greeting all of Sandy's sheep, introducing them to his blade of grass.

"He's fine." Micah gave a distracted wave, still mulling over what Sandy had said about the marks. Had another shepherd marked his sheep with the intent to claim them later? Why would they do that? It would have been easier to just grab the sheep and run. Then again, his sheep would have protested either way, which would have awakened him.

"So what happens if some shepherd comes up to me and says I stole his sheep?" Micah asked.

"Then you have to give them to him."

"But what if I don't want to?"

"You'd go to prison for stealing. Seriously, it's not worth fighting over a bunch of dumb sheep. They're just a hassle to deal with anyway. They're dirty, and stupid, and ungrateful." Sandy swung a wayward kick at one of his own sheep as if to prove his point. "If it wasn't for their wool they'd be useless. Trust me, I've been a shepherd my whole life."

A tinge of anger flared up inside Micah. "Don't treat your sheep that way." He tried to keep his voice calm.

"What way? You mean don't kick them?" Sandy snorted. "Whatever you say." He shrugged, bent down, and inspected Jordan's coat.

"But seriously, *your* sheep are kind of nice, as far as sheep go . . . I'll buy one from you."

"No!" Micah took a step back at Sandy's audacity.

"Aw, loosen up. I'll buy that little lamb over there. She looks kinda sick anyway."

"No," Micah said more firmly. "I won't sell any of my sheep to you."

Sandy shrugged again. "I can give you quite a bit of money; I've been saving."

"I don't care." The entire idea made Micah queasy.

"They're not for sale," Bart told Sandy, looking up for a moment.

"Well, okay, if that's what you want. But there was no harm trying, right?"

Micah didn't answer. He wanted to end this conversation. "You've been a great help, Sandy. Thanks for stopping."

"Yeah well, you come to me first if you ever want to sell one of your sheep."

"Sorry, it's not going to happen."

After shaking hands they headed in opposite directions and for a second the two groups of sheep diverged and mingled, but with haste they separated in pursuit of their respective shepherds. Micah counted his sheep just to be sure.

A couple of hours later, Fidell rose into sight. Unlike New Serragin, where the walls of the city had been clear-cut and containing, here the houses of various sizes and conditions popped up and grew in density until they lined either side of the pathway headed straight for the city gate.

He took a deep breath as they walked along. Maybe they should have plotted a course around the city. He shook his head. *It's just some crowds. You'll be fine.*

The guards nodded them forward without question, and they passed through the arches. Inside of the city's stone walls, buildings of different heights and materials lined the streets, and people were heading everywhere. The misaligning streets, to his comfort, reminded him of the village of Sampter from back home. Cracked cobblestone with dirt-filled gaps met his feet.

They wandered through the crowds.

You're fine. Doing good.

The crowds condensed, and with it pressure grew on his lungs. He fought the fear with deeper breaths.

People passed through and among his sheep, and he whirled around and around, afraid that someone would snatch one up at any moment. The swirling commotion slowed his thoughts. He stopped walking and pressed his hands to his ears to block out the chatter. A sign perched over a doorway, hanging into the street. Ted's Tavern.

"Let's go in there!" He hadn't intended to say it aloud.

Bart scowled. "Where's there?"

"The tavern. Let's—just, let's eat some real food."

He rushed his sheep into a nearby stable, upon which a sign reading "Public Stable" had been nailed to the eave. Even the relative quiet of the stable calmed him considerably. The sounds of the animals and the smell of manure didn't bother him. And then he realized that he had no money for food. Maybe the owner would allow them to wash some dishes for food.

He closed his sheep inside an empty and somewhat clean pen. "I'll be back soon." He glanced over his shoulder from a few steps away, expecting at least a few of them to bleat. But they remained calm. Perhaps this stable reminded them enough of the stable back home that they did not feel abandoned.

When they reached the street, he glanced back again, but they still appeared to be fine. The stable had guards, so no one would steal them. They should be fine for a few minutes.

Bart and Micah crossed the street and entered the dimly lit tavern. The sound from the streets immediately softened. Dirty white candles were glued to each table by wax droplets streaming down their sides, but their flickering flames did little to permeate the smoky darkness. A few men smoked pipes in corners, and a quiet conversation took place at the edge of the room. He didn't see a bartender anywhere.

"Let's sit down," he whispered to Bart as he sat at a table adjacent to the conversation, easing the wooden chair out to avoid disrupting the atmosphere.

Bart didn't follow his example; he dragged his chair and the worn wood scraped across the stone floor, an abrasive screech filling the room. People glared in their direction and Micah winced.

Bart sat in his chair, wiggled around for a comfortable position, and endured a brief moment of silence. "That's a loud chair," he informed the room. His voice bounced off every corner.

Micah placed a hand on his forehead. He considered apologizing, but thought better of it. Besides, the three people in the next table hadn't even noticed, they were so deep in conversation.

"I just can't get over it." A man with hair like a horse's mane shook his head. "We have no idea how lucky we are. I mean, he had it in his *hands*. He'd learned how to use it. Just imagine if King Darius hadn't captured him."

"Yeah, well it ain't over. Don't you forget, he ain't been hanged yet."

"It is too over. I've bet my fortune on it. The Marauders are crafty, sneaky little devils. But they're not going to break him out of a dungeon like that."

"Y'whole fortune? Y'mean all of two silvers then?" He laughed. "Tha's good. Won't sting too bad when yeh lose it all. I heard a rumor—" The smaller man put his bandaged fist to his mouth and hacked and wheezed. He took a breath. " . . . 'bout a man who *did* escape."

The horse-maned man grinned. "You're not talking about that pirate cook, are you?"

"I—n'er heard the details."

"It was an act of God that he tasted a single breath of fresh air. Two guards were struck by sudden death the moment they opened his door to see if he had died. He ran up the stairs to the top of the tower. If two more guards hadn't missed their shift, they would have caught him long before he made it to the top. He leaped off the tower out into the sea." The man whacked the table top with the palm of his hand. The sound of his hand hitting the table jolted the table's third resident from sleep. The mugs hopped from the impact. "The sea is harder than a rock when you jump from that high."

"Ah, but see? He escaped jus' th' same. Kestrel would o' gone down."

"Where there are four times as many guards? Besides, the Castle doubled the security after that. Once that cell door shuts, it won't open for anyone or anything. Not until the criminal is long dead."

"What are you two harping about? Kestrel?" The third man said in a raspy voice, still blinking. He cleared his throat and spoke in a clearer tone. "I have some information."

The other two glanced at him.

"Wh' kind?"

"You know, about Kestrel—the flute."

"I'm not spending another coin on scams like this, so you can forget about it."

"Just listen—I don't claim to know where he buried the flute. If I did I'd have dug it up already." He paused. "But I *do* know where they captured him."

The other two men leaned in.

"Of course," he went on, "it makes sense that he'd have buried it close by. Maybe he saw the King's Guard coming and buried it in a hurry."

"Not for sure though. It could be twenty feet down in the middle of the Garan Desert for all we know."

"Fine, you go ahead and try there. I was just wondering if you men would be interested in helping me dig the *most likely* place."

A deep, hearty laugh bellowed from the shadows at the far end of the room. A broad shouldered man with shoulder length blond hair emerged.

"Westock." The three men spoke almost at the same time. Each of them straightened in their chair.

"Don't listen to this gull brain." Westock swaggered up to their table. "He's just trying to steal your money." He spoke loud enough for everyone in the room to hear, his hands firmly on the table's edge.

The man trying to scam the other two kept his eyes on his lap, his face red. "Sorry, Westock."

"Besides," Westock continued, "if anyone should know where Kestrel was captured it's me." He paced in front of them, his head high and chest puffed out. A twinkle appeared in his eye. "I did, after all, single-handedly catch James Kestrel."

Two of the men jerked their heads back in surprise. The third's mouth fell open.

"Why dinchya kill him?" one blurted then looked down.

"King's orders," Westock didn't miss a beat as he inspected his fingernails. "Our good king knew that he might be able to discover the whereabouts of the flute if Kestrel was questioned."

"Did he say anything?"

Westock shot them a contemptuous glare. "Of course not." He paused. A dazzling white smile flashed across his face. "He didn't need to. His eyes told me everything."

Bart leaned toward Micah. "Uh-oh," he said in a loud, raspy whisper. "He's *ly-ing*."

At first Micah assumed he hadn't heard Bart correctly. Then Westock stiffened and slowly turned around.

"What did you say?"

"You're lying." Bart shook his head then dismissed him with the wave of his hand.

Micah couldn't find words.

"Who is this impudent fool?" Westock roared, knocking aside chairs as he flew up to the table, leaned across it, and glowered down at Bart.

"Oh, I'm Bart," Bart told the face inches from his own, as though introducing himself at a feast.

Micah groaned inwardly.

A man, presumably Ted, appeared behind the bar at the far end of the room. He bore a potbelly and wore a dirty apron. His crossed eyes and unsteady walk looked ready to fail him at any moment.

"I think," he hiccupped, "we're out of ale." He collapsed in a heap.

Westock ignored him, reached across the table, and put a muscled hand around Bart's collar. Micah pulled his crook from under the table.

"Leave him alone. He doesn't mean you any harm," Micah suspected he was about to get a few more bruises.

Westock grinned. "What's this, a little shepherd boy? Are you going to beat me to death with your stick or command your sheep to trample me?" His mocking laughter filled the room, and the three men behind him laughed nervously.

Ted snored.

"Take your hand off him and we'll just leave." Micah rose to his feet. Bart stared down at the hand clutching his shirt as if it were an enormous spider ready to pounce on his face at any moment.

"Oh no. Not today, little shepherd boy. Nobody gets away with insulting Westock. Your fat friend is going to have to pay. And if you try to interfere, you will too." With his other hand, Westock reached toward his belt and unsheathed a long, glistening sword. A metallic ring sang out and faded into complete silence. "Either you leave him to his punishment or stay here and die."

Micah didn't move.

Westock scoffed. "You're going to die for some fool's mistake?"

Micah tensed himself, but he noticed the sharp edge of Westock's sword. How would his sheep fare, stuck in the stable in the middle of a strange town, if he died? Probably as roast mutton.

Help! Bart's wailing voice from New Serragin rippled through his mind. The image of the man clutching his stabbed chest spurred Micah to action.

Out of the corner of his eye, he saw that Bart had pulled his chair out way too far and was clear from the table. Without giving it another thought, Micah dropped his crook and thrust up on the end of the table as hard as he could. It flipped easier than he'd expected and bowled into Westock. Westock lost his grip on Bart's shirt as the table knocked him backward and flattened him into the jumble of chairs and tables.

"Go! Go!" Micah grabbed his crook off the floor and yanked Bart toward the door. He didn't want to think about how angry Westock would be now.

"Loud chairs!" Bart called back to the tavern as they exited. The two raced into traffic, heading toward the gate from which they'd come. A horse drawn cart turned sharply and almost flipped over as it avoided the two runaways.

Micah had no idea where he was going. He shot a backward glance to see Westock emerge from the tavern, his sword glinting and face so red it looked like it was on fire.

"You're dead!" Westock screamed.

With Bart hobbling close behind as fast as his bobbing belly would allow, Micah swerved into a side street, then another, and another. His plan, he told himself, comprised of getting as lost as possible in the maze of streets and alleyways. Weaving through people and wagons, winding their way through the crooked streets, they fled with Westock always close behind. Stone and wood buildings blurred by, and Micah couldn't help but worry how they would ever find their way back to his sheep.

He drew to a stop and Bart slammed into his back. Micah had to lean back in order to keep from running into a lady walking with her children. "Excuse us," he called back as they zipped by. They sped around the corner, but stopped short at a dead end. Micah whirled around just as Westock appeared, blocking their only escape.

"Stop this instant. You're making it worse for yourselves!"

Micah glanced around the nearby buildings and spotted a single, shabby black door in the stone wall to his right. Heavy rot bulged out from its peeling paint. He yanked on the handle. The hinges popped loose, and the door collapsed inward. With no time to scrutinize the darkness within, he charged inside, Bart right behind him.

The door squished beneath his feet as he ran through the thresh-old. They dashed through a room holding large shelves on either side lined with barrels. The dank dimness left everything barely visible. Micah leaped over a snoring body sprawled on the floor. It wasn't until mid-flight that he recognized Ted, who was still asleep.

They had somehow come right back into the tavern.

Bart stumbled on poor Ted's unprotected gut. Ted jolted, cough-ing and spluttering.

A backward glance revealed Westock dashing after them, though he stepped on a cork just visible at the edge of the door's sunlight and nearly lost his balance.

Micah and Bart climbed over the bar and dashed through the room, ignoring the three dumbfounded men staring at them as they ran by. Bart grinned and waved.

The two raced out the open doorway. A slurred complaint bel-lowed from the tavern as the cooler outdoor air washed over Micah. "Blimey, someone stole all my ale. These was plumb full!"

Micah glanced over his shoulder. Westock waved his sword in great arcs, as though carving an enormous fish on the run. Then a bouncing, tilting wagon attached to two thundering horses came between him and Westock. The driver whipped the horses while his wife clutched her seat, her face white. The wagon was coming up from behind them.

"Bart, jump on that wagon!" It jounced up beside Bart's right side. Bart squeezed his eyes shut and jumped, somehow managing to grab onto the wooden railing in the back, and hung there. Micah veered over and grabbed onto the ledge beside Bart before the wagon got away. He pushed up on Bart with his free hand until he was over the railing. Bart hit the wooden deck on the other side with a thud.

Micah glanced back to make sure Westock had seen them board the wagon. His crestfallen expression could be discerned even from a distance. Bart scrambled to his feet and pulled Micah over the rail. Micah hit the deck in the same manner that Bart had. As soon as Micah was over, Bart settled into a cross-legged sitting position and looked ahead to the approaching gate.

Micah pulled him back to his feet. "We're not done yet," he yelled over the din of the city. "We can't leave the sheep, and we're headed in the wrong direction." He checked back to see Westock's dot of a face swallowed by shifting traffic.

"Now!" He raced under the canopy to the front of the cart, and stepped on the bench between the man and his wife. She gasped and latched her fingers to her wooden seat, staring straight ahead. The man hazarded a glance from the road ahead and then back again, as if trying to decide if he was going too fast to fit in a couple punches without causing a disastrous wreck.

Micah clambered down to the leading edge of the wagon, the horses' legs churning up dust beneath him. The wagon jostled and he nearly fell face first into the road. He beckoned to Bart, who groaned then climbed after him, bobbing pardons on his way down.

The wife swooned at the sight of Bart. Her eyes fluttered and she started to lean over. Then her eyes regained their light and her hands regained their grip on her seat. She clenched her jaw.

Bart sidled up beside Micah as they watched the blur-stained wagons, people, and buildings fly by. Micah glanced at the wagon's course. The city gate approached quickly, where traffic flowed freely in and out. He checked behind them to make sure Westock couldn't see them, but he was nowhere in sight. He looked forward again. A slow moving, uncovered wagon rolled along in the opposite direction. It held a pile of hay in the back.

Micah pointed to it and made sure Bart understood. Bart nodded and tensed. "Now!" Micah felt he was a split second late even as he said it. He closed his eyes and jumped, feeling Bart jump beside him. Then, before he knew it, he hit hay—scratchy, and smelling of horse droppings, but it cushioned his fall. A rustling sound signaled Bart's landing beside him.

The bouncing and pitching wagon they'd jumped from raced through the city gate. His new ride headed back for the heart of the city. A tall, elderly man held the reins and a grizzled llama pulled it, hanging its head as if half-asleep.

Bart wiggled through the hay to Micah. "She was a nice lady."

Micah smiled, suppressing a laugh so the cart driver wouldn't notice them. He put a finger to his lips and crouched beneath the railing, signaling Bart to follow. From there he kept a watch out for Westock. As he looked between the driver's feet, he spotted him standing in the middle of the street, his sword hanging limp. He was staring toward the city gate, mumbling. As the cart rolled closer, Micah held his breath; Westock stood a foot away, on the other side of the solid railing.

". . . but they'll be back. And when they do," the whirring of metal through air interrupted his monologue, "I'll be—"

Had Westock stopped speaking? Micah strained to listen, praying they hadn't been detected.

"Carl," Westock said. To Micah's horror, the cart eased to a halt.

Their cart driver gave a nervous wave. "H-hello Westock."

"Do you have something for me?"

"N-no, sorry, but it's coming. I'll have your gold next time, for sure."

"Hmmm, maybe you have something with you I'll accept as payment."

No! Micah thought. *Please don't look.*

"Uh, no, I've got nothing with me."

"I know you too well, Carl. Let me see what's underneath this hay."

Micah's gut gave an involuntary wrench. He hauled Bart up, climbed over the haystack and leaped from the wagon onto the street on the other side. "Run!"

"Traitor," Westock growled at Carl before launching after the two, ignoring Carl's pleas of innocence.

Micah and Bart dodged into the nearest alleyway. But when Micah careened around the corner, his feet skidded to a halt. Bart bumped into him from behind.

Haelus sat before them upon his gray steed, his group of mounted thieves behind him.

It can't be!

"There they are!" Haelus cried, his face a picture of incredulous joy. He drew his sword. "After them!"

Grohm's groan could be heard even above the singing swords and roars of enthusiasm.

Micah whirled around and grabbed Bart by the arm, but Westock appeared, blocking their escape. The walls of this alleyway, hodge-podges of wood and stone, had no doors. They were trapped. Bart and Micah stood, helpless, as the thieves surrounded them, swords pointing.

"What's going on, here?" Westock lunged forward with his sword outstretched. "These are mine!"

"They know where the C—" Sparns managed to say before Haelus kicked him hard in the shin, buckling him to the ground.

"Ow!" His sword clanged to the cobblestone as he grabbed his leg with both hands.

"You're outnumbered eight to one." Haelus glanced from his men to Westock.

"Maybe, but a bounty hunter is worth at least ten men, and I'm no ordinary bounty hunter."

"Who are you, then?"

Westock puffed out his chest. His voice deepened an octave. "I am Westock, mightiest of the bounty hunters, and if you thieves don't scram you'll share the same fate as these gulls."

Micah scanned the alleyway, searching for some means of escape. The thieves holding him at sword point glanced back and forth from Micah and Bart to the bounty hunter, but they weren't distracted enough to warrant a break for freedom. Micah surveyed the thieves. Who was the weakest? Maybe if he charged in just the right way—

"Hey, drop the sword!" one of the thieves called out in a panicked voice. Everyone turned in unison. Bart held Sparns' sword in a double-handed grasp, with the blade tip resting on the ground, a fierce expression on his face. The thieves surrounding him closed in, pointing their swords at eye level.

"Bart, put the sword down!" Micah eyed the thieves.

Bart ignored him. "I challenge—" His sword clattered to the ground as he removed one hand from the hilt to point his finger. He stooped down and picked it back up. "I challenge you, Westock," he paused, a daring grin spreading across his face, "to a duel."

"Bart, no!" Micah surprised himself at the volume of his voice. It echoed through the alley and scattered several pigeons. He wanted to bust through the thieves and wrench the sword from Bart's grasp.

Westock broke into a loud, clear laugh. "You want to duel me? What a fool."

"No, he—"

"Silence!" Westock paused. "I accept your challenge, and after seeing my skills on display, I'm sure the rest of you will gladly hand over the boy to me."

The thieves looked toward Haelus, who chewed his lip for a moment, then nodded. They backed away, forming a broader ring around Bart and Westock. Micah rushed at Bart, but the thieves dragged him kicking and struggling to the edge of the ring.

Bart and Westock stepped toward each other. The silvery magnificence of Westock's sword far outshone Bart's dull and rusty blade. Westock's weapon also appeared to be about a foot longer. And with a grin that reflected a demeanor at ease, Westock brought his sword forward. It gleamed as he whirled it on either side of him until it became nothing but a smear of silver. In a feat that brought a small gasp from the onlookers, he mixed in jabs and cuts, mere flashes of reflected light that downed imaginary foes all around him. Pivoting and leaping, he caused several of the thieves to cringe as he drew near them. But with a final flick the sword became still, pointed at Bart and poised for battle.

Groaning, Micah gazed upward, out of the alleyway, past the rows of pigeons observing the event from the building tops, and prayed for Bart.

With Westock's display complete, Bart yanked his sword point from the ground. But he did so a bit too zealously and smacked himself in the side of the head with the flat of the blade. As if to clear the dizziness, he shook his head and delved into an attempt at a fearsome expression which just made him look ridiculous.

A cynical groan came from the thieves, a collective recognition that this would be a short contest.

Bart and Westock circled one another, swords outstretched. In a playful gesture, Westock tapped Bart's sword with his own—just enough force for Bart's sword to veer off to the left. Like a farmer trying to pull back a runaway donkey, Bart stumbled after it to regain balance while keeping it from falling all the way to the ground. But he overcorrected and veered several steps back the other way.

"His sword's too heavy for him," a thief next to Micah said under his breath.

Micah clenched his fists.

Westock leaped forward and sliced. Micah started. But Bart's sword slipped down from his limp grip and managed to impede the strike. A clang ricocheted off the alley walls. Westock whipped his sword back and jabbed again at another opening. But Bart lost his footing and his sword leaped up to block the second attack as he waved it an attempt to keep his balance.

Westock paused and shrugged. Then he plowed his sword into Bart's and pushed him backward. Bart fell head over heels, rolling backward several times. Swift as a fox, Westock rushed forward and stabbed downward.

Micah's heart plunged.

The stab glanced off Bart's sword and sank a good two feet into a dirt-filled crack in the cobblestone. Resembling an upside down turtle struggling to regain its feet, Bart rolled away from his attacker. Just as he climbed, breathing heavily, to his feet, Westock managed to yank his sword out.

The battle wore on for several minutes, Westock expertly swinging hit after hit. Every time Westock's blade slashed forward, Micah tensed. Although Bart was as slow and cumbersome as could be, he found a way to avoid every attack. With every swing from Westock, Bart should have died, but he blundered through it, stumbling and veering like a drunken hippopotamus. His sword somehow managed to be in perfect position every time.

"When's his luck gonna run out?" Sparns demanded.

But as Micah watched, recognition dawned on him. At first glance, Bart appeared to be an oaf who could barely keep his sword aloft. But as he managed to survive, time after time, clang after clang, Micah wondered if Bart might not be the novice he seemed. A subtle consistency shone through his clumsiness. After a while his accidents, however ridiculous, didn't look accidental.

For the first time in the match, Bart attacked. His sword, after blocking a swipe from Westock, swung like a pendulum and came back around right at the bounty hunter. Westock just managed to raise his sword in time to block it.

"Th-that was hard." Westock's face showed weakness for the first time. Sweat had drenched through both of their garbs and dripped from their faces. But Westock breathed heavier than Bart. With a grunt of effort, Westock pushed the sword away. But it swung around and into Westock from below. Westock just managed to stop this attack as well. Now his face tightened.

Bart kept bringing the attacks, spinning and slashing. He looked as though he barely managed to hold onto his sword, forced to follow its momentum wherever it swung. But each clang pushed Westock back until his back hit the wall. Bart's final swing of the drive looked powerful, drawing a stir from the spectators. It struck Westock's sword on the hilt, sending it flying into the sky. Bart looked up and then down again.

"Here," he said in a hurried voice, shoving his blade into Westock's hands, "you take this one." Then he stepped back and caught Westock's sword. The hilt plunged almost to the ground after the catch, causing Bart to hobble several steps off course before he managed to gain control.

He turned toward Westock, but the white-faced bounty hunter dropped the sword and sprinted out of the alleyway without a backward glance. Bart straightened, reclaiming the attempted fierce expression he'd worn at the beginning of his duel. "Anybody else?"

Nobody moved.

Bart took a deep breath. "Tornadoooooooo!" He spun in place with his sword outstretched. Faster and faster he spun, yelling all the while, until the whirling storm of Bart started toward the thieves.

Thundering footsteps signaled the thieves' flight as they scrambled to squeeze out the narrow alleyway opening, punching and kicking to get away. "No! He's coming!" The one at the back of the pack screamed with a horrified glance over his shoulder. None of them dared stop to pick up Sparns' discarded sword in their flight.

Bart eased to a stop. His head swam from side to side. He veered sideways in one direction, then the other. Then he stood upright.

Micah beamed, though a little afraid to approach Bart himself. "Bart, that was incredible!"

Bart shrugged and let the sword fall to the ground. "It was nothing." But his beaming face said otherwise.

They rounded up the sheep from the stable and left Fidell before sundown, setting up camp a few miles to the south. Bart gave an in-depth account of his battle to the sheep as they walked. ". . . and then I gave him my sword, 'cause his was shinier, and I caught his sword." Bart widened his eyes to demonstrate his seriousness and nodded as if to quell any doubt. "Right out of the sky!" He waited for several seconds, allowing the sheep time to wrap their minds around this, before continuing.

That night, with the sheep asleep within their fold and a healthy fire casting a warm glow over them, Bart and Micah lay upon the grass, gazing up as the stars pierced the darkening sky like blooming white roses on a vast, mysterious hillside. But the moon was nowhere to be seen—it had finished waning, and would start waxing the next night, growing into the full moon. *Time goes by so fast.* Before he knew it the moon would be full, and he would be at the castle. If he survived until then.

Micah turned his attention earthward. After so many nights spent in the open lands of Gable, the owls' serenade sounded peaceful and comforting to him now.

He puzzled over Bart. Did the emblem on his chest mean that he was part of some secret society adept with swords? Why would the emblem be on his sheep? Or had the dual been some kind of elaborate good fortune? Or divine intervention? Then there was the clay castle Bart had constructed, and the fact that he'd been so certain Westock had been lying.

"You're just full of surprises, aren't you, Bart?"

"That's what my mother said," Bart yawned before completing the sentence, "when I put a toad on her head."

Micah laughed. "I'll bet."

"What are your parents like?" Bart asked, his voice heavy with drowsiness.

Micah hesitated. "I'm not sure. I never knew them."

The hooting of owls filled the gap in conversation.

"Do you wonder about your family?"

"Sometimes . . . but it's not something I dwell on or anything. I used to a lot more," Micah thought about it some more, "but then I got my sheep."

Bart reached over and patted him on the head. "You're a good boy, Micah." The next breath that came out of Bart's mouth was a snore.

A few seconds later Bart was mumbling in his sleep. Micah listened and realized that Bart was going through the list of letters, over and over again. He looked over and saw with a smile that Bart clutched a twig against his chest, the one he had used to write in the dirt.

❦

Days of journeying passed by, days filled with regular reading lessons and lots of walking. The rolling hills settled into plains and the marsh woods climbed up the emerging Dogtooth Mountains. They soon found themselves following the main road, a wide dirt line that curved around the trees much more than it needed to. The party encountered more fellow travelers and the population thickened, resulting in several smaller villages. However, keeping Sandy's advice in mind, Micah avoided other shepherds when he could.

As they traveled, what started as a small twinge in Micah's shoulder, where the Aegre Bird had attacked, grew stronger each day. The injury turned various ugly shades of purple and swelled. Whenever he touched it a chill ran down his spine. But he did his best to ignore it. There was nothing he could do but submerge himself in the cold water of the streams they happened upon and attempt to ease the pain with his limited knowledge of roots and herbs; he didn't have any gold for a doctor.

Ariel's young legs grew tired from the long journey, and Micah had to carry her on his good shoulder more often than not. With each passing day she looked more and more like the sickly lamb she had once been. He monitored her diet, making sure she consumed as much food and water as she should. But there was little else he could do for her, except pray.

He was carrying Ariel on his shoulder when the party came to a split in the road. Everyone came to a halt. He studied the obstacle before them. No signs or explanations. The road split into two, with each one heading off in a different direction, neither one worn more or less than the other.

Micah scanned his mental image of the map Grixxler had given him. "We need to go left." He looked over at Bart for a consensus.

Bart's face twisted with concentration. "No—I remember. We need to go right."

Micah didn't know what to say. If they went right it would lead them west, to the ocean. "I can't go to the ocean, Bart."

"It's the fastest way."

"Can't we just go left, even if it'll take a little longer?"

"Right is the fastest way."

Micah didn't know how to explain to him that Grixxler had ordered him to stay away from the ocean. "I-I can't go right. The ocean's dangerous."

"Well, I must go right."

Bart and his stubbornness. "But—that means we'll have to split up."
Neither one of them talked or moved for several moments.

"The ocean's dangerous; you don't want to go that way."

"I," Bart threw his hands up in frustration, "I have to!"

"Then," Micah hesitated, "that means—"

"Good bye, Micah. Meet me at the castle." Bart said farewell to each of the sheep, giving them all a last rub on their heads, and waddled down the path to the right. Twenty paces down the road, he stopped, turned around, and waited. An uncertain expression masked his face.

Micah's resolve swung like the needle of a broken compass. Ignore Grixxler's advice or part ways with Bart? With his feet and crook moving as though made of stone, his grudging steps headed down the path to the left. He couldn't help but notice the abandonment on Bart's face. It felt as it had when he'd left his sheep to find Ariel. *Please let Grixxler's warning be false.* But what if it wasn't? What if Bart had just made the decision that would lead to the death Grixxler warned of?

CHAPTER 12

ONE MARAUDER'S MISERY

Isaac Ganthorn sat on the withered tree stump for hours, his head hanging. His hands cupped his face, as if to keep it from falling into the mist-lined lake at his feet. The hem of his cloak lay in the water. The water's surface quivered with every shift of his cloak and every tear that slid through his fingers.

His thoughts and emotions flew around like frenzied flies, never landing in his consciousness long enough for him to make any sense of what was happening. Why did he feel so alone, so afraid? He removed his hands from his face and blinked as his eyes took in the reflection before him. How he hated even to look at himself. Of all places, why had his mindless getaway from the shepherd boy ended at the edge of a lake?

He shivered as he thought about that other lake so many years ago, where the burst of lightning had revealed his chalky face. He clenched his eyes shut, grabbed his temple and roared to the sky. "Get out of my head!"

A flock of nearby geese flapped into the low hanging clouds.

He brought his head back down and, upon seeing his reflection, crushed the image with a booted foot. Water leapt up and tossed around, distorting the picture to his satisfaction.

But seconds later he again stared at those streaks of silver hair, and those tired and hopeless eyes; they could have belonged to a dead person. Ganthorn groaned through gritted teeth as, for the millionth time, the innocent, infant eyes flashed through his mind. Then the shepherd boy's followed. They hadn't changed much.

He looked down again, deep into his own eyes. He wished he'd disobeyed the king that night, and never taken the first step on that mission. Then maybe he wouldn't be afraid; the nightmares would never have started. Then he could get proper rest, and he wouldn't have to endure reliving his crimes from his victims' points of view every time he fell asleep. He wouldn't see those cursed infant eyes every time before he woke.

Isaac sat up and breathed deep. His voice cracked with the breath, betraying the sobs hidden just beneath the surface. Why couldn't he die right there? Just lie down and let everything slip into sweet, beautiful blackness? But no, he had a meeting with the king, and it would be far from pleasant.

He rose to his feet. "Pull yourself together!" He'd let himself become upset over his silly nightmares again. He'd let himself become panicked; that was the problem. There was nothing at all to his woeful thoughts. They were products of his imagination.

He reached for his dagger but stopped himself as he realized he'd left it at New Serragin. Instead, he stared himself in the face without blinking an eye. "You, Isaac Ganthorn, fear nothing."

After noting the sinking sun, he turned west and strode for the ocean. Already, his confidence was flowing back and his worries were shrinking. He walked through a short stretch of forest and emerged at the ocean's foggy edge. He hadn't stood there long before a slapping noise broke the rhythm of the waves. A dinghy appeared from the fog with three black-robed figures inside. All three stared at him with wide, timid eyes.

See? They know the real Isaac Ganthorn.

The dinghy landed aground, scraping against the rocks. Isaac stepped into the boat and sat down. They pushed off in silence, and the fog engulfed them. After several minutes of rowing in uneasy stillness, the dark hull of *Lady Midnight* materialized out of the nothingness before Isaac was mentally ready for it.

He leapt out of the dinghy and grabbed a rope hanging from the deck. The dinghy pitched violently in his wake, but the other Marauders dared not protest as they fell over each other, attempting to steady the vessel.

Isaac ascended onto the deck. Several heads turned at his arrival. He averted them with a stone cold glare.

"Captain Ganthorn." Lewell hailed him from across the deck. "Our King would like to speak with you."

"Excellent!" Isaac forced an eager smile and passed through the hallway to the king's lounge without breaking stride. His confidence gained an extra boost from Lewell's crestfallen expression. He paused before knocking upon the decorated door. As he waited he couldn't help but note an eerie absence of noise. He turned and saw, to his surprise, the iron door with heavy hinges hanging ajar, revealing the shadowy metal pen within. A stench wafted out that cut Isaac's breath short.

So, they unleashed the beast.

"Come in."

Isaac heard it just barely through the decorated door. He turned and swung into the smoky room. As he entered, he tensed himself for an attack. One never knew when entering the king's chambers if the king would attempt to behead them by flinging some gold-encrusted knife or diamond-hilted scimitar from the collection of exotic weapons that lined the walls.

The king sat upon his ornate chair, the brightest object in the dreary room. Before him sat his wooden desk, covered in maps, charts, a sextant, a telescope, and a compass.

Isaac forced himself to look into the king's bleak eyes, each one like a solitary arctic island. "Your Highness." Isaac bowed from where he stood. He walked across the room and sat in the wooden chair before the king.

"Captain," the king said stiffly, "do you have a parcel for me?"

Isaac hesitated. "I was unable to find the location of the Caelum Flute." He braced himself for a storm.

The king closed his eyes, no wrinkles yet troubling his face, but Isaac could sense the fiery passion being pushed back within.

"That's fine, Ganthorn." The king opened his eyes. "I didn't expect you to find it, not yet. The secret will remain locked away with Kestrel in the dungeon. For now."

Isaac couldn't suppress a small exhale.

The king lifted the telescope off the table, rose from his seat, and walked around to the window behind his chair. He peered out through the telescope. "Did you discover any clues as to its whereabouts?"

"No, Your Highness."

"Any valuable information about the castle?"

"I'm terribly sorry, Your Highness."

"Did you dispose of all those you questioned?"

Isaac withdrew a crumpled scrap of parchment with a list of names scribbled upon it from his cloak and placed it upon the desk. "I was able to kill all but one, My Lord."

The king snapped his head away from the telescope, the islands of his eyes catching fire. "You failed?" He threw the telescope on the table. "Head Captains do not fail, Ganthorn!"

Isaac couldn't help himself; he cowered—slightly.

The king's eyes flashed to Isaac's belt. "Where is your dagger?"

"I—lost it."

The king's face darkened several shades. "Why am I suddenly reminded of your botched infant delivery in the Heather Mountains?" he snapped. "You will never be half the Head Captain that Kestrel was. Never!"

The king turned back to the window with his telescope. "I must warn you, Ganthorn. I hope this isn't a return to that disastrous form. Your career can't take another blow like that. Lewell is breathing down your neck for your position."

Isaac tightened his fist, withholding a rush of anger. "You and I both know what a fool he is compared to me."

The king turned away from the window. "Yes, I do know that somewhere inside you there is a talented Marauder worthy of your position. But right now all I see is a man who fails to deliver anything but excuses." The king turned back to the window, peering again through the scope. "Who is the one you failed to murder?"

Isaac paused. If he could survive the coming rage, he knew his chance at redemption followed—his remaining testament at authenticity. He took a deep breath. "Bart."

The king lowered the telescope and sighed. His shoulders sagged and his head tipped back, revealing the bald spot inside his crown. He addressed the window in a grave, colorless tone. "Why? Why were you unable to kill such a simple fool?"

"He was with the shepherd boy." Isaac impressed himself with how well he hid his triumph.

The king whirled around. "*The* shepherd boy? Micah?"

Isaac nodded.

"So then he's made it to New Serragin. Was he well? Were his sheep with him?"

"They are all fine and accounted for," Isaac lied. He didn't remember seeing any sheep in his mindless flight. "I did manage to stab Bart, but it wasn't fatal."

The king gasped. "Did the boy see you?"

135

Isaac jerked back. "No." He spoke perhaps a moment too hastily.

The king squinted at him. He lifted the telescope and turned once again to the window. "I may have judged you a bit quickly, Captain Ganthorn. News of the shepherd boy pleases me."

"What pleases you pleases me, Your Highness." Isaac bowed.

The king squinted into the telescope. "I have a pesky problem, though."

"What might that be?"

"A ship has been following us since we left that inn. It troubles me for obvious reasons. If they know . . ." he trailed off, and then composed his words again. "We can't have them blabbing our plan, it would ruin everything." The king stared at Isaac.

Isaac could feel his gaze slicing into him, examining him for worthiness.

"I want you to dispose of the ship—and its company."

"Yes, Your Highness."

"Still on the topic of the Heather Mountains incident . . ."

Isaac swallowed, barring thoughts of his nightmares from exploding through his mind.

"I'm giving you a crew, and I expect you to bring it back to me." He waved Isaac away with his hand. "Now go."

Isaac rose from his chair and walked to the door.

"And tell Captain Lewell that all lookouts are to meet Crab on deck instantly," the king added as Isaac passed through the doorway, "to pay for their incompetence."

⚬⚬

The wind nipped at Robbyn's hair as she stood by the wheel, gazing through the telescope. Darkness settled over the water.

"They're stopping for the night." She handed the telescope to Drift's eager hands.

He gazed through it for a few brief seconds before saying, "We'll keep our distance." He cranked the wheel. "The winds are pretty lively. Wonder if we'll get some rain."

"I hope so. Anything that'll help us get by unnoticed."

In minutes the night became impenetrable and the winds gathered momentum. Rain peppered them and the boat pitched back and forth a little. Robbyn sidled closer to Drift.

A flash of light lit up the sky, but she reacted too late to see where it came from. A crack of thunder followed.

"A storm's brewing," Drift said.

Robbyn took a step closer to him.

ex3

"This lightning's going to give us away, Captain," the helmsman hissed.

"What can they do? Run?" Isaac laughed. "It doesn't matter if they see us or not. They're doomed."

"You sure this is a good idea? I can't see a bloody thing. We should wait 'til morning."

"Which one do you want, light or no light? If you plan on making a long career out of this Marauder business, I suggest you learn to adapt to adverse conditions."

Another flash occurred, followed by the crash of thunder.

"I saw them," Isaac said. "Did you?"

The helmsman gave one quick nod without breaking his gaze.

Isaac turned to the crew positioned at various stations around the deck as the thickening rain pattered around them. He raised his voice to be heard above it. "To starboard side. Prepare to board."

He fingered his newly granted dagger, staring out through the rain. Within minutes it came down in great sheets, drenching them all. The lightning struck again, and Isaac saw the bright prongs fork down from the sky and disappear. The thunder roared as if from just beside him.

"The storm does complicate things," he muttered.

◈

Robbyn wiped the rain from her sodden eyebrows, blinking the water out of her eyes. She had her arms hooked through the railing to keep from being thrown overboard. Drift had both hands braced against the wheel. He peered into the darkness, squinting against the battering wind and rain. The lanterns hanging under the eaves of the cabin banged and clattered, emitting a faint and flickering light.

"Robbyn!" Drift's neck sinews bulged as he bellowed over the storm. "Tie that rope around your waist!"

She grabbed the rope and attempted to wrap it around her waist without unhooking her arms from the railing, but the rocking platform of the boat made it quite a task. The flash of light came again, and she saw something dark on the water quartered by the jagged trace of lightning. Rain blurred the image heavily, but she'd seen it—a ship. A terrific crash of thunder accompanied the sinking of her heart.

"Drift!" she called. But the storm snatched her call and drowned it in the deafening rain.

Meanwhile, the mighty wind kept their ship shooting through the water at a breakneck speed. The rain flew by, pelting her face and stinging her hands, now white from their grip on the railing.

The wind roared stronger still, and she fought to keep from being blown overboard. Drift blinked away the rain and cast her a worried look. With a last glance at the sea in front of them, he transferred the wheel to one hand and secured the rope around her waist with the other.

Drift didn't look forward when the lightning struck again. But Robbyn did, and she saw the large outline of a ship right in front of them.

"Drift! Drift!" she screamed, pointing at the ship. But he could not have done anything even if he'd heard her. When darkness replaced

138

the brief lightning, it seemed as though the ship had disappeared. But a festering knot in Robbyn's stomach remained. It was there and they were on course for disaster at a ridiculous velocity.

The collision happened sooner than she expected. Thunder exploded from the bowels of the ships. The impact sent both her and Drift hurtling over the railing.

For a few seconds she floated through the sky. The deafening sounds of creaking and splintering wood rang up to her ears as the ships crumpled each other. Drift flew into the night sky, still clutching the broken wheel, and disappeared from the meager lantern light. A sharp yank tugged at her waist, squeezing the air out of her. All of her momentum ended. She plummeted and collapsed on what must have been the lower deck. The two ships continued to plow into each other, spraying shards of wood. The floor beneath her trembled and arched toward the sea. For a moment she thought the incline would continue until it spilled her overboard. But then, with a final moan, everything eased to a halt.

Lightheaded, she clawed at the knot at her waist while she rose to her feet. Her eyes could only register a dark, whirling image of mangled wood. The floor beneath her still pitched enough that she had to cling to a chunk of wood to keep from tumbling over.

"What happened, Captain?" a voice sputtered above the beating rain.

She ducked, still fumbling with the knot.

"Be quiet, fool!"

A gasp of pain came from elsewhere.

As Robbyn regained her bearings, another flash of lightning shed light on her predicament. The ugly remains of the two ships had wedged together. Two figures standing at the other ship's wheel wore black cloaks.

"Marauders," she breathed. Where was Drift? She *needed* him now.

"Captain, we're at the mercy of the sea! We need to—" A snap sheered off the Marauder's sentence. A mourning groan followed, heralding the main mast's drop. It smashed into the deck feet from where she sat. She covered her face as a shower of wet splinters rained on her.

"Where are the rest of the men?" the other Marauder demanded, holding onto the railing to keep his balance.

"Either dead or lost."

"What now?" the Marauder at the wheel asked.

"We finish the mission, you gulls! Find those spies and kill them!"

Robbyn untangled the knot and pulled herself from the woodpile. She crouched, having no idea where to go. The option of jumping overboard crossed her mind. But a flash of lightning quelled that thought.

A mammoth wave rose above them like a stealthy predator.

"Brace yourselves!"

Before she could think about why or where, she turned and ran. She raced past where she had seen the Marauders, slipping and stumbling on the flooded deck. She could sense the wave pressing down on them. She could feel the Marauders cringe and hold on for dear life behind her. But she dared not look back, or up.

Then the ground disappeared beneath her. Bludgeons of water hit her as she fell downward into nothingness. With a thump she hardly felt, she hit something hard and roughly as narrow as her waist. She held on tight as the full force of the water collapsed on top of her. Water shot into her mouth and up her nose.

With a creak and a groan, the entire ship turned over, and she clung tight to what must have been one of the ship's ribs as it pulled up out of the water, carrying her far above. She took a deep breath and held tight for several moments, dangling like a dying leaf in an autumn windstorm.

Don't let go! Don't let go!

A swoosh and a crash sounded from above, signaling the fall of another wave over the unfortunate ships. A tremendous crunch rose above the sounds of the storm. At that moment her fingers gave, and she plunged, kicking and screaming, into the water. From there the twister of wood and water that surrounded her swallowed all notion of direction, and she had no idea where the surface was.

She writhed around until frigid air blew over her hand and she struggled toward it, inhaling breaths as large as her lungs could stand. The waves of the storm seemed several times bigger now that she floundered among them, desperate for something to hold her up. She darted glances around. No sign of the ships, or anything for that matter. She snuck in a last breath just as another wave pushed her under. Her head bobbed back up into the rain, where she spotted a broad, flat piece of wood. She swam toward it and tackled it. She had to hold on. It was her last hope.

But a subtle force drew her toward what she could only think of as sleep. Each whip of the cold wind nudged her in that direction. Her thoughts slowed and then her mind buckled into darkness.

CHAPTER 13

The Storm's Havoc

Micah peered out at the calm, windswept scene from beneath the thick branches of a stunted long-dead tree. Still wet and cold from the storm he'd endured the night before and exhausted from the flight into the Marsh Woods, he considered what to do next. Sparsely garlanded trees surrounded him and his sheep—not very useful for keeping a storm out. And now they had to find their way out of this gloomy recess somewhere in the heart of the Marsh Woods.

The high notes of various birds twittered from a nearby meadow, celebrating the morning, but he couldn't see any of them. He was just grateful that a monster hadn't devoured him and his sheep even though he hadn't been able to start a fire. Apparently the storm had been enough to drive even the night creatures away.

Water coated every groove and crevice of every tree in sight. Giant pools of muddy water stained the forest floor.

He counted the sheep huddled around him. They were dirty and wet, and they'd certainly smelled better, but all were accounted for.

He stared up at the dark gray sky. It made no guarantees to hold its water. Three days had passed since Bart departed their company. Had he been able to find shelter from the storm? Could he be lost and alone among the endless hills of Gable? He had taken the path toward the ocean. The storm had probably been worse there.

Micah prayed for Bart's safety. Then he grabbed his dripping crook and his soaked pack and rose to his knees, gathering resolve to complete the day as he did so. But as soon as he leaned on the trunk to stand, a fiery pain like he'd never felt before engulfed his shoulder. A roar of agony ripped from his throat. As his voice echoed away, he grabbed his shoulder and squeezed it as hard as he could. If he had been strong enough, he would have crushed it. His knees wobbled and he winced, tears collecting in his eyes. With a shudder, he realized that his coldness didn't stem from the damp air.

He pondered seeking help from a doctor in the next village, but he had no coins. After several minutes of steady breathing, he inched his way to his full height, careful not to provoke his throbbing shoulder. His sheep stared at him, unmoving.

"It's time to go." The words felt strange in his mouth, the only part of him that felt dry—and uncomfortably so. They sounded even stranger to his ears, being the first human voice he'd heard in awhile.

With a breath of moist air, he took a step southward, navigating the enormous pools of water. "Just go south," he told himself. His sheep followed.

They pushed through the woods, the birdsong fading behind them. As he burrowed through the floating white fog that rose from the water-laden forest floor, he couldn't repel the sense that he was feeling his way blindly, rather than navigating.

The pain in his shoulder grew as the day progressed, treading on the edge of his mind. It spread through him, sapping his energy. He didn't find any roots or herbs in the desolate Marsh Woods, but he doubted they would have helped. As midday approached, threads of cloud-strained light weaved down onto the forest floor, and Micah felt colder than he had in the morning. When he touched his skin, drenched in a sticky blend of sweat and rainwater, it felt hot.

An hour later, he no longer avoided the steaming puddles but trudged through them, leaving his sheep to wander. The sky had darkened to nearly black; the sun had disappeared. Could the storm be returning to finish them off?

Trying to keep his shoulder steady, he hobbled forward in a light-headed stupor. The forest wobbled around him, as if a slow earthquake were trying to shake him to the ground. Somewhere in his foggy, reeling mind he realized that he needed help.

A fine drizzle came down, hardly noticeable among the prevalent dampness already there.

He ignored the pounding in his head and the urge to vomit as he constructed a sheepfold. His limbs moved themselves, without the residency of his mind. He merely let his muscles follow the process countless previous sheepfold-building hours had ingrained. He gathered branches and boulders, and placed them against the giant, gnarled roots of an oak tree. It wasn't his best work, but it would do.

The drizzle thickened, shooting pinholes in the fog. Micah placed his crook and pack inside the sheepfold. "Go inside."

The sheep stared at the entrance for a moment, bleating uncertainly.

"Inside," he repeated louder, wincing as the pressure in his forehead mounted.

They filed in and he rolled the last boulder into place with a great deal of effort. The sheep bleated in protest. But he ignored them.

Find help. The two words bounced around his mind. With heavy eyelids, he lurched through the forest.

The sheep strained their voices, but their sheepfold disappeared into the clutches of the wilderness behind him, and so did their calls.

He made his way forward, each arduous step like pulling his foot from a pool of tree sap. His vision melted into a blur. An exposed root snagged his foot, and he stumbled into water. He struggled up, his shoulder screaming in agony from the flailing, and he swallowed a mouthful of muck before he climbed out.

As his strength drained away, he resorted to clawing his prone body forward with his good arm. Finally, his trembling fingers stopped. Unable to go an inch farther, he turned, stomach upward, receiving sprinkles of rain in his face, cooling his scorching temple. His eyes closed and his body sagged into the soggy mud, limp.

⚬⚬

Pale light glowed through Robbyn's eyelids. Her body rocked back and forth like a cradle in time to the sound of the ocean caressing the beach. She clung to that hazy phase between sleep and consciousness, unwilling to choose either one.

But wakefulness overtook her. Her feelings and thoughts trickled back. She opened her eyes to a gray sky. Her back ached with stiffness as she sat up.

What a night. She found herself sitting on the section of wood she'd grabbed the night before, drifting forward and back in the shallows of a beach, with a line of trees farther ashore. Upon closer inspection, she discovered the chunk of wood was a section of wall from their cabin; the corner had been defaced by Drift and his Marauder's dagger. She stepped onto the sand and rose to her feet. How blissful the firmness of the ground felt.

With bleary eyes she surveyed the ocean, inhaling the charged, clean air. *What happened to everyone? Where's Drift?*

There, upon a craggy cluster of rocks on the horizon line, perched the pitiful remains of the shipwreck. A jagged patch of white sail fluttered in the breeze.

The chilling thought that she might be the sole survivor surged through her mind and down her spine. She looked down the beach. Scraps of wood and floating barrels of goods littered it, but no people. She looked up the slope, toward the trees.

Someone lay in the sand.

Cautiously, she approached, but it didn't take long for her to recognize the body as Drift's. She ran to him.

His burly arms were still wrapped around the ship's wheel. His hair was matted, his features unconscious and pallid. Overall, he gave off the impression of a beached whale.

"Drift." She slid to her knees, placed a hand on his shoulder, and tried to shake him awake. Solid as a lodged boulder. But his heart thumped with a strong beat.

"Robbyn." His furry eyebrows rose and his eyes flickered open. He sat up, letting out a deep, bear-like groan.

"Drift." She backed away, even though she wanted to throw her arms around him.

He pried his arms away from the wheel and hurled it into the trees. "Quite a storm, eh?" Glancing around at the scattered debris he added, "What happened?"

Thoughts of the flashing lightning and towering waves still lingered fresh in her mind. "We crashed into a Marauder's ship." She scanned the horizon. No sign of Marauders. "I think they were hunting us."

Drift rose to his feet, releasing a cascade of sand. "Hunting us?" He looked about the beach with a new sense of urgency. "Why?"

"I don't know, but if they know that we know what they're doing . . ."

Realization washed over Drift. His face regained its color. "We've got to go."

"But Drift," she protested as he lifted her off her feet and bundled her up in his arms, "we don't have the weapon anymore. We don't have any proof to show King Darius."

"We can't stay here." Drift pounded into the forest, weaving through the trees. "You aren't safe here."

They flew through the trees, Drift thrashing through the undergrowth at a speed that rivaled that of a horse. His arms shielded her from the whipping branches. She wondered how far away the Marauders could be, and how long Drift's stamina could last. But his

146

massive, comforting rib cage heaved against her. She closed her eyes and held on tight as the hours of Drift dodging tree stumps and leaping ditches went by. He proved to be adept at running long distance and didn't stop even once to rest.

"A storm is coming," Drift grunted to her at one point.

"Again?"

"This one'll be worse."

"Worse?" She opened her eyes. The clouds had darkened, but she didn't know why Drift thought this storm would be worse. In fact how could any storm rival the previous one?

Minutes later they burst out onto a shallow, slow-flowing creek. Drift hesitated at the water's edge to catch his breath.

"The creek'll cover our tracks." He plowed into the water, kicking gushes of water onto the rocky banks. "Sorry, m'lady." He turned downstream, crashing through the water in arching, one-legged leaps.

"So . . . we must beat them to the castle, then?" Robbyn asked.

Drift grunted in agreement.

◯◯

Isaac's eyes shot open, his chest pumping furiously. He struggled to his knees, still shaking as the last fragments of the nightmare flickered through his mind. He inhaled deep, calming breaths. Wet sand caked his body and he averted his gaze to keep from looking at the widespread furrows from his tossing and turning. With every blink, those infant eyes stared into his, peering into his mind. Did he know? Could he see how terrible Isaac felt?

He sighed. Sleep, his formidable adversary, had held a grip on him longer than it had in years. He placed his forehead in his gritty hands, cold and empty, as if the storm had drained the life right out of him. His only feeling was a gnawing in his chest, a yearning for his crimes to disappear, to never have happened.

How could he go on? He had no hope, nothing left. That rock

147

down the coastline had more right to live than he did, and more desire too.

With his heart weighing him down, Isaac climbed to his feet. He gazed left, then right, down the beach. Nobody. Nothing but shards of wood and debris lay strewn across the sand.

He gazed out at sea. To the far right a tiny, forsaken pile of caved-in lumber lay on the tiny, forsaken rock.

As if his Marauder body had taken over, leaving the real Isaac alone in the sand, he trotted down the beach, searching the ground. Numbness pervaded his mind, distancing him from his own thoughts and senses.

A humongous human outline imprinted the sand. It didn't belong to a Marauder. Isaac placed a hand on the ground. A subtle warmth still radiated from the print. He followed the cluster of footprints until the smaller set of prints disappeared. The large prints set off into the forest. The distances between each print were incredible.

"He was definitely running," Isaac mumbled. He stood and looked toward the direction the prints had made for—a wide hole disrupted the vegetation of the forest.

He dodged through the trees. When he came to the creek, he studied the steps leading in and turned downstream.

He raced alongside the water. *It'll only be a matter of time.*

❧

Drift kicked through the water, keeping to the shallows. Thunder rumbled from the sky. At least this storm was giving them fair warning.

Suddenly, the bushes rustled, then a twig snapped. Robbyn held her breath and Drift ran harder. The rustling continued. Robbyn's heart beat faster. But then the head of a deer emerged from the foliage. It stepped cautiously to the water's edge, and Drift veered over to the far side of the bank. Robbyn let her breath out, though she wondered how far behind the Marauders were.

A short while later the green trees gave way to dying, blackened ones. A dense, white fog curled out of the creek, though a sparse rain pushed it down.

As if spurred by the rain, Drift clambered up onto the bank opposite from the one where they had entered the creek. With no water to slow his feet, he ran faster.

The rain thickened, lit by flashes of lightning. Drift charged away from the creek, into the malevolent recesses of the Marsh Woods. Or at least she thought it was the Marsh Woods; it certainly fit the descriptions visitors at her inn had given.

"Drift," she said as the rain became painful, bringing back memories of the night before, "we need to find shelter."

"A friend lives nearby," Drift said as the rain hardened into stinging hail pellets. "It's not far."

The wind resisted them, but Drift bulled through it, partially sheltering her from the weather. In his speeding rampage, he stumbled over something on the ground and almost reeled into the mud but managed to stop himself.

Robbyn gasped. "Is that a—?"

A sodden, bedraggled boy lay upon the ground face up, the hail piling on and around him. His skin looked so pale that at first that she feared she gazed at a corpse. She dropped from Drift's arms and put a hand to the boy's clammy forehead.

"He needs help." She looked up at Drift. "The storm will kill him if we leave him."

"As you wish." He reached down and scooped the frail body up in his arms. The mud sucked at the boy's body as he pulled it from the ground that had claimed him.

Drift cast a glance behind them. "We need to go, now."

Robbyn stood and the force of the wind bowled into her. She stepped forward with legs numb from not moving for so long. She nodded, and they raced deeper into the Marsh Woods.

CHAPTER 14

A Legend's Birth

I'm comfortable—that was Micah's first semi-lucid thought after so long a spell of darkness, like a single, leafy sprig sprouting from a barren desert. He found himself lying down, and kept his eyes closed. He had no strength, but he felt warm, dry, and calm. The distinct crackle of a fire, the sound of rain tapping on a roof, it reminded him of the rainy days he'd spent cozying next to the fireplace in his cabin.

Wearily, he opened his eyes, his thoughts still sorting into place. Thick, wooden rafters held the roof up above him—nearly five times larger than the ones in his cabin.

A cottage of some kind. Another bed sat beside the one he lay in, three wooden chairs tucked around a circular table, and decorative quilts and blankets hung in most every available space of wall, piled in the corners, and lining both beds in several layers. Wooden contraptions occupied a third of the room, and a fire licked upward in the river stone fireplace set in the wall. Overall, the cottage had a shabby but comfortable air about it.

"He has awakened," a cracked voice exclaimed.

An old woman sat in an oversized chair beside the fire. She smiled at him. A walking cane, similar to his crook, but much shorter, rested in her lap.

A sudden, shocking realization hit him. "My sheep!" he cried. He had fallen from a cloud and hit the cold, hard ground of reality. Scolding himself for not realizing sooner, he pushed away the layers of blankets to climb out of bed, but the exertion drained him almost immediately, as if his arms and legs had been hollowed. He fell back onto the straw cushion and groaned.

"Your sheep are well cared for, and you're lucky to be alive. If Drift hadn't happened upon you and your sheep, you'd have died two days ago."

Micah didn't know quite what to say. "What? . . . Where am I?"

"Well, you're in an old geezer's cottage, of course. Anyone could have told you that." She laughed—a cackling kind of laugh, full of good humor with a hint of mischief. It carried on several seconds longer than it should have.

"Yes, but how did I get here?"

"Well, if I were you, I'd blame myself. What were you thinking, running around with an open wound? You can't imagine the time Robbyn and I've had clearing the infection while keeping your temperature down."

Lifting his blankets, he found a white cloth wrapped around his shoulder. He was bare-chested, though he still wore his pants. Images came floating back to him, snatches of fitful wakefulness in which the old woman and a reddish-brown-haired girl tried to spoon water into his mouth.

"Not to mention keeping you watered," she added, as though she'd heard his thoughts.

"Two days?" He frowned. "Hasn't the storm passed yet?"

"Oh no. Do you remember that storm the day before you were found?"

When had he been found? His sense of time was muddled. He did recall a storm though. "Yes."

"That was just a warning," she said in a low, ominous voice.

"These last couple days have been bad enough, but they're just a warm up. A storm beyond your imagination will be here before tonight, and I'd get comfy in that bed, there, because it's going to stay awhile."

He didn't know what other choice he had but to stay in bed, regardless of the weather. "How do you know?"

Her tone remained heavy. "Have you ever heard of the Undying Storm?"

"No."

"It's a big storm that never dies. Now you know." She laughed her cackling laugh again. "It has plagued the ocean around the Green Isles for as long as I've been alive, and I suspect it always will. You can't sail very far out into the ocean without meeting a solid wall of storm. It's what cuts us off from the other lands, like Serragin. That and the Wilderness."

He took a moment to absorb everything she'd said. So that's what existed beyond the ocean's horizon—a wall of storm. That figured.

He looked about the cottage. "Will your house hold?"

She cackled longer than ever, as if such a question were unbearably ridiculous, until it faded, and she recovered with a good-humored sigh. "This cottage's built sturdier than you might think. My husband built it with such a storm in mind."

Indeed, upon closer inspection, he realized the shabby house had been sturdily built. Humongous supports held up the roof, with extra bracing in places one would least expect them, such as the chimney, and his bed post. The maze of woodwork reminded him of the support system of New Serragin.

"But the storm still managed to end his life while he was away at sea," she continued.

"I'm sorry." He paused. "But thank you for your hospitality. Wh— What's your name?"

A mischievous grin spread across her face. "If you want a title, I'm Gretchen, Our King's Royal Wool Spinner." Her smile broadened.

"But you can just call me Gretchen the Great, or Your Majesty." She winked.

A guttural noise escaped Micah's lips, as though he'd been punched in the gut. Grixxler's instructions surged through his mind.

"But—the—I." His words fled him. "Why aren't you at the castle?"

"Oh, well, six months ago, our King declared that he likes Asian silk better than wool." She shook her head. "He sent me home."

"Could King Darius have possibly hired a new wool spinner?"

"Pshaw!" Gretchen dismissed that thought with the wave of her hand. "King Darius may find wool a bit scratchy, but he isn't foolish enough to question my skill at the loom." She looked toward the door, then leaned toward him. "Why do you ask?" She penetrated him with her sparkling blue eyes.

"I—" He hesitated. He had one more question. "My master said you won't accept wool unless it's fresh off the sheep. Is that true?"

Gretchen chuckled. "I may look crazy, but I still have a few apples left in the basket." She winked.

Micah groaned. *What's happening?* He dropped his head into his hands. "I'm supposed to bring my sheep's wool to the castle, to take the wool to King Darius' Royal Wool Spinner at the castle. The king himself ordered it."

"I very much doubt it."

Micah closed his eyes, overcome with sudden weariness. Now, on top of the strange emblem in his sheep's coat, the Royal Wool Spinner hadn't really sent for him. Had Grixxler been fooled? If that was the case, then what lay ahead for Micah and his sheep? Should he even continue his journey to the castle? But if he returned home without finishing the journey, Grixxler would probably kill him on sight. And as he thought about it more, he realized that he wasn't even certain of Grixxler's innocence, which sparked a lonely thought; could he trust no one? He sighed. Why had he been sent on this journey? Nothing made sense.

"But you haven't told me your name."

He opened his eyes. "I'm Micah."

"Everything will be fine, Micah. But I'm beginning to wonder about Drift and Robbyn."

She gave him a look as if expecting him to share her sentiment. "Oh right. You don't know. They're using this short lull in the storm to tend to your sheep and see that the townspeople are well, before the Undying Storm unleashes its full force."

"Where are the townspeople staying?"

"Most of them are staying in the old lighthouse. It'll last. The storm is actually south of us. It'll only glance us." She rubbed her hands together, grinning. "But it should still be pretty exciting."

He groaned. Things just kept getting worse. Grixxler popped into his mind, shouting at him for getting too close to the ocean and hurling curses at him every other word. "Lighthouse?"

"Certainly. Claghorne was once a major harbor city. But as trade declined, the lighthouse was abandoned, and most of the town left as well."

"I've drifted too far west. I'm on the ocean," he whispered. He buried his head in his blankets.

"Is something the matter?"

He started to speak, but his stomach revolted. After several seconds of silence he resurfaced and complied. "My master told me to stay away from the ocean at all costs. He said it's too dangerous."

Gretchen squinted. "Well, if anyone can attest to the safety of being near the ocean, it's me. I've managed to survive here longer than just about anyone."

"What if he was trying to warn me about the Undying Storm?" He had led his sheep right into danger. "Are my sheep safe?"

"They are the safest animals for miles. My husband and I moved here even before Claghorne was founded, so we got the best plot of land, and it happened to have a cave in the side of the hill, burrowing deep underground, which is where your sheep are." She smiled at him. "You certainly are a tight fella. As my ma used to say, if you don't relax you're going to lay an egg." She cackled.

At that moment the door swung open. A rain-filled gust of wind swished into the room.

A flurry of copper hair followed—a girl. He recognized her as the one who had helped care for him. Behind her an enormous man blotted out the view of the storm. He stepped inside and latched the door, having to duck considerably to fit in the doorframe. His size took Micah's breath away. Their soaked clothes dripped water on the floor.

"He's awake!" Robbyn pulled off her cloak and hung it on a peg next to the fireplace. Her attitude of familiarity unsettled him, even though he knew why she knew him. Drift hung his cloak on the rafters and stacked three more logs onto the fire.

"Robbyn, Drift, this is Micah. He thinks the ocean wants to kill him."

"You might be right, the way this storm is brewing." Robbyn rubbed her arms and shivered.

Drift grunted as he placed his massive hands in front of the fire, casting large sections of the cottage into shadow. He gave a courteous nod in Micah's direction and turned to the fire.

"I must say," Robbyn grinned, "you chose an interesting place to take a nap."

"Are my sheep all right?" Micah struggled to sit up.

"They're fine," Robbyn said. "That little one is really cute."

He glanced at the door behind her. Perhaps he should drop his suspicious attitude, she seemed sincere. He could trust her. "Thank you." He let himself fall back.

"We found your possessions in the sheepfold," Robbyn nodded toward the wall beside Micah's bed, where his crook, pack, and clothing lay, clean and dry.

"Let me ask you, though, Micah," Gretchen said, "how did you get into such trouble?"

Micah was still trying to puzzle out a reason for being sent to a wool spinner that didn't exist. "It's a long story."

"Time isn't a problem." Drift's deep voice burst from beside the fire, and Micah started at the voice. The giant didn't even turn around.

"You'll have to forgive Drift," Gretchen said. "He doesn't like being stuck in one place much. But tell us about your journey."

So Micah shared his tale, starting all the way back at the Heather Mountains, where Grixxler had sent him off with the cryptic instructions. At first he chose his words carefully, leaving certain parts out. But as the minutes passed the story came easier, and he let it flow. He told them about the indifferent city of New Serragin, where he had met Bart, and the Marauder who had run away, terrified at the sight of Micah. He told them about their run-in with the thieves, the attack of the Aegre Bird, teaching Bart to read, the duel with the bounty hunter, and so on, until his story arrived at the cottage.

"And that's it," Micah said.

The storm gathered its strength, as signaled by a whistling wind, dramatic claps of thunder, and beating rain. Yet a sense of safety resided in Micah as he lay nestled within the confinements of the cottage, protected from the storm raging outside. Drift and Robbyn had completely dried off and comfortably seated themselves in wooden chairs, facing Micah.

"That's quite a tale." Gretchen cleared her throat.

Micah nodded. "Yes, it is."

Robbyn leaned forward. "I wonder why that Marauder didn't kill you."

They listened to the storm beating against the cottage. Micah tried to imagine the chaos it would accomplish outside.

"There's something," Robbyn glanced at Drift, "we should share. I wasn't going to tell you, for your sake." She nodded at both Micah and Gretchen. "But someone else should know, in case the Marauders catch us." She paused. "It's a dangerous secret."

Drift looked from Robbyn to Gretchen to Micah.

"Tell us!" Gretchen's eyes gleamed. She leaned forward.

Micah wasn't as enthusiastic, but he didn't object.

Robbyn explained how the Marauders had burned the inn to the ground, and stolen the ships. She described the weapons that had been mounted on each ship, and their capabilities. Then she detailed the monster's export from the ship, the shipwreck, and the race to the cottage.

"And now we think they're chasing us."

"They are chasing us," Drift said.

Robbyn continued. "We know they're going to destroy the castle, and they know that we know."

"That's a bold plan," Gretchen said, "but I see one possible weakness. The King's Navy patrols the waters surrounding the castle, even at night. So the Marauders will have to launch their attacks from a long ways away."

"Trust me," Robbyn looked at Drift out of the side of her eyes, then back again, "that won't be a problem."

"Yes, but a very thick fog shrouds the castle and the waters around it for miles, every night. They won't be able to see a thing from a distance, and therefore won't be able to aim their weapons."

Nobody said anything for several moments. "Even so," Gretchen continued, "the Marauders are too clever not to have thought of that."

"So," Micah began organizing his thoughts. "The Marauders are going to tear down the castle with these weapons in order to set James Kestrel free?"

Robbyn nodded. "That's what we think, anyway."

"Why is everyone fighting over the Caelum Flute?" Micah began to wonder if Sandy's explanation of the flute was true. "Those thieves were going to kill us because they thought we had it. It seems like everyone's after it. Why's it so valuable?"

At first nobody said anything.

"It's an ancient flute rumored to have the power to converse with the birds," Robbyn said. "I have no idea how it was made to do that. There probably isn't a person alive who does."

"Actually," Gretchen smiled more widely than necessary, "it isn't nearly as old as you'd think. I remember quite well how it was made."

Silence ensued. Robbyn's mouth fell open. Drift turned around.

"Of course, I suppose that doesn't necessarily make it not ancient." She chuckled, and began her story . . .

‏ જ્જ

Samuel Kamloop arrived at the outskirts of Burella early in the morning. The town was quiet, slow in appearance, much like his home town of Chesterton. The wide dirt road paved straight through, with cottages lining each side. But even in the still of the morning a high-pitched *ting, ting, ting* wafted over to him. It came from a tent toward the end of the row.

This is it. This could be the day!

He quickened his step. His bulging, cumbersome pack swung back and forth behind him. He paused, sighed, and hitched it up his back; after three days of hiking he was more than ready to dump the burden.

But that didn't matter now. This endeavor was going to make him the wealthiest man in Gable. In time all the Kings of the Green Isles would pay handsomely to get their hands on one of these flutes.

Samuel hesitated at the opening of the tent. He eased forward to take a peek inside. A forge sat at the middle while multiple benches and shelves lined the walls, filled with tools, metal, rocks, and trinkets.

The man who stood inside didn't look much like a Byronian. Sure, his head reached roughly Samuel's shoulder, and his figure resembled Samuel's pack, but this guy looked mean. Broad shoulders, a hunched posture, and scarred, leathery skin—all of these, no doubt, the result of decades spent at the forge. A reddish-gray beard, rugged and uneven, hung from his chin. Rumor had it that he let the forge singe it to length. Samuel didn't doubt it.

"Samuel Kamloop." The man looked up from the yet unformed lump of silver. He set his hammer atop the pile of tools scattered over his bench and wiped his dirty hands on his filthy apron.

Samuel stepped inside the tent, warmed by the small fire burning in the forge. "Tell me you've got it, Gordon."

Gordon cast a speculative glance at Samuel's pack and pulled the cloth away from an abnormally shaped lump sitting on the shelf.

"Byronian silver," he said in a reverent voice as he produced a gleaming cloud constructed of harsh lines. It drew what little light glowed from the forge, creating a scintillating aura around it. It seemed to float, rather than rest, in the little man's hands. Samuel couldn't tear his eyes away.

"Is it really Byronian?" He pushed the question through his light and fuzzy thoughts.

Gordon nodded. "I personally harvested it from the very heart of the mine in the Kakotine Mountains. It's a rare chunk of metal." He looked again at Samuel's pack. "It'll cost you."

Samuel drifted out of his daze, dropped his pack on the ground, and opened it. He dug through the mounds of paper, casting aside several wooden flutes, some of them snapped in half, and withdrew the one he sought, model seventeen. Then he withdrew several scraps of paper, and, slowly, beneath Gordon's eager eye, the sack full of coins.

"You're absolutely sure it's Byronian? Nothing else will do."

Gordon scowled. "I know my metals."

Samuel hesitated. No one he had talked to had disputed Gordon's reputation. He could only hope it would be enough. He lifted the sack and spilled half of the copper, silver, and gold coins onto the table beside the forge.

"I'll give you half now, and the other half only if you can make it perfectly."

"It makes no difference. Show me what you need."

Samuel drew his attention to the notes and sketches, explaining to him the exact dimensions, referring to the wooden flute, but making clear the variations from it.

"Don't purify it; don't melt it all the way. A mold won't work; it must be done by hand. Do you understand?"

Gordon gave Samuel a meaningful look. "It won't take long, though it will be difficult. I have no doubts in my ability as a silversmith, but as for speaking with the birds—"

"It will." It had to.

Gordon pumped away on the bellows, raising the fire to a satisfactory roar. He took the raw silver and placed it over the fire, but according to Samuel's request, he didn't melt it all the way.

In the painstaking hours that followed, Gordon lived up to his lofty reputation. With the expert use of his array of oddly shaped tools, the silver was clay in Gordon's fingers, eager to become what he willed it to. Each passing hour seemed like minutes in retrospect. Gordon worked tirelessly, paying attention to each agonizing detail. And as the day wore into evening, Gordon, sweating profusely and swelling with pride, produced the magnificent flute.

"It's *perfect*," Samuel breathed, shivering with delight as the cold metal graced his fingers. He absentmindedly plopped the sack of remaining coins beside the pile. Turning toward the cool air, he held the flute up to his practiced lips. How long had he yearned for this moment? It no longer mattered. He took a deep breath and began his song. But what came out was not the pure sound of a flute, but of a bird, a robin singing a song in timely, patterned notes, a hybrid between bird and instrument. The song was colorful and lively, reaching up into the highest of notes.

The resonance continued to ring through the air. Samuel stopped.

He lowered his flute and waited, his heart pounding with fervent anticipation. Silence ensued. Gordon watched on.

Out of the corner of his eye, Samuel saw Gordon's hands drift closer to his pile of coins with each passing second of stillness. Nothing happened. Then, in an instant, a red-breasted robin alighted on Samuel's shoulder and twittered out its own call. Then another landed on his other shoulder. Samuel's excitement couldn't be contained. He stretched his arms out like a scarecrow, laughing like a gold miner with an armful of gold.

The robins kept coming, landing on every part of him available. When they consumed that estate they perched on nearby branches, filling up whole trees. A symphony of robins sang their shimmering song. People emerged from their cottages and stared wide-eyed at all the robins collecting outside.

Samuel took up his flute again and joined in. Using his knowledge of their language, he asked the robins to fly up into the sky and perform a loop. As one cloud they fluttered high into the sky and performed a giant circle. Samuel lowered his flute and brushed it with a fond finger.

"The Caelum Flute," he declared to himself. He reentered the tent and restored the wooden flutes and his papers to his pack. He took one last surveying glance around the tent to make certain he hadn't left even a scrap of paper. His eyes fell on the dumbfounded Gordon.

"Your skills are amazing, Gordon Silversmith. I may need other flutes in the future."

Gordon merely nodded.

Samuel shouldered his pack and left. The robins dispersed to their former business. The people lined the streets of the village, staring at him as he walked by, particularly the silver flute that shimmered in his hand. He wouldn't have felt prouder if he'd been seated upon a tall stallion and dressed in silk, with a royal procession following him.

His legs couldn't carry him fast enough back to Chesterton, to Gloria. A smile spread across his face as he pondered what her reaction would be.

ভেত

Two days later, he arrived. Eager to get home, he broke into a sprint for his house and burst through the door, the flute hidden behind his back. Gloria was sitting in a wooden chair, and Gretchen, a wool spinner from faraway Claghorne who was getting on in her years, sat adjacent to her.

For a moment, nobody spoke.

Gretchen chuckled, shaking her head. "You are in some deep trouble, young man."

Gloria blushed, and looked from the ground to Gretchen to Samuel. "I—I know you took the money, Samuel."

"I know, it was wrong of me, but—"

Gloria shook her head, deflecting the apology. Nobody said anything for a few more seconds.

Samuel bit his lip. He waited for the perfect moment to reveal the flute, but it never came. This wasn't how he'd imagined it.

Then Gloria looked up, and put on a brave smile. "Gretchen has come with good news; King Darius has asked her to become his Royal Wool Spinner."

"That's good." Samuel itched to pull the flute out, to make Gloria happy.

"I'll be off to the castle before winter," Gretchen added.

"I'll go with you," Samuel blurted. The words flew out before he could check them. The ill-fitting statement inspired a silence.

"What?" Gloria reacted first. She sounded ready to cry.

"No! I mean I have something King Darius must see." Samuel pulled the flute in front of him.

"Samuel, what did you—"

"It's the Caelum Flute. I've done it Gloria; I can speak to the birds!" He surveyed Gloria for her reaction.

She stared blankly at the flute. "That's what you spent the—"

"Watch, I'll show you." Samuel opened the door and ran outside, gesturing for them to follow.

They shuffled out, surveying the entire area around them.

Samuel held the flute up to his lips and played his second song. The screech of an eagle echoed from the instrument. The notes rang piercingly high. Samuel's fingers fluttered gracefully along the spine and he swayed to the rhythm. Perfect.

When he cut off the song, the eagle didn't take long in coming; it swooped and sent a rush of air over the party of three, then climbed back upward, pumping its majestic wings. It cried in answer upon reaching a pinnacle and plummeted back downward, where it leveled off and landed on a nearby tree limb.

Samuel took a cautious step toward the eagle. He recognized it. It lived nearby and he'd spent many long hours studying its voice. He took another step. The eagle didn't move, but it kept a sharp eye on him. Samuel inched forward until he stood beside it. Still, the eagle didn't move. Making sure to avoid making any sudden movements, Samuel lifted his hand up and placed it on the eagle's back. He stroked its feathers. The surrealism of the moment made Samuel dizzy. He backed away and watched as the eagle sprang into the air and disappeared.

He looked back at the dumbfounded faces of Gretchen and Gloria. Gloria's open mouth formed into a smile as her eyes met his.

"You did it!" She squealed and ran toward him. He swept her into his arms. They embraced each other for several gratifying moments. George watched from the inn doorway, his eyes wide and a mug on the ground below his hand. Samuel's smile widened and he turned away from him, still hugging Gloria. *What a wonderful recovery.* He couldn't have imagined it better.

The months that followed flew by so fast that at their end, Samuel could only recall brief snippets, wondrous, blissful snippets—dancing in a cloud of sparrows, singing in a ring of meadowlarks, flying through a starlit night on the back of a giant condor, with Gloria beside him as always, her head resting against his shoulder. And these snippets ran together, as if his life now consisted only of uninterrupted happiness.

But now, in a meadow similar to the one in which the idea for the Caelum Flute had been born, he had some deep thoughts to consider again.

He sat in a chair, turning the flute in his fingers, thinking about Gloria's smile. But he couldn't enjoy it fully, not when her comment from the previous day had troubled him so much. *'They're sure agreeable creatures, aren't they?'*

It had been the first time such a thought had been voiced, but Samuel sensed it had been bothering him from some buried corner of his mind for some time. *There has to be a simple answer.* He raised the flute to his lips. The rush of excitement he received in doing so still hadn't faded.

He produced a Northridge grouse's call and whistled in soft tones to himself until a chestnut colored grouse strutted out from the undergrowth. Samuel hesitated. Did he really want the answer to this question? Then he took a resolved breath and asked the grouse through flute song to swim out into the middle of a nearby pond, a task no sane Northridge grouse would ever attempt. But the grouse jumped to obey and, to Samuel's horror, plowed into the pool, flapping and kicking to reach the center.

Samuel sat stunned for a moment, then rushed to the water's edge and pulled the struggling fowl from the water. He set it on the ground and became lost in his hapless conclusion; he hadn't discovered how to converse with the birds, he'd discovered how to control them.

But why hadn't he noticed it before? The birds might have sung with him, but they'd never spoken back in intelligent verse, at least according to the "language" he'd "discovered". He had been deceiving himself; he'd invented a device that put the birds in a trance, and any objective observation would have told him as much long before.

Like a blot of ink spreading from a toppled inkwell, the realization tainted all of his memories with Gloria over the past few months. He clenched his fists. His life had become so *perfect*.

He sighed and released the grouse with a brief twiddle of the flute. The grouse took to the sky at a sharp angle, sending hollow reverberations through the air with its wings. But it didn't enjoy freedom for long. An arrow sliced out of nowhere and knocked it out of its flight pattern. The fowl hurtled downward and plopped at Samuel's feet. It didn't move.

Samuel spun around in anger, scouring the forest around him.

A man, younger than himself, appeared from the woods not far from where the grouse had emerged. His left hand clutched a bow. He had long dark hair, and a flowing black cloak. Samuel cursed under his breath. A Marauder.

"That was amazing." The Marauder smiled. Samuel followed his gaze to the Caelum Flute hanging in his hand. He had to be careful; Marauders didn't usually travel alone, and he certainly didn't want to get involved with a group of them. The Marauder strutted forward, pulled the arrow from the grouse, and slung the bird over his shoulder. He smiled and pointed to the bird. "The King will enjoy this."

Samuel said nothing.

The Marauder offered his hand. "I'm Isaac Ganthorn."

Samuel inspected the hand—clean and soft. But he didn't offer his own. This was very unusual Marauder behavior, but his confidence suggested he wasn't alone. Samuel scoured the trees behind Isaac again before settling his gaze on Isaac's face. "What do you want?"

"I want to buy that flute." Isaac dropped his friendly demeanor.

Samuel studied him for several long seconds, an inkling of

realization sparking in his mind. "Buy it? You're a Marauder. Wouldn't you prefer to kill me and pry it from my fingers?"

"I'm in a generous mood today." His voice darkened. "Don't spoil it."

Samuel actually laughed out loud, his mind snapping the pieces together.

"I know what it really is." Samuel sneered. "You haven't been a Marauder long and your king doesn't trust you yet, not even enough to get an audience with him. If you told your superior about the flute, he'd go himself and steal your glory. So here you are, all by yourself, trying to buy it from me and feigning confidence to scare me."

Isaac's features went icy. "I could still kill you."

In response Samuel whipped the flute to his mouth and sounded a complex call, an attempt to squeeze a full song into the space of a few seconds.

Isaac swiped at the flute too late and Samuel knocked him to the ground with a kick to the chest. The giant condor arched down from the sky. Samuel clambered up a tall boulder, continuing the song as he did so. Isaac struggled to his feet and rushed after him. As the condor swooped by, Samuel leaped onto its back and sailed out of reach.

A look of hatred twisted Isaac's face as he notched and shot an arrow. It fell way short and he threw his bow to the ground. "I'll get it sooner or later!"

Samuel wanted to scream. The Caelum Flute had been discovered, and by a Marauder no less. Worse, Samuel knew its true power now . . . and so did the Marauder. Samuel shivered, but not from the cold air rushing past them; whoever got their hands on this flute would have the power to rule the world. Why had he been so foolish, flaunting it about? But it was too late to be mended. He could only console himself with the thought that perhaps Isaac wouldn't find him again. Maybe he should take Gloria into hiding. No, he couldn't put her through that.

When he got home he pushed the memory of the experience out of his mind and told Gloria nothing about it. He didn't want to burden her, and telling her about it would make it more real, more of a threat in his mind. By hiding it from her perhaps he could prevent anything more from happening. And the next morning the sun rose again.

ೕ

Samuel stuck his hand out and caught one of the snowflakes drifting to the ground. It melted immediately. The flurry of snow ended just as fast as it had started, with nothing left to prove it had ever existed. *Still, winter's coming fast.*

Any day now he would have to make a decision, whether to go with Gretchen to the castle, or wait, a decision made harder by Gloria's recent illness. Plus, how would the king react? Samuel couldn't bear to think about what would happen if the flute ended up in the wrong hands.

He sighed and strolled down the path toward home, fir trees on either side of him. *Just focus on getting Gloria better.*

But as he neared his village, he heard shouts. Smoke rose above the tree line. His heart froze over with a sudden, painful understanding. A cluster of unintelligible sounds twisted into a knot in his throat and went unspoken. He dropped the notes he had collected and broke into a sprint for the village. The noises of people crying grew louder as he approached. He skidded from the forest to the sight of houses aflame and people huddled together in the middle of the street, wailing.

"No." Samuel sprinted through the village.

George the bartender stepped in front of him, waving his blood and dirt spattered arms, his eyes wide. "Sam, the Marauders came!"

Samuel shoved past him, barely comprehending his words in his focus on his own house. Fortunately, his cottage had not been set aflame. Gloria sat on the ground outside the front door, dirty and bedraggled, crying into her self-hugging arms. Nothing had ever given Samuel as much pain as that single, heart wrenching moment. She looked up and spotted him with red eyes. He ran to her and swept her up into his arms.

"Gloria," he whispered. That one word couldn't relate his feelings, but no others could have helped.

"The Marauders," she choked into his shoulder. "They—they d-destroyed everything."

He pulled her tighter. A fine scarlet line marred her neck. "Who did this?" He traced a trembling finger along it.

"He-he said his name was—" She sobbed, each break in her words a stab to Samuel's heart. "Isaac Ganthorn. He-he made me tell you—he's c-captain now." Samuel clenched his fist and closed his eyes. Hatred filled him like boiling water.

Much as his leaden limbs willed him not to, Samuel pulled away from Gloria. He walked into the cottage and straight to the bed. Bending down, he found, as he expected, the shattered strongbox. The house had been ripped to pieces from the inside out. Samuel's notes covered the debris like snow.

"Did they take any papers?" Samuel asked.

"No . . ." Gloria frowned from the doorway. That gave Samuel slight relief. He gathered up all the papers and tossed them into the unoccupied fireplace. Then he lit the edge and watched them crumble away.

"The Caelum Flute should never be made again," he declared to the brief fire. He walked back to the doorway and gazed into Gloria's eyes. He was about to do the hardest thing he'd ever had to do.

"Gloria, the flute . . . it controls the birds. With it the Marauders will be powerful enough to take over the Green Isles. I—"

"Samuel, wait, there's something I-I-"

Samuel shook his head, holding back tears. "I must—go and retrieve the flute." He couldn't believe he'd managed to squeeze the words out.

Gloria widened her eyes. "No, Samuel, you can't. What will you do? Don't go!" She was begging, and Samuel's will teetered on the verge of shattering.

"I . . . must . . . hunt the Marauders and find a way to steal it back."

Gloria shook her head and opened her mouth, but words didn't come out. Samuel embraced her once more for several long moments, like a traveler in the desert drinking his last sips of water. Finally, he let go and broke his gaze away. He turned to the path out of the chaotic, burning village, unable to look back at the forlorn figure of his wife watching him leave. But he could hear her sobs even after all sounds of the village had died away behind him.

CHAPTER 15

FORSAKEN

Micah drifted back to reality.

Gretchen folded her hands in her lap.

Robbyn blinked, wiping her wet eyes. The storm had escalated to a furious pitch, yanking at the cottage relentlessly, but it seemed to rage in the distance, unable to penetrate the quiet atmosphere of the cottage.

"Never heard that before," Drift said.

"What happened to Samuel and Gloria?" Robbyn sniffed.

"Samuel was never seen again, to my knowledge. I can only guess that the Marauders killed him or he died before reaching their ship." The storm slammed against the cottage, as though fueled by this trace of malevolence.

"And Gloria?" Robbyn sounded afraid to ask.

"She was killed in a later Marauder attack. It's a sad tale, indeed, but I suppose it's not surprising that such an evil tool would be created in such circumstances. The flute has caused heartache even from its very beginnings."

"But why doesn't anyone know about this story?" Micah asked.

"Because when I left for the castle a few days after the attack, I took these secrets with me. I only tell it to people I trust, people who will keep it to themselves." She raised an eyebrow at each of them.

Drift cast a sideways glance at Micah.

Gretchen chuckled. "I assure you, this shepherd boy can be trusted, old friend."

"But why must we keep it secret?" Micah said.

"Gordon Silversmith—the Marauders can't find out about him. They would force him to remake the Caelum Flute. As of now he hides deep in the Kakotine Mountains, as I told him to do." She raised her eyebrow at each of them again.

"But why doesn't Gordon try to remake the flute himself? It could be used to drive away the Marauders—it could be destroyed afterward." Micah quickly added the last part. His interest in the subject had been piqued.

Gretchen frowned. "A second flute? Why destroy the world twice, my boy? Besides, without Samuel's notes, Gordon will never be able to make the flute. Samuel was wise to burn them."

The noisy shift of Micah's stomach interrupted the onset of shame. He placed a hand to it beneath the blankets, hoping no one had noticed.

But Gretchen smiled at him. "You must be terribly hungry, Micah. We have plenty of bread, cheese, and water, and little else until the storm is done."

A chunk of wet bark would have tasted good at that moment. Micah ate and drank his fill, especially the white wedges of cheese—so packed with flavor—then went back to sleep.

He awoke to another great crash of the storm but found the inside of the cottage unaffected, though Drift had planted himself in the middle of the floor and grasped the convulsing overhead beams. Gretchen sat with her head lolled to one side, asleep. Robbyn sat at the table with her hands folded, her head tilted toward the door. Thunder pealed out amongst the howling and banging of the storm. She smiled at him, and he fell back to sleep.

In the following days, the storm's noises escalated to waking him thrice more, each time only for a few hours at most. After waking up the third time, he felt as healthy as his normal self—even more so, in fact—and eager to continue his journey. But the storm continued.

A snort sounded through the room. Gretchen lifted her head, her eyelids floating open. She smacked her lips for a few seconds. "It's time."

A gust of wind battered the cottage. Rain still beat the roof.

"I beg your pardon?" Robbyn said.

"The storm's over."

Micah and Robbyn looked at each other.

From the fireplace, Drift tilted an ear toward the door. "She's right. It's moving on."

Micah pulled his shirt collar to the side to find a pink scar there. He lifted his covers and scooted off the bed onto his bare feet. The rush of colder air made him pause, and his legs wobbled as he walked around to retrieve his things, but moving again invigorated him.

Everyone rose from their seats.

"I'm afraid you can't afford to wait until it dies completely." Gretchen laughed. "So hold onto your hats!"

His feet sandaled, his back cloaked, and pack and crook in hand, Micah made his way toward the door, each step more stable than the last.

Robbyn and Drift grabbed their cloaks.

"One more thing," Gretchen hobbled over to them with the aid of her cane. "I want you three to travel together. Perhaps whatever prevented that Marauder from attacking Micah will keep the two of you safe as well."

Drift glanced at Micah and nodded.

"What about his sheep?" Robbyn cast an apologetic glance at Micah. "I don't mean to be rude, but if we have Marauders after us—"

"Take my cart," Gretchen said, "and my horses."

Micah sighed with relief. With the storm's delay, he didn't know how he was going to reach the castle before the full moon.

Drift shook his head. "We won't need your horses."

A smile crept onto Gretchen's lips. "I didn't think so."

Robbyn didn't seem as puzzled as Micah by this bit of conversation, so he didn't ask.

Gretchen turned to him and wrapped one arm around him, her left hand still holding her cane. He hugged her back and allowed her to lean on him for support.

"I'm not sure what the mystery surrounding your journey is about, but I think it's safe to assume it's more important than some robes for the king. Be careful." She released him and hugged Robbyn. "Thanks for all your help, and take courage."

"Thank you for your hospitality," Robbyn said.

"Yeah, thanks." Micah fidgeted.

Then Gretchen turned to Drift. She reached up and patted him on the back. Even if her back had been straight, her head wouldn't have reached much taller than Drift's waist. He lowered a hand that covered Gretchen's back.

"Take care, big fella." Then she backed away and made a motion as if to brush them away. "Now off with you. I'll be praying hard."

Drift opened the door. Wet wind blew in around it. Robbyn rushed outside, and Micah followed her into the charged wet air, then Drift shut the door behind them.

Micah donned his hood against the rain and wind and surveyed their surroundings. Toppled trees and splayed branches, everything drenched, a sight made gloomier by the still gray sky. A cottage had collapsed in the distance. He had expected to see the ocean, and though he did smell salt on the air, the tree line blocked his view, and for that he was grateful.

He turned to find no cottage at all, only a shabby door planted in a hillside.

"This way, Micah!" Robbyn called.

He turned again, completing a circle, to see her following Drift into the wind. She squinted and held her forearm in front of her, but Drift didn't react to the weather. Micah followed them to a nearby hillside similar to that of Gretchen's cottage, but this one had a boulder wedged into it.

Drift rolled it aside and bleating sheep spilled forth. They surrounded Micah, and he knelt down to embrace them. The realization of how much he'd missed them hit him at the same time as their nuzzling heads.

"Whoa!" Drift spread his arms to prevent two tan-colored horses from escaping the cave, and he rolled the rock back into place.

They lifted the sheep into a nearby cart, and Robbyn and Micah climbed in as well. Then, to Micah's surprise, Drift strapped the reigns to himself.

Robbyn climbed into the seat as Drift fastened himself. With an impish grin, she grabbed the reigns. "Let me know if I get too hard on you."

Drift's beard shifted into a grin, and in response he bolted forward. Both Robbyn and Micah nearly toppled backward.

"Likewise," Drift called back to the bumping and jostling wagon. They careened along the trail at a speed far superior to that of two horses. The trail ended up following the coast.

Sea shells of different colors popped up and down along the beach.

"They're sandhoppers," Robbyn said. "Gretchen told me about them. Apparently they're related to grasshoppers, but they wear seashells to protect them from the birds, and they like cold water. Gretchen said at the castle, where the water's frigid, they absolutely cover the beaches."

Micah spotted a cluster of seagulls studying the leaping oddities with obvious intent.

As the day progressed, the trail curved back into the mainland, and Drift maintained a breakneck pace. At this rate, Micah realized, it wouldn't be long before they reached the castle, if the Marauders didn't reach them first.

⚬⚬⚬

The soles of Isaac's feet squished miserably as he trekked through the muddy sod of the Marsh Woods. The white fog magnified the effect of his tired, blurring eyes, making it difficult to see very far in front of him. Cold, tired, and nauseated by the stench of his own root breath, he trudged onward. The past few days had been bitter and depressing. He'd been very lucky to find the hollow tree in the midst of the forest, however tight the fit had been. Who knows what the storm would have chosen to do with him if he hadn't found shelter. The storm had also wiped away all signs of his prey. But Isaac knew that ultimately their aim was the castle. So he trudged southward as if in a trance.

"No one can help me," Isaac told himself grimly. The fog that surrounded him was depression itself, folding in on him, swallowing him up. But it slowly dispersed, and he strolled into sunlight, though it did nothing to alter his dark mood. He looked back into the swirling white fog. It seemed to have a life of its own, devouring the remnant moisture of the storm, always thickening. And it left an insidious trail of white behind him, as if it had been unwilling to let him go.

A shabby cottage built into a hillside stood before Isaac. At his feet lay, to his surprise, an array of footprints, amongst which lay the giant's unmistakable boot mark.

I've found them. He traced the footprints backward. They'd come from the cottage.

They'd stayed with a villager. He withdrew his dagger. It sang with the motion, a vicious prelude to death. But far from vicious, he felt cold, empty, and distant. He didn't care anymore. He didn't care whether he lived or died or whether anyone else lived or died. He opened the door, slipped inside, and shut it noiselessly behind him.

Micah lay upon the wooden bed of the wagon. The pitching and rocking had forced him out of his prone position and onto his forearms. Whenever the ride softened, and he lowered himself to the floor, he was rewarded with multiple whacks to the head as the rocking motion flared up again. His sheep swayed and bumped to the rhythm of the cart. Rachel disliked it the most. Long after the other sheep had accepted their fate and lay down to rest, she kept up her steady stream of bleating. She lost her balance with every major bump. He grinned at her stubbornness.

He glanced ahead at Drift, still plowing ahead as evening faded. The sinew bulged from his stump-like neck and the leather strap cut against his chest. His heavy legs churned at a blur. Never before had he seen anything like this giant.

Their route led away from the ocean until the forest swallowed them. Fortunately, this forest, in contrast to the dead, swampy wood, consisted of healthy evergreen. Almost like home, although flatter. It smelled like it did when he stood outside his cabin after a rainstorm. He welcomed the gush of warm nostalgia.

With a pang, home felt very far away. Casting a look in the direction of those familiar mountains revealed nothing but crowded, wet trees fading into darkness. He looked about for reassurance and found it in the white, fuzzy bodies strewn about him. He patted Rachel on the head.

The wagon went airborne and he gritted his teeth before it crashed to the ground. He wondered for the last time that day whether wagon maintenance concerned Drift. But although the wagon swayed, creaked, and shimmied—sometimes to hair-raising degrees—it remained intact.

They slowed to a stop, and in the disappearing light Drift stopped pulling and jogged to the declining pace of the wagon. Micah climbed stiffly to his feet, as did his sheep and Robbyn. Drift tossed aside the straps, breathing deeply. After a brief stretch, Micah leapt from the wagon and walked around, stomping the circulation back into his legs. As he walked by Drift, a wave of humid air passed over him. Sweat had drenched through Drift's clothing and was streaming off his water-laden beard.

"I'm going to find some water," Drift announced as he pulled a couple of buckets out of the wagon.

"No, you just sit down. I'll get the water." Robbyn took the buckets from his hands and made her way into the forest. Drift sighed and sat on a stump.

Micah understood how Robbyn felt; he wanted to do something as well. "I'll make the sheepfold."

He surveyed the area around them. In the scarce light, made scarcer by the surrounding trees, he made out a grove of sorts. In the middle sat a ring of small stones and the blackened charcoal of past campfires. Flattened vegetation covered the fairly level ground. Not far from the fireplace lay two horse-sized boulders separated by a narrow gap perfect for a sheepfold entrance. He pulled the hood of his cloak over his head to fend off the fast approaching cold and went off in search of building materials.

✑

Isaac surveyed the room, his eyes adjusting to the dim light—lots of wool blankets and clothing, a fireplace, and a tiny old lady with a stick, sitting in a chair that held her feet aloft. She stared straight at him with piercing blue eyes.

"Ah, there you are, Isaac. I'm Gretchen. Welcome to my humble cottage."

Isaac started at the sound of his name and the familiarity with which she said it.

"You're very late, you know," she said in a tired voice, as though

177

he'd been keeping her waiting. "And here I thought Marauders were always early."

Isaac said nothing. He couldn't look away from those bright, youthful eyes. They cut right into him and laid bare his darkest secrets, even more so than the King's did.

"I sense something the matter with you," she said. "Do you feel well? You certainly don't look well. If I didn't know better I'd think you were dead."

"Be quiet," he snapped, raising his dagger.

"Oh, you can put that knife away. I won't be serving dinner." She laughed—a crumbling laugh that showed her age. Like the rustling of paper.

"Stop it." He took a step forward.

Her laughter trailed off. "Have a seat." She indicated a single wooden chair facing hers. "We have much to talk about."

He crept over to the chair without removing his gaze from her, like a prowling wolf. But he didn't sit down. "What do you want?" He glared at her through narrow eyes.

"I already told you; I just want to talk. If you must know I get quite lonely sometimes." She laughed again. Each rustle of her voice pushed his nerves closer to the edge.

"Stop!" He lunged forward with the knife.

She stopped, and gave him a bored, disapproving look. "I'm Gretchen, by the way." She looked away from him, over at the fire. When she looked back and found the knife still in her face, she sighed. "Put that away, please. I'm sorry, but this is just getting tiresome."

"How do you know I won't kill you?" Isaac inched the knife forward.

Gretchen smiled, raising her eyebrows, daring him to proceed with what he'd come to do. The expression infuriated Isaac. He gritted his teeth and pressed the knife forward. "How do you know I won't kill you *right now*?" he spat. He hoped he looked as crazy as he felt.

Gretchen rolled her eyes. "Do you really want to dream about this? Do you really want to see the old lady who seemed unfazed by your threats, chiding you, laughing at you, every time you close your eyes to rest? I'm annoying enough as it is in real life."

Isaac inhaled sharply. "H—"

"Oh, come now, Isaac. Isn't it obvious? Those tired, swollen eyes, the shaken demeanor, the dejected posture." She paused and gave him an imploring look, as if waiting for him to finish the thought. "You've been having nightmares for years. I've seen it before. And judging by your surprise, you probably think the Marauder King doesn't know about it." She shook her head. "You know, there's a name for what you've been feeling. It's called guilt."

"I'll do it!" Isaac screamed, waving his knife around. "I don't care anymore!"

A shadow enveloped Gretchen. Her smile disappeared. "You think you're alone, don't you?" She spoke in such an ominous tone that Isaac staggered back several steps.

The shadow on Gretchen's face intensified, and the spunky old lady who lived a humble, quiet life disappeared. The eyes of this new person were distant, and glazed—full of sorrow and pain.

"You think you're the only one."

Again, Isaac took a step back. His leg knocked into the wooden chair.

"You think you're some kind of freak, that somehow everyone else in the world is perfect and innocent, not a worry in the world." She sounded disgusted. "Did it ever occur to you that you're not the only one who needs rescue?" She paused and leaned forward, glaring into his soul.

Isaac sat in his seat with a thump.

"I've done terrible things," she said in a tone so low it was little more than a whisper. The sorrowful lines around her eyes deepened. "And so has everyone else."

For a few long moments neither said anything. Isaac listened to the dying fire. He just wanted out of this house.

Gretchen leaned back; the old lady in her had returned. But her tone remained serious. She spoke in a hushed, intimate tone. "They either suffer in silence about it, like you have, or hide their feelings from themselves, or stuff something such as drink or work in that hole in their heart." She paused, a smile creeping onto her lips. "But there is true healing, Isaac. You can be forgiven. I've found it, and so have others, but not nearly enough of them. There is someone who wants to take your burden and shoulder it for you."

Her eyes sparkled, and Isaac felt as though he was being whispered the elated secrets of a little girl. He was not impressed. He knew where this conversation was headed, and it annoyed him.

"Who?"

"He is known by many names. The Hero, Savior, Messiah, Yeshua . . ."

Isaac sighed. Just as he thought. He already knew about the Story. His mother had read from it to him every night. He looked at the door, then toward the fire. He started to rise from his chair, but then his eyes fell on Gretchen. Her silent gaze compelled him to sit back down.

"How does He do that?" Isaac sighed. *Just get up and leave, Ganthorn.*

Gretchen rose from her chair, snatched her walking stick from beside the fireplace, and hobbled her small frame over to a cupboard in the corner. She opened it, reached in, and pulled out a battered leather book. "Read through this." She dropped it in his lap. "The Hero was killed by the very men He went to rescue. And in doing so—rescued them. His death," Gretchen planted a bony finger in Isaac's chest, "was your punishment. And mine. And everyone else's. He took it for us."

"So, it's done then?" That did relieve him. Not that he believed in the Story, or God, or Messiah. But in the off chance that he was wrong, at least he was covered.

"No, you have to choose. It's up to you to accept the Gift or not, whether to turn from the life that caused your guilt and accept the Gift. Again, read the book. It's my favorite story."

He examined the book in his hand. Just looking at it brought his mother to mind. And that did make him feel a little better. But still, this lady . . . her behavior . . . He knew he wasn't going to kill her. He sheathed his dagger and ran a finger over the title. He rose to his feet and drifted toward the door.

"Come back for dinner sometime. But I'll provide the silverware," she said with that cackling laugh.

Isaac opened the door, but Gretchen reached up and grabbed his shoulder. He turned and found himself looking again deep into those earnest blue eyes.

"Isaac, He *loves* you."

It took several seconds for Isaac to tear his gaze away and exit the cottage. He walked for several minutes before he looked up and fully realized that he was headed back for the designated meeting spot, to be escorted to the King. He still had no idea what to do. The King might kill him; in fact, it seemed like the likeliest possibility.

Although he walked at a slow pace, it wasn't long before he arrived at his destination—a short, rocky beach closed in and hidden by vegetation. Just past it the shoreline began its southward ascent into what would eventually be the steep cliffs that surrounded the castle. The thick, steamy fog pressed hard against the bank, like a wall. And there, beside a wooden dinghy on the water's edge, stood a cluster of black-clad Marauders.

"Ganthorn, is that you?" called one of them as Isaac continued the shallow descent to the beach. He stashed the Story in his shirt.

"Aye." As Isaac drew nearer he saw that Captain Lewell had been the one to address him. He greeted Isaac with that same twisted sneer that always quartered his face.

"What are you doing here?" Lewell's eyes filled with suspicion.

Isaac climbed into the dinghy. "Take me back to the ship."

The creases in Lewell's face deepened. His eyes widened. "You're all that's left?" With no answer from Isaac, Lewell's look of surprise shifted into an evil, knowing grin.

"You're through, Ganthorn," he rumbled in a low, provoking voice.

Isaac said nothing as Lewell motioned the remaining Marauders into the dinghy. They scraped off into the water. It didn't take long for the milky fog to surround them. Two low-ranking Marauders worked the paddles as Lewell taunted and smirked at Isaac the whole trip. The rest of the Marauders aboard watched with wide eyes.

"You're lucky that storm hit, or we wouldn't have even been there when you arrived," Lewell said as Isaac held his unbroken gaze on the wall of white at the helm of the dinghy. "His Highness is angry enough as it is. What, with the storm forcing us to regroup and repair, this wretched fog, incompetence among the men, the spies that got away—oh yes, he knows; you weren't the only survivor—not quite!"

Isaac didn't even wipe the flecks of spit spattering his cheek.

A sly grin lit Lewell's face. "I wonder if a man can reach a certain point," his tone softened to a whisper, "where he simply goes mad with rage." He paused. "I suppose if it can happen to anyone, it can happen to the King."

The familiar black hull emerged.

He didn't mind Lewell's rants, but he wondered with a fluttering heart how much worse the King's would be.

The dinghy slid into place beside a waiting rope ladder, and Isaac climbed it.

"Idiot!" Lewell called up the ladder. "You're done for! Your days are numbered!"

Isaac climbed over the railing and strode in the direction of the king's chambers. The Marauders, wielding hammers and saws and planks, all paused in their repairs to stare at him. He ignored them, as he did two other Captains' looks of surprise as he passed within inches of them down the narrow hallway.

He placed a hand on the handle of the king's chamber door. The longer he stood there, the harder his heart pounded, so he took a deep breath and yanked it open.

"Who dares—" The king stopped mid-sentence and set down a map.

"Ganthorn, where did you—how?" The king paused and gathered himself. Arrogance regained control of his features. "How did your quest go?"

Isaac averted his gaze to the floor. "Why are you doing this? You know how it went."

The king stirred. "Did you hunt down the spies?"

"I'm—I'm done being a Marauder."

Heat sprang to the king's eyes. "You what?"

Isaac didn't move, didn't speak, didn't breath.

The king let loose a roar that could have belonged to the beast once housed next door. With every vein swelling from his face and neck, he grabbed the edge of the oak table and heaved it forward. It crashed to the floor, shattering wood and glass.

Isaac covered his face, and when he removed his arm the broken table had submerged into the floorboard.

The king stood on the other side of the table, clenching and unclenching his fists, breathing fast. His eyes were so filled with hate that Isaac couldn't help but avert his gaze. A guttural noise escaped the king's throat as he leapt the heap of rubble. Before Isaac could react the king grabbed him around the neck and slammed him up against the wall. Knobs of various weapons dug into his back.

"You are banished from the Marauders, Isaac Ganthorn!" he spat.

Isaac couldn't gather enough breath to remind the king that he'd quit.

"You're a disgrace!" the king screamed as he swung him by the cloak and hammered him into the floor.

Pain shot through Isaac's head, and he clutched it as he rolled over.

"I'm sorry I ever allowed you to be a Marauder!"

Isaac hauled in air through what felt like a caved-in windpipe. Yet he forced himself to look into the desolate eyes of his former king and managed to choke out, "Me too."

The king threw open the door with a bang and screamed out to the crew, "Take us to Marooner's Island, *now!*" Holding open the door with his foot, he grabbed the prone form of Isaac again by his cloak and hurled him out into the hall.

"Take care of this waste of flesh." The king ripped Isaac's dagger out of its sheath and tore the cloak off his back, hacking and ripping it to shreds all the while. He threw the cloth remnants to the floor, gave a final spiteful glance at Isaac and shut himself in his chamber with a slam that resounded down the hall.

A muffled sound echoed through the door and it took Isaac, now clad in gray shirt and pants, a moment to recognize it as sobbing.

Just as he climbed to his feet, two Marauders peeked into the hallway and listened for several seconds. They nodded to each other at once, stole down the hall, and grabbed him by both arms. Isaac considered running. Busting away from these two rookies and diving overboard wouldn't be too difficult. *But where would I go?* It didn't matter any longer whether he rotted in a cell, wasted away on an island, or lived in freedom. He didn't care anymore.

They lugged him down the hall, into the sunlight for a moment, and dragged him down the stairs. The light faded and the moisture thickened as they descended to the lowest level. Barnacles and mold appeared on the warped walls. The smell of mildew lined the air. They turned into a narrow hallway, and the wooden walls gave way to rusty bars.

They heaved Isaac into the first cell on the left, and he landed face first in a layer of slime. A clang sounded behind him, then footsteps clomped back up the stairs.

He didn't pull himself from the slime for several minutes. He hoped the king really did go through with taking him straight to Marooner's Island. But he knew the king wouldn't; he would cool down and realize that it was too foggy, repairs still needed to be made, they needed to stay on schedule.

He sighed, lifted himself off the ground, and wiped the slime off his cheek with his sleeve. He pulled the Story from under his shirt and set it in his lap. *Foolish old lady.* It had probably been her only copy. He wished he'd left it with her.

He surveyed the prison, trying in vain to blink away the ghostly images of faces locked behind the bars. He squeezed his eyelids shut. *It's empty. It's empty. Nobody's here!* When he opened his eyes, the images had vanished. How ironic; in his nightmares he endured his crimes from his victims' perspective, and now he shared their predicament in real life. Now he truly could not escape his nightmares, not even in wakefulness. But those people had only been slotted for slavery; he would face a slow and painful death. *But a deserved one.*

Whatever happened, though, Isaac resolved to not drink the water. The slaves hadn't known what went into that stuff, but he did, and it made his will all the stronger for it, if not his stomach.

He shook his head and grabbed up the Story. He hadn't read a book since training, but he needed something to take his mind far away. The crusty wall beside him held a speck of light. He pushed the Story in front of the ribbon, caught the speck and used it to begin reading, one highlighted word at a time.

ᏜᎧ

Isaac trembled as the Marauder's silhouette approach the cell. His parched tongue caressed his upper lip. But he had to be careful this time; he couldn't afford another spill. A hand slid the bowl of murky liquid between the bars, and Isaac pounced on it. He brought it to his lips and downed it—three gulps.

Then, with a clink, the cell door swung open. "Git out, slave." Isaac squinted up at the meaty Marauder escorting him. How fast things changed; he'd fallen from Head Captain to below the slave waterer.

The Marauder pulled him down the hall and up the steps. At the sight of the light at the top of the stairway, Isaac had to avert his gaze to the steps in front of him. As they climbed the light grew brighter and brighter until, when they reached the top, he had to scrunch his eyes as tight as he could and follow his escort blindly across the main deck.

He chanced a glance and squeezed them against the flash of dazzling light. But after a few moments, through brief snatches of rapid blinking, he discerned that the King was not in attendance, though almost everyone else was. Spectators covered the deck. Isaac squinted out at the rest of the fleet. Their inhabitants watched as well. He picked out Lewell from the crowd, beaming at him. But nobody spoke; only the sound of the wind and Isaac's footsteps could be heard.

Isaac could only recall a few times a Marauder had been banished to Marooner's Island, and never a Head Captain, or even a Captain, for that matter. Such thoughts didn't comfort him as he stopped at the edge of the railing. Then he saw it, Marooner's Island, little more than a solitary sandbar with a lone palm tree planted at its center.

No land existed in sight in any direction. The baby blue water of the shallows looked serene and quite enticing. He leaned over the edge of the ship, peered at the much darker water beside them, and remembered that these waters were deceptively frigid.

With a backward glance that revealed nothing but hundreds of faces he wished he hadn't seen, Isaac stepped atop the railing and plummeted overboard. Before he had time to think about it, he plunged into the water.

An icy chill grabbed him as soon as he breached the surface—much colder than he had expected. Reaching upward, he climbed to the negligibly warmer surface and struck for the island, shivering. It took clamping his teeth into his tongue to prevent himself from gulping in the salt water.

It wasn't until his tired feet touched ground that he felt the full extent of his exhaustion. He crawled onto the warm sand. The Marauders had already turned to leave. He wouldn't be a part of their grand voyage, or their celebration to come. But then again he wouldn't be there to suffer the destruction that followed, either.

He trudged up the beach, toward the tree. The island was bigger than it had appeared from the ship, though still small as islands go. He expected to find skeletons at the base of the tree, but there were none. Of course not. The storms would have washed them away.

Soon his skeleton would follow. Chances of rescue, and therefore survival, were nonexistent. None of the ship routes passed the island, and if a ship did happen by, nobody would be naïve enough to pick up a Marauder.

Isaac sat at the base of the tree and pulled out the Story. It was soaked, but the letters were still legible. If he routinely flipped the pages the sun would be able to dry it out. He looked up—in futility, he knew—for a coconut. No such luck. So he watched the black ships shrink away, trying not to think about the various possibilities for his eventual death.

CHAPTER 16

It Dwells in the Water

Micah looked up past the outlines of the evergreen trees flickering in the firelight at the moon, which had revealed itself in the twilight. He cleared his throat. "It's almost full."

Drift sat hunched over the fire, frowning. "Three more nights."

"I have to get there before the full moon, according to my master." He cleared his throat and coughed.

Drift raised one eyebrow. "Us too. That's when they hang Kestrel." He glanced at the piles of logs formed in a circle around the boulders—the completed sheepfold.

Micah followed his gaze and peered through the space between the boulders. His sheep still slept soundly. He coughed again, and put a hand to his throat. He sucked in a breath of air and gagged.

"Something wrong?"

"I'm just thirsty." He twisted around, searching for the buckets of water. But they had disappeared.

Drift sat up, a hand on his dagger. "Where's Robbyn?"

A piercing scream rose over the owls and crickets. "It's the Beast! It's the—" *Kersploosh!*

"Robbyn." Drift sprang off the ground and thundered into the woods, his massive bulk snapping tree limbs and ripping through undergrowth.

Micah leapt up, rushed over to the sheepfold, and rolled a stray log into the opening. He started to run back into the forest but hesitated. Should he leave his sheep alone?

Another scream, mingled with splashing and gurgling, rang out.

He fought his way into the tangled vegetation of Drift's wake. Terrible images raced through his head as he battled against the constraints of the forest. He could see, filtered through layers of bushes and branches, the distant form of Drift bulling through the forest like a dragon through a cloud cluster.

"Hold on Robbyn! I'm coming!"

Drift's roar spurred Micah's heart faster.

More splashing, a mangled scream, and then more splashing.

"Hold on!"

Drift disappeared from sight. Two seconds later the loudest splash of the night ripped outward.

Micah pressed forward, tripping and falling, through the moonlit forest. The darkness made it difficult to protect himself from the back lashing branches. Finally, with a last whip to the face from a thorn bush, he stumbled into a clearing with a wide pool of muddy water, a small waterfall at each end.

Drift appeared to be in the midst of a tussle with some sort of red water beast. Robbyn was spluttering and thrashing on the surface of the water, a few yards from the battle.

Although Micah couldn't make out much of the tumultuous cascade that was Drift and the beast, it was clear that Drift was attempting to fend the creature off with one hand and grab Robbyn with the other.

Throwing off his cloak, Micah plunged into the water. It deepened and he pushed off, paddling and kicking toward Robbyn. She took a deep breath before her face followed the rest of her body under. He dove under and reached for her. From beneath the water, only moonlit murkiness could be discerned, as well as a few floating insects near the surface.

He kept kicking forward, and Robbyn's sinking body materialized, motionless.

Wrapping his arms around her, he pushed off the bottom. Robbyn surfaced, but he couldn't position himself to reach the surface without lowering her. He had to keep his legs kicking hard to prevent her from sinking them both. He tilted onto his back, aiming for the bank, but she drifted underwater again.

He caught a frighteningly clear glimpse of the beast through the murk and his heart skipped a beat. It looked to be the size of a large dog, red with jagged black stripes. The long, twisted teeth of its wide mouth protruded from its lip at every direction. Micah winced as it writhed up to them.

Where was Drift?

Its face passed within inches of his before the rest of the scaly, slimy body slid by. The beast's spiny, fluttering tail followed, sliding the beast through the water, swishing water in Micah's face. The unmoving, unblinking eye, a perfect white circle with a pupil as black as its stripes, fixed on him as it circled them ever so slowly.

Micah did his best to keep Robbyn above the waterline as he kept his feet flailing beneath her, in the colder reaches of the pool.

But he needed air—fast; his lungs begged for release. He clenched his jaw against his lungs' pain and turned his head to keep his eye on the predator. Then he caught sight of the teeth marks in Robbyn's leg and the curls of blood dispersing into the water from it. He jerked his head back to the beast to see it break into a lightning-quick streak for Robbyn.

He let go of Robbyn, brought his body into a tilted ball, and unleashed a two-footed kick into its nose with his sandaled feet. He felt hard contact and the creature exploded into a twisting, looping dance of confusion.

But the effort burst open Micah's lungs. He sucked in a deep draft of water, and tried to cough it out, but couldn't. Panic spread from his paralyzed lungs, and he flailed. Robbyn drifted away, and one hand snapped in her direction, but he couldn't—he needed air. The more he struggled to breathe the more the water poured down his windpipe.

Then something yanked him upward, and once he breeched the water's surface he coughed it all up. Sweet, blessed air. Even as the water spluttered from his mouth he looked up to see Drift, his hand holding Robbyn and Micah by their collars and his other hand clutching the writhing monster—by the teeth. His face was so contorted and red that at first it looked like one of the beast's appendages. He leaned back and hurled the beast. It wriggled as it sailed over the small waterfall, and splashed into the next pool.

As if nothing had happened, the woods fell quiet, save for the owls and crickets. Drift waded to the bank and plopped Robbyn and Micah down.

Robbyn fell to her hands and knees, still coughing up water.

"Are you all right, Robbyn?" Drift asked.

"I-I'm usually a good swimmer. But it pulled me under and I ran out of air—I panicked."

Drift clenched his fists and pressed them into his forehead. "This is my fault. I should never have lost sight of you. How could I have forgiven my—"

"N-no . . ." Robbyn dabbed the hem of her skirt into the beast's bite. She looked up. "Please don't beat yourself up. I-it was my foolishness. I didn't think anything would happen if I hurried. I was just really thirsty. It's thanks to you two that I'm still alive."

Micah didn't see how he'd helped; he'd ended up needing rescued as well.

"You don't understand," Drift said. "It's not your fault. Those things—they hunt deer by releasing a spore that tricks the mind into thinking it's thirsty, which lures them to the stream—humans, too, sometimes."

Micah nodded. That must have been what plagued him.

"It just kept getting worse," she said. "I thought my throat would catch fire."

"Aye," Drift said. "Next time—run."

Robbyn sighed. "Thanks again, Micah. I would have drowned. Truly."

"Aye, she would have." Drift had his regretful gaze on the mossy river stones, and he appeared to be trying to crush one in his right hand.

Robbyn glanced toward the pool. "I thought it was *the Beast.*"

Drift shook his head. "If it had been you would have died before I reached you."

He hoisted her into his arms and started back into the forest. He gave Micah a hearty slap on the back on the way by. "You did good, Micah."

With a final look at the deceptively peaceful brook, Micah followed them.

✑

Isaac sighed through cracked lips. He lay against the base of the palm tree, careful not to move so as not to invoke the wrath of his sunburns. It felt like weeks ago that he'd been left to die, but not even a night had passed. He would have given anything for a ship to stop by and take him back to the mainland. For that matter, he would have given anything for a glass of water.

But for the most part, his thoughts dwelled far from his current predicament. She's right. *It really does feel like a burden.* And how heavily it weighed now, for he had no distractions, no options. Nothing could shield him from the victims floating around in his mind.

He winced. So much distress—why had he caused that? He wished he could start over, be born all over again. He would do everything differently the second time.

He loves you. The memory of Gretchen's voice cut into his thoughts.

With as little muscle movement as possible, he reclined his stiff neck and looked up along the trunk of the palm tree. *Do you? Do you really?* If there was a God, it didn't make sense that He would love Isaac. What was there to love? He was a cowardly, murderous thief.

Isaac closed his eyes, trying to imagine the Hero-Messiah, bent double beneath the weight of a wooden cross he dragged to his own death. He seemed to have a big enough burden without Isaac dumping his own on the poor guy's back.

He clenched his eyes shut and groaned as the shepherd boy's eyes flashed through his mind.

"Make it stop!" The words slipped out before he could stop them. He concentrated on listening to the waves caressing the beach for several minutes.

Then he turned his head to scour the beach, but stopped short.

For there, on the sand only feet away from him, perched a ship—weather beaten and in need of repair, but the sails were nearly perfect. Isaac could not believe it. He had a ship. He could sail to the mainland and— Was this some kind of temptation? Or maybe just a mirage. He pulled himself to his feet and walked up to it with dizzy steps. He skimmed his hand over the wooden side. No, this was definitely not a hallucination. His shaking fingers traced the weather-worn words: "*The Wooden Swan.*"

"Are you lost, old girl?"

How long had it been there? Isaac couldn't be sure; it had been so long since he'd turned his head in that direction. But it didn't matter now. He placed his hand on the rail and started to pull himself inside, then froze. Where would he go? He could hide away in the mountains—he shivered—*not* the Heather Mountains.

Then, with a terrible sinking sensation, he knew he couldn't. He let go of the railing and backed away. He couldn't force himself to pretend nothing had happened. The nightmares wouldn't quit. He would be leading a haunted existence; he'd be *guilty*, even if he found a way to hide it beneath the surface. It would be just as miserable out there as it was here. He turned to face the palm tree, but made no move toward it.

Just as miserable.

He was trapped, nowhere to turn, no way to fix what he'd done.

Isaac collapsed. The weight of his guilt should have plunged him into the depths of the sand—buried him. But it didn't. It clung to him, squeezing ever tighter.

He needed to let it out. It threatened to burst. All that heartache, and it was his fault. He couldn't contain it all. He needed to tell someone. It needed out.

"I've done terrible things." The words came much louder than he had intended. He paused . . . No echo. But he did feel a little better. "I—I have these dreams—nightmares—I—they—" No, he needed to start at the beginning. Isaac took a deep breath, but then he exhaled without speaking, so he took another one. "I was born in a small coastal village, to a young gypsy. She had brown hair and eyes, and she had an amazing singing voice. Sometimes, when I had trouble sleeping . . ."

CHAPTER 17

The Gable Kingdom Castle

The morning sun had hardly cleared the horizon when the Kingdom came into view. It came suddenly; one minute the Drift-drawn cart weaved through the crowds on the forest roads, the next it jostled over a grassy plain. The plain dropped into the ocean via steep cliffs on every side save for the forest behind them, and those cliffs narrowed to a point—Gable's southernmost point—where the castle stood. The dark ocean met the line of the cloudless sky in every direction, and hundreds of patrolling ships dotted its surface.

The castle sat at the far end of an enormous walled city, at least ten times larger than any Micah had seen. But the castle itself is what held his eye. Its gray stones shimmered in the sunlight. Arching walkways connected the densely spaced towers high into the sky. He could not wrap his mind around the fact that mere men could have constructed such a majestic fortress.

"This is it." Robbyn took a breath. "We made it."

Lines of people and vessels of all sorts trailed from the wide stone walkways leading to the city gates.

"They must be coming to see James Kestrel's hanging," Micah said.

"It's so sad," Robbyn said. "They have no idea what they're walking into. Look at them."

One tower stood up above the rest—the dungeon. Micah peered up at it. Somewhere inside that stone cylinder James Kestrel awaited his hanging, now just hours away. It felt strange to be so close to Kestrel, as if Micah hadn't fully believed in the stories about him until that moment.

The wooden, archway-shaped doors leading into the city lay wide open, and it took the party some time to reach them. But when they had parted the crowds and found themselves rolling into the city, the guards with chain mail and emerald green capes let them through without question.

Inside the city walls, shops of multiple stories lined the tidy, intersecting streets. People of every stature and color poured in and out of these. Guards, both on foot and on horseback, waited at every corner. Wheeled, iron-barred cages accompanied many of them. Every once in a while, one of those cages held a few prisoners. Enormous emerald green banners with gold trim stretched across the rooftops.

"Welcome"

"To"

"The Gable Kingdom"

Drift inched the cart forward; traffic moved painfully slow, especially for carts, but Drift's cart benefitted from the fact that nobody wanted to stand in front of him.

"How do we get to the castle?" Drift spoke through clenched teeth, his body almost as rigid as the city wall.

Micah found it difficult to hear him over the crowd noise, and the nauseating density of people put him on edge.

"Just look up," Robbyn said.

Micah did so and found that the castle remained always in view as they navigated the streets. Even as the tallest of city buildings drifted between them and the castle, at least the dungeon tower remained in view. The closer they drew to it, the tenser he got.

"How much for the big, hairy horse?" someone jeered from a second story window.

Robbyn glanced at the man and opened her lips as if to say something, but did not respond.

Drift ignored him and pressed on. Although he received quite a few curious looks, no one within reach spoke to him.

The street opened into the town square. Several marble statues of men in various noble and valiant poses lined the eastern wall.

As they traveled past them Micah read the inscriptions in the gold plates at each of their feet. *King Koreus, King Stein, King Graham* . . . Micah looked up and, sure enough, a crown topped each of their heads.

Also in the square, three fountains spewed water nearly as high as the wall in giant, graceful arcs. Throngs of giggling and squealing children surrounded them with upturned palms, splashing around in the puddles. The stonework of the square, as seen in the few areas void of people, glittered with exotic color and Micah felt certain that some pattern could be made out if the square had been empty.

At the end of the city square the crowds thinned, and the walls of the castle—taller than those of the city—rose in front of them on the other side of a moat and drawbridge. The single gate stood taller as well. Although a few wheeled vessels journeyed in and out, it was far from the whirlwind of people at the city's entrance.

A group of guards checked each and every person and item before allowing them in or out of the gate. As they waited in line, Micah squinted up at the towers of the castle looming over them. They'd seemed enormous from a distance, but up close their height boggled his mind, as if a breath of wind would knock over one of the tower roofs at any minute and send the whole thing toppling down on them.

"Let's unload the sheep." Drift lifted Logan and Jordan off the cart, one in each hand.

"Are you sure you need to do this, Micah?" Robbyn wrapped her arms around Hannah and hefted her to the ground. "We don't know how much time we have. Maybe you could do this tomorrow, after we save the castle."

"No, I must obey my master. It won't take long."

"All right, then. Once you get through, Drift and I will put the cart in the stable and attempt to reach the king, or at least someone with influence. Once your sheep are sheared, meet us back at the stable."

"That's it?" Micah said.

"I'm afraid so." Robbyn clutched her bandaged wrist. "We'll have to be really persistent."

Drift scanned their surroundings from beneath furrowed brows. The guards had already begun glancing at Drift out of the corners of their eyes. Their capes were of a darker green than those of the soldiers and guards in the city. And they wore breastplates, rather than chain mail.

"Say your prayers," Robbyn said softly as the last party ahead of them entered through the gates.

Micah tightened his grip on his crook and started toward the guards, but froze mid-step. For on each of the guards' breastplates an emblem had been emblazoned—the emblem of a bird perched upon a cloud.

Micah's heart plummeted. *No!*

"Business?" The front guard with a mustache jutted out his bare jaw.

No words came to Micah's mind. What could he say? "I—"

A second guard knelt down and started parting the wool on Rachel's left hip. She tried to wriggle away but the guard held her tight in his arms. Micah's innards curled as he tried to mentally brace himself for what would come next.

"Business?" The guard with a mustache spoke in a louder tone.

Micah looked from him to the other guard. Could he run? No,

that would only further incriminate him, and he wouldn't make it far.

"I—these sheep are to be sheared—their wool—is for King Darius."

"Taxes, eh?"

The guard on the ground looked up, scowling. "These sheep bear Our King's mark!"

Several glances shot in Micah's direction as two guards rushed forward and grabbed him by the arms.

"Thought you would steal the Good King's sheep and offer them back as tax, did yeh?" The mustached guard shook his head in disgust. "Off with yeh, you slimy little thief!"

The guards dragged him through the gate. He started to protest, but could think of no way to make his argument that made any sense. Nothing he could say would cancel the obvious evidence against him. They threw him into a wagon identical to the ones he'd seen earlier, and he bounced off the iron bars of the far wall. The door clanged shut.

Micah scrambled back to his feet and brought his face to the bars.

"Take them to the chamber of evidence," the lead guard ordered, pointing to the sheep.

With a lurch the wagon rolled forward. The guards led the sheep, bucking and bleating, in the opposite direction. The last image he saw before turning the corner was Robbyn's concerned face on the other side of the gate. Micah threw his fist against the bar. Then he tucked it into his armpit in pain. It hadn't even yielded a bang, which made him feel more helpless. People stared at him as he rode by, just as he had stared at the criminals in the other wagons.

The wagon turned off the main cobblestone road, along the inside of the wall, away from the people.

It had all happened so fast. He still didn't quite understand. Who would want to frame him as a thief? Grixxler? He pushed the thought away. It didn't matter. He had to focus on a way to escape. But how? He turned toward the approaching dungeon tower. Nobody had ever escaped before. What made him think he could? He looked everywhere, wracking his brain. The driver—he could plead with the guards guiding the wagon.

Then he noticed that his crook still lay beside him. There were only two guards. They were both much taller and more heavily armored, but he surely stood a better chance of escape against them than once locked in the tower, even if all he had was a crook. He crouched into a ready stance and waited for his opportunity.

But his heart sank when a cluster of guards hovering around the only dungeon entrance came into view. And his last hopes dashed to pieces when, upon the opening of the iron wagon door, four guards drew their swords and held them out.

"We don't have to let you live," one of the guards raised an eyebrow.

Micah rose to his feet and climbed out of the wagon.

One guard ripped the crook from his limp fingers. "Hey look, the sheep thief has a bit of brain left after all." The guard cracked him across the back of the head with it. They pushed him along into the dungeon.

Once Micah crossed the threshold, the sunlight evaporated. He might never feel the warmth of the sun again. Spider webs, shadowy stonework, and a horrific smell summed up the inside of the dungeon. They hauled him like a sack of wheat up the crooked, spiraling stairs, past countless criminals who glanced at him with eyes sucked of all hope.

Despite his predicament, he couldn't help but wonder which one of these shady characters was James Kestrel. The cells consisted of nothing but narrow nooks separated from each other and the walkway by tightly-spaced, vertical iron bars thicker than those of the wagon. On the wall of each cell hung a window barred with identical iron bars. The light that filtered through these windows appeared dim and washed of color.

They arrived at an empty cell. One guard released his hold on

Micah's leg to fish out his ring of keys. After fumbling briefly he picked one out and sprung open the door. They hurled Micah against the stone floor. He rolled onto his elbows.

"What's this?" Another guard arrived from the steps above and leaned against the stone wall opposite the cell. "He tried to sneak a weapon in?"

Another guard appeared from behind him and spat between Micah's legs. "It's no weapon. Just a shepherd's crook. 'Sides, scrawny little kid like that, he's gonna need it to defend himself."

The guard holding Micah's crook entered his cell with a grin. "He was going to use it as a weapon though." He glance over his shoulder. "You should have seen him, Bock, holding it like some sword. What'd you think, thief? Were you gonna beat your way to freedom with this stick?" The guard's eyes gleamed. "Not even going to honor us with a knife?"

"Disrespectful whelp!" A guard hollered from behind.

Micah scuttled backward, the muck of the floor collecting on his palms. He willed the guard to turn around and leave him be.

"No, please, just leave."

"Not as tough as we thought, are we?" The guard raised the crook and brought it down hard on Micah's face. *Thwap!*

Cheers broke out from the guards behind.

Micah curled up and covered himself with his arms. The blows kept coming, stinging and snapping. It took effort each time to keep from crying out. With every strike the chorus from the guards grew louder. They brought the butt end of the crook down on his back and ground it in, finally eliciting a cry of pain.

"Mmph." Micah writhed away.

"I'll teach you!" The guard rammed his booted foot into Micah's stomach.

His lungs emptied. The sting of tears gnawed at the corners of his eyes as he rolled back and forth, gasping for air.

The crook clattered to the ground beside him. Micah stopped rolling and lay still, his forehead pressed into the stone floor, his whole body flashing with pain.

Micah closed the voices out, reducing them to a low drone until a clang broke through. He turned over to see the guards dispersing, his cell door closed. Closed forever.

He rose to his knee, wincing. He clutched his back and pulled himself up the wall for a view out his window, which showed only the wide blue ocean dotted with ships. But when he pressed his face against the bars and looked sideways he saw the cliffs, and atop them, the road he'd arrived on earlier that day. In fact he could see the exact spot from which, in freedom, he'd gazed up at the tower. Long lines of crowds still filed into the castle city at full force.

Coming to their doom. Sighing, he slid back onto the floor, unable to imagine more dire circumstances. Someone had framed him. But who? Grixxler? Why would he do that? It didn't make sense. And nobody could help him now, not even Drift and Robbyn. Even if they somehow possessed the ability to set him free, they needed to focus on reaching the king; they were Gable's last hope.

His helplessness ate at him like a pack of vultures. He limped the length of his cell, pacing back and forth, back and forth. The stinging of his beating softened until he could walk straight again, and he kept pacing. He plopped onto the ground, his thoughts still spinning at full speed.

Micah lay in this state for what felt like an hour. He watched the guards march the stairway, never leaving a cell out of sight for long. Time crawled by. Every time he looked out the window the sun didn't appear to have moved.

He closed his eyes, but quickly opened them when he heard a voice echoing up the stairway. "Seven hundred sixty-seven, seven hundred sixty-eight . . ." A background of groaning and cursing followed the voice. The protests grew louder until they came from cells adjacent to his.

As Micah listened, it dawned on him that he knew that voice. And as it drew closer and closer his excitement grew until, when the speaker emerged, he popped to his feet, unable to believe his fortune.

"Bart!" Of course. He'd completely forgotten that Bart wore the bird and cloud on his shirt. Micah ran to the bars facing the stairway.

". . . seven hundred eighty-one . . ."

"Bart, it's me! You made it!"

Bart stopped next to Micah's cell, looked up from the stair he stood upon, and turned to him. His face exploded into joy with a smile wider than Micah had ever seen. Then he gasped and clamped a hand over his mouth. He took two steps back, looking down at the floor of Micah's cell. He looked up the stairs and down them, then back at Micah. His expression devolved into sadness, and for a moment Micah thought Bart would start crying.

"Oh, hello, Micah," he said in a low, colorless voice. He gave a small wave. "Your cell is on stair number seven hundred eighty-two." With that he turned back to the steps and took another step upward. "Seven hundred eighty—"

"Bart! You have to let me out of here! They think I stole my sheep. Somebody framed me!"

Bart turned to Micah again. "Prisoners have to stay in their cells." That tone didn't belong to Bart. It was as if he were playing back someone else's words.

Micah took a step back. "Bart, I was framed! You don't understand. The Marauders are going to attack the castle tonight! I need to get out! We need to warn the king!"

Bart shook his head. "Prisoners have to stay in their cells." He turned to the steps and continued to count his way up the tower.

Micah couldn't believe it. He went back to the wall and sat hard upon the floor. Bart didn't understand. It wasn't his fault. And Micah realized that there really wasn't anything Bart could do to help him escape. Unlocking the cell door would only get him so far. But it still hurt that Bart had regarded him so coldly.

He burrowed his head in his arms and sat there for hours, never bothering to look up, praying and thinking. Had Drift and Robbyn been able to reach the king? Had the king believed them? Would an alarm be sounded, warning the people to flee the Kingdom and, in effect, causing instant and widespread panic? Or would the king try to subdue the Marauders stealthily, keeping his own people in the dark about their predicament?

As late afternoon rolled around and no sound came—and the people continued to file into the Kingdom—somehow Micah knew the truth. Nobody had believed Robbyn and Drift. Thousands of people were about to die.

"Micah," a voice hissed from the shadows.

Micah jolted upright and searched for the source of the voice.

"Come here." It came from the cell next to his.

He could only make out an abundance of shadows through the iron bars. He hesitated and took up his crook. The voice definitely didn't sound like Robbyn or Drift's. Cautiously, he crept forward, attempting in vain to pierce the darkness.

"How do you know my name?" Micah whispered. He waited briefly and heard nothing.

Was this someone trying to help him or harm him? He didn't have anything to lose . . .

He closed the fingers of his free hand around one of the bars. He could just make out the outline of a person inside, slumped against the wall.

A pale hand shot out of the darkness and locked around his wrist. He yanked back against the steely grip, but to no avail. He dropped his crook and pulled with his other hand in panic. But as fast as the arm had appeared, it shot down, snatched the crook, and whipped it into the darkness.

Micah scrambled away until his back clanged into the bars on the other side of his cell, his heart pumping furiously. He heard nothing but silence. A guard walked by, and as soon as the echo of his footsteps faded away, a hooded figure appeared in the meager light of the thief's cell, holding Micah's crook. With a flick of the wrists the hood fell away, and Micah recognized the man instantly. He gasped. The sight jerked his memory back to the day he had first acquired his sheep. For there, before him, stood a dilapidated version of the old man who had once given him that shepherd's crook.

Micah couldn't breathe. "You're that—that kind old—"

"James Kestrel," the man said in an icy voice. He slid his hands up and down the crook, pausing every once in a while, as though feeling for a pulse.

"But—I—how?" It couldn't be. That old man who had treated him so kindly was a disguise? He wished his cell were wider so he could back farther away.

"I knew you'd make it, Micah." Kestrel's smile revealed several missing teeth. He wedged the crook between two of the iron bars and heaved back on one end. The fibers yawned and creaked until a rich crack echoed down the stairway. Sand poured forth from the broken end of the crook and spilled over into Micah's cell. Then a flash of silver emerged. Kestrel placed his hand over the end, and with a gentleness fit for an infant, produced a slender, silvery flute, shining brilliantly even in the sparse light, as if Kestrel held not a flute, but a sliver of moonlight.

Micah gasped. His vision spiraled. It couldn't be. "The Caelum Flute," he breathed.

Kestrel gave a long sigh of contentment, his eyes entranced with the trinket. "My old friend, it's been so long." He stood up, his fingers already covering the holes. He brought it to his lips and began a melody comprised of what sounded like the cries of vultures, so incredibly vivid that Micah cast glances over both shoulders expecting to find a flock of vultures already there.

Micah regained his senses. "No!" He leapt to his feet and reached for the flute. But Kestrel dodged out of the way, yanked Micah against the bars, and wrapped his arm around Micah's neck without missing a beat. Micah tried to scream, but little air choked through Kestrel's stranglehold. And with Kestrel's torso pinning his arms to the bars, he couldn't move either. He kept a trained eye on the walkway, choking on his breath, praying that the overdue guard would turn the corner soon.

Finally, Kestrel released Micah and dashed away from the stone wall. A moment of silence, then two enormous black talons slammed into the bars of Kestrel's window. A rumble spread from the window through the tower. A gigantic black wing flapped up and down just outside Micah's window, sending vibrations through the air. The stone around the window crackled and shuddered. In a shower of gravel, the chunk of wall busted away. A spectacular amount of sunlight shone through the hole, blurred by the clouds of dust.

"Guards! Help!" Micah yelled. Distant footsteps rushed up the steps. But they would be too late. Kestrel ran toward the hole and launched himself into the sky. Micah ran to his window and slammed his head against the bars to see Kestrel dip toward the ocean on the back of an oversized vulture. He flew beneath ground level, hidden by the cliffs, past the lines of oblivious people, and disappeared into the forest.

Micah's legs buckled. He slid down the wall, hit his knees, and clutched his face in his hands. He had just freed *James Kestrel*.

"What happened?"

Micah whirled around. Several guards had arrived, one of whom was racing through his keys at the door of Kestrel's former cell, unsuccessfully punching them in at random. Most of them looked back and forth from Micah to the hole in the wall. Bart stood at the back of the group.

"You have to listen to exactly what I have to say." Micah stood up.

"Shut up, prisoner!" one guard snapped—the same mustached guard from the gate. "You two." He jabbed a finger at two nearby guards. "What happened?"

"This was after my shift."

"Me too, sir."

"Then who was on shift after you two?"

They both pointed to two adjacent guards who raised their arms in defense.

"It wasn't our shift yet, sir."

"You bumbling fools! How did this hole get here?" None of the other guards said a word.

Micah spoke up. "Sir, please, I saw what happened!"

"I told you to shut up!" He picked up a loose stone and hurled it at Micah. It missed him by several feet and clattered off the iron bars of the window behind him. "For all I know you were an accomplice!" Now red faced, he turned to his troupe. "That goes for the rest of you as well! You'll say nothing of this matter to anyone! We're going straight to King Darius."

"Please sir," Micah tried again, "tell His Highness that the Marauders are going to attack tonight! They have the Caelum Flute, and ships with powerful weapons!"

The guard glared at him, turned, and left down the stairs. Everyone else followed.

Now alone, and at a new level of frustration, Micah kicked the sand in his cell, noting only as he did so that the broken shepherd's crook, the only piece of evidence in his favor, had vanished. Micah dropped to the stone floor with a thud. How could he have been so foolish? He'd been set up, used as a crucial cog in the demise of all Gable. He'd seen all the warning signs and forged ahead anyway.

"Stay away from the ocean?" He snorted. Of course the Marauders hadn't wanted him to run into The King's Royal Wool Spinner. Vivid images of the people running around in panic as sections of the castle exploded around them and the towers rained down took residence in his mind. He wandered from wall to wall, reaming on the iron bars, and kicking at the stone wall. There had to be a way to escape. But nothing yielded. Sore, and ill with disgust, he shook his head and slumped again to the floor.

Evening approached when a noise stirred him—Bart's voice echoing from the halls below. "Food time," he repeated again and again, adding, "This tower has one hundred and eighty-five cells, one thousand one hundred and sixteen steps, and one hundred and eighty-six windows," every once in a while. Prisoners who hadn't yet received their meal groaned and cursed. Micah sat up and watched as Bart threw loaves of bread wrapped in cloth to the prisoners before him.

Micah could see the area around him better with the sunlight coming in through the hole in the wall.

"Did you warn the king?" Micah asked, afraid to even hope for a positive response.

But when Bart arrived at Micah's cell, he didn't even acknowledge his existence; he tossed the loaf of bread through the bars and continued onward. The bread hit the stone floor at Micah's feet with a thud. He stared at it for a few seconds, much too sick to eat. He lay back down, his eyes misting over. But then the noise of the bread hitting the floor rang through his mind again. *Thud.*

He sat up and examined his dinner more closely. Something wasn't right about it. The package was large and misshapen. Anticipation beginning to rise in Micah's chest, he snatched it and unwrapped it, his fingers blundering. The contents of the package spilled out, and he paused, unable to believe it. He looked up the stairway, but Bart had gone.

There, upon the stone floor, sat a gleaming, brass key. Next to it sat a large coil of rope. But the item that Micah couldn't bring himself to look away from was the dirty cloth, for scribbled on the inside in meandering, haphazard letters were the words, *God Bles Yow*. Micah sat speechless, cradling the gift. How could he have ever questioned Bart—his closest companion?

A second key tumbled from the cloth. What were the second key and the rope for? Maybe to climb up onto the ceiling and— That didn't make sense. As he pondered this, Bart's voice echoed back to him from up the stairway. ". . . One hundred eighty-five cells, one thousand one hundred sixteen steps, and one hundred eighty-six windows. . ."

Micah covered the rope and keys with the cloth, rose to his feet and paced. He could almost hear his thoughts whirring. "One hundred eighty-five cells, one hundred eighty-six windows," he murmured. Bart had told him that back when he had given him a tour of the clay castle. *But why did . . . ? Could it be?* He rushed over to the window, bringing up Bart's clay replica of the castle in his mind. Mentally, he walked around Bart's sculpture, scrutinizing the dungeon. Comparing the arrangement of stones around his window with the stones around the windows on the replica, he spotted his cell facing the ocean near the top of the tower. He leaned in closer to the clay castle, inspecting every stone, crack, and crevice. If Bart was correct . . .

And then Micah saw it—a window with no bars over it, three windows below his cell.

"That's it!" Micah's hope erupted. "One hundred and eighty-five cells, and one hundred eighty-six windows. One window doesn't have a cell!" He knew what he had to do.

Fazing back to reality, he grabbed his items and hurried for his cell door but stopped when he realized he should wait for the next guard to pass. He stuffed the items back under the cloth and waited, attempting to appear as normal as possible, until the guard on watch turned the corner. His heart pumped all the while.

Then he sprang into action. Shouldering the rope, with keys in hand, he slid his arm through the bars and wiggled the key into the keyhole. He tried to turn it both ways, but neither worked, so he switched keys and, with a click, it snapped into place. Micah turned his wrist, swiveling the key easily to stop. He pushed on the cell door. With a moan that set his teeth on edge, it swayed outward, just a little. He squeezed through the opening.

A prisoner in the cell across the stairway from his watched him with beady eyes but said nothing.

With a glance down both ends of the stairway, he shoved the other key into the keyhole of James Kestrel's old cell, opened the door, and slipped inside. Any second now the guard would turn the corner. He tied one end of the rope to a cell bar, his fumbling fingers resistant to doing his bidding. Finally, he completed the knot. After two violent tugs at the rope to test its strength, he threw the coil out the hole.

He didn't wait for it to unravel as it sailed forth into the evening sky; he knelt down. A brief, dizzying glance into the dark waters of the ocean gave him pause. But he swallowed and, without any more hesitation, clutched the rope and eased himself over the side. Keeping his eyes trained in front of him, he descended one step after the next, trying not think about the fact that nothing stood between him and the deadly waters below. The cracks between the stones offered little for footholds, and his feet skidded more than once on thick carpets of moss. But the rope made the descent easier.

With brief glances to the side, he counted the windows on the way down until he arrived at the level with the fourth window—unbarred, just as Bart had depicted it. From there he wrapped the rope around one hand and pulled himself sideways along the wall with the other. He grabbed a chunk of moss that fell away from the wall, causing him to swing like a pendulum in the wrong direction.

He looked up, imagining a guard peering over the edge and slashing the rope. That's all it would take. Almost certain death.

On the swing forward, Micah clutched the wall again and crawled forward. Once on the window ledge, he leaped inside, only too eager to be rid of the rope and have his feet on firm ground.

He was in a dark room drenched with spider web upon spider web. He clawed his way through the sticky mess, but when he reached the room's center, he realized it had no door.

A strange crack caught his eye, and when he focused on it, he found it to be shaped in an arch—a door made of stone, or at least made to look like stone, to blend into the wall. But a wooden door in the floor claimed Micah's attention. He opened it up, and it creaked as he did so. Black spiders scattered as the scant light poured down on them. A ladder descended into darkness. Micah took a deep breath and stepped onto the first rung and it held his weight.

As he descended, he kept his head up, focused on the steadily shrinking square of light, stepping down to a steady rhythm. When the square had almost shrunk out of sight, his foot hit something solid. He swung it beneath him, sending echoes through whatever chamber he stood in. Satisfied that he'd reached the ground, he stepped off into total darkness. He felt his way along the wall and realized, based on Bart's replica, it headed straight for the city.

"Bart," Micah told the echoing tunnel, "you are one clever man."

༄

"Please! You don't know what you're doing." Robbyn watched yet another group, this one with a llama-drawn cart filled with rolled up tapestries, pass through the castle gate ahead of them.

Evening had snuck up on them, and shadows were beginning to thicken in the corners and crevices. Before long, the sun would dip below the city wall and disappear from the pink-orange sky.

"We're telling you the truth! The Marauders are going to attack any minute!"

The brightly dressed little man ignored her, and informed Drift instead, fear in his sunburn rimmed eyes. "I'm done arguing," he squeaked, taking an aggressive step forward and then several back. "His Highness has the safety of the castle well under control." The man gave Drift a reproachful glance. "And he doesn't need some giant to tell him what will or *will not* happen!" With that he turned around and scurried back over the drawbridge and through the castle gates.

"What now?" Robbyn turned toward the square. Most of the people had left. Four chain-mailed guards were rolling a wooden platform with a noose into the center of the square. Soon the people would start filtering back from the city to witness what they'd come to see.

"Now we fight, m'lady."

"And pray. Maybe we can try and warn people to flee while they can."

"Shh," Drift cocked his ear toward the north. "Do you hear that?"

Robbyn paused. She heard a faint, wailing voice but couldn't make out what it said.

"They're here!" Drift roared.

The guards nearby stopped in their inspections and stared at him. "What? Who's here?"

A black horse and a rider bearing the bird and cloud on his breastplate galloped into the square. The sounds of yelling and banging rose from the streets behind him. "We're under attack!"

Panic struck as those on and near the drawbridge attempted to force their way into the castle. Those too far away ran in every direction. The gasping messenger leaned on his horse, panting. People fled all around him. "It's the Marauders. They've already broken into—the castle. Close the drawbridge!" One group of guards shoved people back across the drawbridge as another group set to work pulling it up.

☙☙

"They're here!" The sound echoed into Micah's alley and gave his heart quite a jolt. He recognized that roar.

No! It's too soon!

He climbed out of the trapdoor, noting as he did so that he was bedecked in spider webs. As soon as he let go of the door, it sprang shut. A cobblestone covering lined its top, causing it to melt into the cobblestone street just as well as the arch-shaped door in the secret room.

Micah dashed off toward the square.

"We're under attack!" Screaming and bellowing followed.

Micah ran harder, burst around the corner, and spotted Drift with Robbyn beside him. They were the only two people not either scrambling to shut the gate and restore order or running for their lives. In fact, they looked lost.

"Were you able to warn the king?"

Drift and Robbyn spun around. Micah crouched and grabbed his knees, trying to catch his breath.

Robbyn looked him over. "Micah! How did you? And you're covered in—"

"No time," Micah said, regaining his breath. "Kestrel's escaped, and he has the Caelum Flute."

Robbyn gasped. "And we weren't able to warn the king."

Drift grunted.

The sun still hung a short distance from the city wall. Micah had to get to the forest and stop Kestrel. But that could only be done through one of the castle gates, through the city. He checked the thinning avenues that surrounded them. The gruesome clanging and screaming of battle reverberated from the streets to the north.

Without a second thought he broke into a dash in that direction, across the now empty square. "He's in the forest. We've got to go now!" he called over his shoulder. But Drift and Robbyn were already running behind him.

"Micah!" Drift bellowed as he sprinted easily in front of him and, as they kept running, pushed him back with a massive hand. "I'll lead. You two stay close."

The three of them ran—Drift in front with Robbyn and Micah at either flank—into the street corridor. Micah didn't know exactly what they'd find, though the long, ominous shadows dancing on the wall gave some indication.

They careened around the bend. An endless mass of battling men appeared in front of them. Micah groaned inwardly, but Drift kept running, so he did too. They flew into the midst of the battle of the black-clad Marauders, the green-clad kingdom soldiers, and a hodge-podge of other colors representing the townspeople.

Arrows whizzed, weapons clashed, and battle horses glided through the fray. People threw pots, pans, vegetables and everything else in between from the high-rising windows that towered over either side of the street. The accumulative roar mingled with the sharp clangs of metal weapons blotted out Micah's thoughts almost completely.

Drift barreled forward, distancing himself from Micah and Robbyn. On his way by he snatched two tall shields off the ground, braced them to his forearms, and held them in front of him. A Marauder poised to stab a townsman received the full power of the giant's charge. The Marauder's comparatively frail body flew away. Drift plowed forward without losing speed, bodies bouncing off his shields. Micah and Robbyn followed the trail of empty space, dodging stray attacks.

Clothed only in wool, Micah felt defenseless against the myriad of weapons swinging around him. A Marauder swung a hefty two-handed sword at Micah's midsection and just missed. As Micah scrambled away he wondered if his belly would have even slowed it.

As they cut through the mêlée, they flew past intersecting streets, and battling masses extended down each of those as well.

Just focus on getting through.

Micah expected Robbyn to shield her vision from the gruesomeness happening all around them, but she looked forward, focused.

Drift swerved just a few feet to the left and right and took out Marauder after Marauder, letting loose a guttural noise with each contact. Then a horse appeared in front of him, with a Marauder on its back. Drift kicked up his speed, spread his shield-laden arms wide, and tackled it. The two tumbled to the ground. The Marauder scrambled away, and Drift pinned the wriggling, neighing horse to the ground with his shoulder.

Micah jumped over the horse and grabbed the reins, but the horse slipped from Drift's grasp. The reins ripped out of Micah's hand, and the horse galloped into the fray.

"Oh well," Micah shouted over the battle. "We need to keep moving!"

Drift readjusted his shields and plowed onward. Robbyn and Micah followed.

A Marauder drew the string on a bow aimed at a townsman less than five feet away. Robbyn swung out her foot and kicked at the backside of his knee on the run. The contact sent her reeling into Micah. But it caused the Marauder to stagger just long enough for a soldier to stab him.

Micah blinked hard and looked away.

A slicing sword interrupted Micah's field of vision; he threw himself to the ground just in time to avoid a beheading. From his prone position, a cluster of arrows chinked against the cobblestone beside his head. He threw himself into a roll away from them only to have a body collapse on top of him.

"Oof." He pushed the heavy, black-clad figure off.

Clambering to his feet, he attempted to gain his bearings. He was in the middle of an intersection, but from which direction had he come? He scanned the heads surrounding him in the hopes of spotting Drift. But a sharp pain spread from the top of his head just as a crack rang through his ears. He hit the cobblestone once again. This time his vision blanked.

ℰℛℴ

Micah awoke to the sounds of the battle still raging, with his face inches from the rough, scarred face of a Marauder lying on him. He pushed the heavy man off and climbed to his feet. As he did so the pieces of a hefty chair fell off of him. He clutched the top of his head but snapped his hand away at the pain. Then he looked up. All kinds of furniture, dishes, trinkets, and food items still poured from the windows.

How long had he been out? It couldn't have been long, for the last rays of the sun still lit the city, and the battle still raged on as boldly as ever, although the immediate area lay covered with the dead and wounded.

He turned completely around, but Drift was nowhere to be seen, and he still had no idea which direction to go.

"Drift!" His vocal cords vibrated but no sound came from his lips that could be heard over the roar of the fight.

A full head of cabbage bounced past his feet. He looked up again, and something caught his eye—an object, floating far above, outlined against the pink-orange sky. It was a bird, growing steadily larger. *Could it be Kestrel?* He dared not remove his focus and lose it, so he walked along the ground in the direction it appeared to be headed.

He was just about to break into a lope when something cold and flat pushed against his throat. He froze and lowered his gaze earthward. The blade tilted until the edge pressed against his Adam's apple, flawlessly sharp.

Something heavy thudded into the square of his back, propelling him forward. He closed his eyes, hit the ground and clutched his neck—unharmed. He turned onto his elbows to find three Marauders standing over him in an alley secluded from the action, though the muffled sounds of battle still filtered into his ears.

The one in the middle, a blond-haired, stubble-bearded fellow, held up his knife, as if to prove that he'd pulled the knife away. A twisted smile slithered across his face. The three advanced.

Micah scrambled backward until he hit the wall.

"How did you escape, Shepherd Boy?" the blond one demanded. The other two drew daggers and slashed them forward until they stopped just before Micah's face. Micah had never seen any of these people before.

What did it matter to them? Kestrel had escaped. Their plan had worked. What did they want with him now?

Micah chanced a look skyward, afraid he'd lose Kestrel if he didn't. The bird appeared to be nowhere in sight; the darkening sky made it difficult to tell, though. Before Micah could discern for sure, a swift foot kicked him in the jaw, nailing him where the guard had already bruised him. He opened and closed his mouth. The Marauders looked up, following the direction of his gaze, then back down at him.

"Where was Kestrel when you left?" the dark-haired Marauder on the right demanded.

Micah glared at each of them in turn. What kind of a game was this?

Another kick to the jaw. "It's a simple question, *Micah*."

Micah clutched his jaw. It felt misaligned. His heart and mind raced simultaneously. Kestrel hadn't met with the Marauders in the forest? *What happened?* Maybe a soldier or a hunter had shot his ride out of the sky and stolen the flute.

"I—" Micah had no idea what to say.

The Marauder raised his foot again.

"No! He had already escaped."

"Escaped?" the Marauder on the right said. "But then that means . . ." Each of them looked at each other in turn.

A stiff breeze blew over them, breaking up the stagnant air. The gentle wind whistled in Micah's ear as he stared down his foes. Then, ever so subtly, the whistle changed note. Then it changed again. He looked over just in time to see a giant mass of red streaking toward them. He rolled over and covered his head just before the bird smashed into the Marauders.

The mass of feathers crunched through a nearby stack of barrels. The shattered wooden shards burst from the collision, and several fragments hit Micah's back. He sat up, wide-eyed.

James Kestrel was running toward him. He had the Caelum Flute clutched in his hand as if it were a dagger he wanted to use to stab Micah. Behind him stood the Aegre Bird, preening its feathers beside the splintered remains of the barrels and prone, black-clad bodies.

"Micah!" Kestrel roared. Micah tried to scramble to his feet and run. But Kestrel grabbed him by the collar and yanked him over to a nearby wooden door. Kestrel glanced both ways down the street, where the battle still raged on, then kicked open the door and hauled Micah inside.

The room was nothing more than a closet with dirt flooring— enough room for maybe six people to stand up inside. When Kestrel closed the door all light vanished.

"You should have stayed in the dungeon, Micah."

Kestrel's dark voice sent shivers down Micah's spine.

Micah imagined a dagger poised above him, ready for the strike. He started to panic and groped in the darkness, but met nothing but air. Where was Kestrel?

Kestrel's voice lowered an octave. "You would have been safe there."

Micah clawed through the air, spinning in circles. He needed to grab a hold of Kestrel and get the flute. He ran face first into something hard and slumped to the floor. A light flickered to life, illuminating the little room.

Micah sat there, his world spinning. Gradually, the blurry outline of Kestrel holding a knife became discernible. The image sharpened, and the knife morphed into the Caelum Flute. Kestrel leaned against the opposite corner, staring at Micah. A lantern hung from the hook next to his head, casting dramatic shadows across his face.

"W-what do you want from me?"

"You don't remember me, do you?"

Micah swallowed. He couldn't wrap his mind around the fact that he was speaking with James Kestrel. "I remember you perfectly. Y-you were that—kind old man—in Sampter."

Kestrel's eyes stared unblinking. "No, I . . ." He shook his head. "It doesn't matter. There's no way you would ha . . ." He trailed off and glanced toward the door. "I only have a couple minutes."

Micah straightened, and frowned. What was this?

Kestrel looked into Micah's eyes again, and took a deep breath. "James Kestrel is not my real name."

What?

"My real name is Samuel Kamloop. I was married to Gloria Kamloop and you are—Micah Kamloop. My s—" Kestrel didn't finish.

All of Micah's breath left him and he found himself unable to close his mouth, let alone respond. "But—then," he managed. It couldn't be. "Samuel" was tricking him into a trap—another Marauder ruse to fool him into helping them. But then again, what more could the Marauders gain from him? They had the flute, they had the explosion weapons. Samuel had taken out those three Marauders with the Aegre Bird.

Samuel glanced toward the door again. "Listen! I wish I had more time, I really do, but the Marauders have a fleet of ships with—"

"I know. I—"

Samuel ignored him. "The Marauder King is in the Castle as we speak, standing on top of the dungeon tower. Your sheep are with him."

"What? Why?"

"Haven't you figured it out yet?" Samuel took the lantern off the hook. "Your sheep are East Plain Sunshine Sheep, a very rare breed of sheep that gives off light. Don't you see it, Micah? The Kingdom is shrouded in fog every night. The Marauders need a target for their weapons, something to break through the fog."

Micah shook his head, still recovering from the fact that he was speaking with his father. "No, that can't be. My sheep have never given off light. This cloak you gave me didn't even—"

"You have to burn their wool. And it has to be fresh."

Micah staggered. "So then . . . that means—"

"Yes." Kestrel's voice darkened. "They're going to burn your sheep alive."

Another wave of shock coursed through Micah's body. He felt as though the wind had been sucked from his sails, and his heavy heart was pulling him into the depths of the ocean. He didn't want to believe it, but he knew it was true. It all made sense. Why had he never thought to try burning some wool?

"We've got to get there!" Micah cried. He shoved past Samuel and stormed through the door.

❧

"I don't know what happened to Micah!" Robbyn shouted ahead to Drift.

Drift slowed to a halt, lowered his shields, and scanned the crowds, his eyebrows, and every other part of him, in fact, soaked with sweat.

Robbyn continued to look around. Night had fallen, and the first wisps of fog had begun to settle over the city, which was now lit by torches. But Micah was nowhere to be seen in the chaos of people around them. In respect to the city gate, however, they'd nearly reached it. "Drift, I think we should go back!"

Drift leaped toward her and threw his shield behind her. A clang rang through her ears and she jumped away in time to see Drift grab a Marauder by the belt and throw him into a nearby prisoners' cart.

"Anything could have happened to him!" Drift said over the battle roar when he turned back around. "Where should we look?"

Robbyn could see the worry in his eyes as he looked out over the battle. But she never got the opportunity to respond.

Before she could take a breath to speak, she heard it. An unworldly howl drowned out the battle. The deep, warbling noise sent tingles down her spine. With each echo of the voice all other sounds grew quieter. That familiar terror struck into her heart. A shiver rolled through the battlefield.

Panic closed around her like a giant fist. "Drift, it's here! It's . . ." But she trailed off at the sight of his narrowed eyes.

CHAPTER 18

The Blade and the Bludgeon

"Robbyn, they're going to use the Beast to clean up this battle." Drift looked over his shoulder. "It's trained to attack the biggest threat first. I have to draw it away. I have to fight it."

He turned his attention to the ground surrounding him and picked up an enormous two-handed sword. The blade, most likely the product of an overzealous smith, had probably been the downfall of its wielder. He hefted it and threw a few practice strokes. Then he hustled over to the destroyed remains of the city gate.

Robbyn followed, trying to think of a way to object.

He burrowed through the rubble of the wooden gate and produced a large, wedge-shaped hunk of wood. Quickly, he hacked it into shape with a few quick strokes. The battle commenced behind them.

Robbyn kept glancing at the enormous, open archway, through which hung impenetrable night, her heart hammering in anticipation of the beast's arrival. "Be careful."

"Listen, Robbyn." Drift refined the piece of wood with smaller strokes. He stole a glance out the archway. "Find something black, wrap yourself in it, and hide somewhere safe." He held his completed bludgeon in one hand, and the blade in the other.

"Drift!" Robbyn screamed. The Beast materialized from the darkness in mid-leap and crash-landed just before them. The force knocked Drift flat amidst the rubble of the gate. It leaped again, chunks of wood and metal flying forth. There it stood, surveying the battle before it, sniffing the air.

The Beast stood half again bigger than Drift. The slick black fur on its back looked like hardened tree sap, though its gray underbelly was made of softer fur. It looked remarkably like a wolf, with pointed ears, a swishing, bushy tail, and panting tongue, though its stocky build more closely resembled a bear.

It leapt forward and hit the cobblestones with a crunch. The loose flaps of fur-covered skin hanging between each of its four legs rippled.

Now that it was closer to Robbyn, she could see the Beast's face. Her heart hammered, and she began to sweat.

Above its full set of carnivorous white teeth, its eyes reflected only one emotion—eagerness. It was intoxicated with its desire to decimate the fight before it.

Everyone within a couple hundred feet of the monster froze, including the Marauders.

The rubble pile shifted and Drift emerged, pulling himself upright. The Beast didn't notice him; it arched its head and let loose another howl. Cringing, Drift brought his arm back and smashed the bludgeon into the Beast's head from behind.

An echoing yelp cut the howl short. The Beast whirled around with teeth bared, its growl an unbroken lion's roar. Drift stared it down, growling right back. All humanity had left him; he looked just as much a beast as the Beast did. His sword and bludgeon hung at the ready.

Without warning, the Beast sprang forward, and Drift blocked its fangs with the sword. With his other hand he crashed the bludgeon into its head again. In the second that it took the Beast to shake its head, Drifted turned and ran. He disappeared from the city's torch-light and into the night.

His pursuer didn't take long in giving chase. It crouched low, its muscles rippling, and launched forward into the sky. Once airborne it stretched its legs outward, snapping the loose flaps of its skin tight, and the Beast shot forward. It sliced into the darkness, gliding at an incredible velocity, like some horrible parody of a flying squirrel.

For a moment Robbyn didn't move, shaking. Her darkest night-mare hadn't imagined the Beast to be that horrible.

She looked back toward where she had last seen Micah and saw only dueling masses. The archway through which Drift and the Beast had disappeared contained only perfect darkness. She had never felt so alone.

She searched the ground around her whilst praying for Micah, then for Drift, and then for everyone, including herself. She picked up a knife about half the length of her arm, and a glowing lantern. Then she ran in the direction of the city archway. The shattered gate proved to be a larger obstacle than Drift and the Beast had made it appear. When she had conquered the mounds of debris, she stood facing the impenetrable darkness, a black wall outlined by the arch of the gate. It dwarfed her. She was so small, so insignificant stand-ing there with nothing but a knife and a shaking lantern to battle the giant wall of darkness and whatever lurked within. But she had to go. She had to chase after them. She took a deep breath and stole out into the night.

ᗶᎧ

Drift powered through the darkness, running as fast as his churn-ing legs would carry him. He couldn't see anything in front of him, and the unseen fog soon swallowed the light of the city behind him. Even so, he sensed the obstacles as he dodged them, and he sensed the Beast closing in on him. But he knew he needed light, and so he kept pounding forward until he broke through the fog and the moon illuminated the plains around him. Drift shot a glance backward to see the Beast emerge from the darkness, its tongue flapping as it ran.

Drift sprang off the grassy plain and hurtled upward into the top of a spry, young inflectos tree. The tree bowed to Drift's weight. He grabbed the tip and brought it with him to the ground on the other side, the tree flexing to his will. Gritting his teeth, he pulled it tight, his eyes focused on the sprinting monster. He let go.

It snapped forward like a catapult and smacked the Beast into the ground just as it launched into a glide. The Beast skidded into the sod. But that hardly slowed it down. It sprang up and took flight again, several barks ripping from its throat.

Drift tore off for the cliffs, casting backward glances whenever he got the opportunity. The Beast dashed after him and launched into a glide. From the air it twisted its torso, propelling itself off trees and boulders with blinding agility. The next thing Drift knew, the barks came from right behind him. He turned and sliced the sword around, but his target leaped away and lunged back. They battled to the edge of the cliff, hacking, swinging, and lunging. Drift stepped back and almost slipped into nothingness. The fiend took advantage; it sank its teeth deep into Drift's sword arm.

He tried to pull his arm away but the Beast twisted and shook its head. With his free hand, he smashed the bludgeon over its head again and again. But it wouldn't let go.

"Aaaaaarrrgh!" he roared into the night sky, sure his arm had been torn off. But the agonizing pain was still there; the arm still held on. The tug of war drifted away from the edge, the Beast's teeth sinking deeper and deeper into Drift's flesh.

He planted his foot on a sunken boulder between them and pulled until the sinews in his muscles threatened to snap. He lifted the Beast painstakingly over the edge of the cliff, sure that his body would crumple with the effort.

As the Beast drifted over the edge, it yanked Drift after it.

After sliding several feet toward his doom, he swung the club underhand and connected with the Beast's neck. The Beast coughed out its hold on Drift's arm. Pulled by the momentum, Drift nearly fell into the ocean after it. He caught a dizzying glimpse of the craggy, wave-washed rocks below. He strained to gain his balance and dove back onto dry grass.

But the Beast didn't fall; it snapped its legs outward, glided out over the ocean and swerved back to the cliff. It smashed feet-first into him.

Drift lay on his back, face to face with a roaring, teeth-lined black hole. Rancid breath spurted onto his face. The Beast's full weight crushed him into the sod, and the two of them teetered close to the edge.

Drift panted. He couldn't withstand this wretched thing much longer.

He grabbed the slippery red tongue from inside its maw and yanked. With a yelp, the Beast leaped away, pulling its tongue free, and sprang back for a second attack. Drift kicked away its snapping fangs, leaped to his feet, raised his sword, and charged.

◈

Robbyn scurried through the night. Her raised lantern offered little illumination of the forbidding blackness that surrounded her.

The darkness hemmed in on her, suppressing her glimmer of light. But not her resolve.

The noises of both the battle behind and the one ahead echoed back to her. The sounds of Drift's battle filled her stomach with fear. The nearer she drew to the Beast, the more rot-filled her stomach felt, the more her instincts screamed to run away. But the continued struggle and furious barking of the Beast assured her that Drift was still alive, for now. And for that reason she had to keep going.

"Please be all right, Drift, please be all right," she whispered. Her heart pounding, she pressed forward.

ↁⱺↁ

Drenched in sweat, slobber, and blood, Drift hacked and blocked, struggling to keep his position as the Beast dove, snapped, and clawed. The fight continued along the very edge of the cliff. Drift swung again and again, like a tireless lumberjack carving his way through an old oak tree. But the swift Beast sprang away time after time. It was too fast for him.

The Beast then made its move. It flew back several feet, and launched off a tree straight for him. Drift crossed his weapons and braced himself as the enormous monster slammed into him and knocked him to the ground. Once again, the Beast's weight crushed him. The sharp claws dug into his skin and the hot, wet breath of its growling snout pressed against his face.

With a roar, Drift grabbed the Beast's front legs and rolled. He managed to free himself from its weight. But the ground beneath him disappeared and a tickling sensation blasted through his stomach as he plummeted. The Beast lost its footing, crashed its jaw into the cliff edge, and tumbled over after him.

ↁⱺↁ

"No!" Robbyn screamed. She let the lantern clatter to the ground. Its light flickered out. She ran to the edge of the cliff. A crash sounded up to her. She dropped to the ground and peered over the edge.

The moonlit outline of Drift lay on a narrow ledge, not moving. The writhing body of the Beast slammed on top of him.

A gasp of pain burst from Drift's lips, but he didn't move. Robbyn couldn't tell if he was unconscious, paralyzed or worse.

The Beast flipped onto its feet. A growl rumbled from its throat, but it was a different sort of growl, almost a purr.

No! Robbyn set her jaw, swallowed her fear, and pulled out her knife with shaking hands. Before she could think about it, she stepped over the edge. Weightlessness overcame her. She flipped over mid-flight and found herself falling straight toward the Beast's back. She held her knife forward. Her target rushed up on her faster than she had time to think. Just before impact, she closed her eyes.

What felt like a boulder slammed into her body. She lost all of the air from her lungs. But when she opened her eyes, she found herself lying on top of the Beast, the knife hilt pressed against its hide, the blade deep in its flesh.

She tried to suck in air. Had it died?

It convulsed, nearly bucking her off. With a quiet whimper the Beast fell sideways.

She scrambled off its back and dove onto the ledge beside Drift as the Beast tumbled into the ocean. A splash sounded up to them, along with a spray of icy water.

Drift sat up, a quiet groan rumbled somewhere within his chest.

"A-are you all right, Drift?" Robbyn asked, still shaking.

A single tear slid from the giant's eye, tumbled down his tough, wrinkled cheek, and disappeared into his jungle of a beard. He wrapped his massive arms around her and held her tight. He said nothing.

CHAPTER 19

THE MARAUDER KING

Micah and Samuel dashed into the city, where the torchlit battle still raged under the last traces of twilight.

"The Aegre Bird can take us to the tower." Samuel pushed the flute to his lips and floated out a song while his eyes darted all around. A rush of wind fell on them as the Aegre Bird hopped to the ground beside them.

Micah's shoulder tingled, but he ignored it.

The bird showed no sign of being entranced. By all appearances it had decided to be calm for the time being.

Micah inched away from it, anticipating a lash of fury at any moment. It opened its beak, and he jumped back a full stride, but the bird screeched softly, almost with affection.

Samuel continued his song, nodding toward it. Micah sidled up to it, his steps slowing the closer he came, until he stood beside it. He plotted the best way to mount it. Even though it didn't move, its eyes followed him.

"Oof!" The song ended on an off-key note.

He turned around in time to see the flute clatter to the ground a short distance away. Samuel lay on the ground; the blond Marauder stood over him, a gash across his red face. The flute rolled and clattered along the irregular cobblestone. All eyes fixed upon it. The Marauder and Micah made a move for it at the same time. But before Micah could take a second step, the Aegre Bird started to quiver. Micah stopped in his tracks and whipped his head around at the bird. It was tensing its muscles, preparing to take off. He froze, unsure what to do. This could be his only chance. His sheep might die if he passed this up. He looked back at Samuel, and made his decision.

Alarm washed over Samuel's features. "Micah! Don't!" But too late.

Micah dove for the bird and latched onto two handfuls of feathers just as Samuel called. His feet probed for a foothold until he found one on top of the bird's ribs.

Without a second to spare, the monster exploded into the sky, nearly tearing Micah's grip away.

"The trance isn't complete!" Samuel's voice called after him. It faded so quickly that Micah could barely hear, "complete."

He held on with everything he had. But the winds battered him as the Aegre Bird sped onward. At this speed, Micah's grip wouldn't last long. And as soon as his grip gave, he would hurtle to the ground.

To gauge his fall, he glanced at the mass of battling ants below, blurred by fog. He couldn't make out anything for certain until a shiny flash drew his attention to the Marauder fleeing for the city gate with the Caelum Flute in hand, Samuel in pursuit.

As they winged higher, the fog enveloped them, and the city below disappeared. Darkness surrounded them. Micah had nothing but the lantern hooked around his elbow to illuminate himself and the bird he rode.

He groped for a better hold with trembling hands. The feathers were like thick, greasy metal wires, and they pricked his skin, burrowing under his fingernails. The stench was nauseating. *What a terrible, terrible idea.*

The Aegre Bird ripped from its course into an erratic dance, flitting all over the sky. Micah's handholds began to slip.

But just as suddenly as it had started, the bird stopped flitting and held a steady course once more. It let out an ear-splitting screech of anguish.

Micah's heart thumped harder. *It's battling the trance!*

Was he going to make it? His stomach performed a backflip as he pictured himself plummeting hundreds of feet to the ground. If the trance broke before he reached the tower he was doomed, and so were his sheep, the kingdom, and the world. Then another thought struck him: *Are we even going in the right direction?*

The bird swiveled its massive neck. Its glowing eyes stared straight into his. Recognition pulsed from them and the Aegre Bird burst into another panic attack. This time it folded its wings and plummeted into a steep, spiraling dive. Spinning towers popped into view, lit up by torchlight, expanding rapidly. Micah felt the pull on every part of him, even his face. Just as he closed his eyes on fear of impact, the Aegre Bird pulled out and shot upward. Micah squeezed the handfuls of feathers as hard as he could, his stomach tingling with nausea. The Aegre Bird leveled off, and though Micah's arms screamed for release, he forced himself to hold tight.

A ring of torches emerged from the fog in the distance. *Just a bit farther. Hold on.* The Aegre swooped into a shallow dive, closing in. It was going to pass right over the tower, close enough to put a torch out with its wake. Micah's heart pounded. He needed to let go at just the right moment . . . *Now!*

He pried his fingers off and let himself fall away. As swiftly as he'd gone airborne, he hit the stone floor, and tumbled to a stop. Still shaking, he raised his head to view the well-lit circle. He'd survived the flight. How gratifying it felt to stand on firm ground again.

His heart skipped a beat. "My sheep!" They were bound, piled up, and dirty, but alive.

"See," an ominous voice said, "it's qualities like this that make you such a terrific shepherd." Micah swung his gaze to a black-robed man with a crown and long, gloomy features. The light seemed to repel from him, as if an aura of shadow surrounded him. "You did well, Micah."

Micah started at his name, still unused to the fact that everyone seemed to know it.

The man's lips curled into a playful smile. He paced, his jeweled hands flashing as he spoke. "Grixxler has been loyal. He trained you well."

Micah backed away.

The Marauder King edged closer. "I'm glad, because our whole plan depended on you delivering the sheep to the castle."

Micah swallowed, unsure if it was wise to speak. He kept a wary eye on his sheep. "I already know all about your plan."

The king stopped.

"I know there's a fleet of Marauder ships with explosion weapons waiting." Micah pointed out into the foggy darkness, gathering courage. "They're waiting for the signal, for you to burn my sheep alive."

At that point, four guards sprawled on the ground entered Micah's field of vision, unconscious—or worse.

The king laughed. "Clever." He spun around, arms stretched wide. "I must admit, I'm quite anxious. I can't wait to see the castle town destroyed. I can't wait to rule from this wondrous castle." The Marauder King's grin widened, exposing several golden teeth.

So they didn't plan to destroy the castle, just the town and all of the people. Of course. Why destroy such a fortress when they could rule from it?

Micah had to act now; he had to take out the king. Without giving it a second thought, he rushed forward and spread his arms wide like he'd seen Drift do to the horse. Another Marauder leaped from the shadows and dove on him. The stone floor ground hit his face first as they skidded to a stop. He struggled until the Marauder whipped out a dagger and pressed it to his throat. He lay still, helpless.

The Marauder King laughed so hard he coughed. "Your rescue

attempts are useless, shepherd boy. It's over." With that he lifted the torch nearest to him and swiftly strode to the pile of sheep.

"No! I-I'll," Micah's mind whirled. "I'll pay you! I'll . . ." He trailed off. How foolish of him. As if he had anything to offer.

The king stopped, turned toward him, and laughed again. "Fool." He shook his head, still chuckling.

The knife edge pressed harder into his throat.

The Marauder King stood before the mound of sheep as they tried to wiggle away from the torch. He straightened and breathed deeply, as if soaking in the power he now had.

Micah felt sick, unable to watch the suffering his sheep were about to experience. He flailed, trying to wriggle free from his captor. For that he received the butt of the dagger to the sore spot on his head. He closed his eyes.

"What was that?" the king demanded. Micah opened his eyes to the sight of the blade several inches away from him and the king scanning the unyielding night around them. Micah craned his neck far enough to see the Marauder on top of him searching their surroundings as well.

And then, all at once, it appeared.

The Aegre Bird swooped down from the nothingness, plucked the Marauder from Micah's back, and disappeared in a flurry of feathers.

But there, where the Aegre Bird had first appeared, stood Samuel, finishing the last notes of a fierce song, his eyes fixed coldly on the Marauder King. With a last, deep note, he pulled the flute from his lips.

"Your plan has failed," Samuel said.

Micah crept into the shadows, taking advantage of the distraction. A frame of concern flashed into the Marauder King's eyes and left just as fast. He narrowed his eyes and whipped the torch to within inches of Ariel's back.

"Don't be a fool, Kestrel," he growled, the features of his dark face flickering in the firelight. "I need only flick my wrist and the castle is gone forever. Gable would never recover. Nobody would win."

Samuel shrugged. "You've got nothing left to gain. You lose either way." Samuel looked skyward. "In fact, you're scheduled to die any second now."

The King ripped his gaze to where Samuel looked, like a mouse watching the skies for a hawk. The torch began to shake.

With a look of hatred aimed at Samuel, he steadied himself. His lips curled into an evil smile. "So be it." Roaring with laughter, he raised the torch, twirled it in his hand, and stabbed the fire into Ariel's side.

Several things happened at once.

Ariel's wool caught fire, and a blinding brightness burst from her, immersing the area in an explosion of daylight; the Aegre Bird swooped down, snatched the cackling Marauder King, and dragged him into the darkness; Samuel took a sharp step forward, stopped himself, cursed, and tore into a rapid song on his flute.

All the warmth drained from Micah's body, leaving him a cold, empty shell. The sight of flame consuming his sheep rendered him helpless, crippled. The image burnt itself into his mind and—

"Ariel!" he screamed, his voice hoarse. He collapsed forward. Paying the blinding light no heed, he fell to his knees, delved his hands into the brightness, and closed his arms around the small, burning body. Bleats of panic filled his ears. He sobbed as he ripped the bonds away, pulled her from the pile, and rolled her writhing body on the ground in desperation. The world flashed dizzyingly from night to day with each flip, but the flames only grew.

He ignored the blistering heat and held the burning body tight to his own. He gritted his teeth and clamped his eyes shut, drowning himself in the unfairness of what had happened, hating the fact that he had to do what he was about to do.

He rose up with Ariel tucked against his chest and ran with wobbling legs. Tears streamed down his face as he barreled past Samuel.

His focus fixed straight ahead—the edge of the platform, the stone half-wall.

Samuel didn't stop his song, but Micah could feel him running after him. Micah pounded forward and leaped onto the half wall.

The notes behind him rose in pitch and volume, blaring at him to stop.

Micah propelled himself off the ledge, out into open space, and hurtled toward the sea. He squeezed Ariel tight.

He would die. A rock—that's what the water would feel like when he finally hit. He might even die before he sank underwater. In fact he hoped he did, because if he didn't, the frigid water would finish him. But he dwelled on the fact that Ariel would have a chance to live if he could absorb the impact from their fall.

They fell slowly, it seemed. Memories poured through Micah's mind, as if they had all burst free and were flashing through his vision as they dispersed into the air above him. He saw every night they'd spent curled up in the cabin, or under the stars, waiting out that blizzard with her tucked close to his heart.

Realizing with a pang that this would be the last time he embraced any of his sheep, he pulled Ariel tighter to himself. He strained to peer through the brightness at his lamb and found her leaning her head against his chest with her eyes closed. The sight broke his heart. Together, they were a sinking fireball, casting a twinkling flood of light—a falling star.

The wind whipped at his smoldering, billowing cloak as they sank. A gentle tug at his heart warned him of the imminent water. He pointed his toes straight downward and pressed Ariel harder into his chest.

"Swim hard, little one," he whispered into a fragile ear.

Then they hit. The water's surface felt like ice that shattered on impact. The crash immediately sent Micah into a stupor. The sudden quelling of their velocity made him realize in some corner of his mind that they had been falling much faster than he'd felt. The shock of the bone-numbing cold overtook and replaced the shock of the collision. He stiffened as the ice-laced water collapsed over him and pulled him under. With a sputtering hiss, the flame died, and the light vanished.

He drifted downward in a state of profound numbness. Where was Ariel? Why was he still alive? The two thoughts bounced around the unimportant parts of his subconscious, but never formed a discernible thought. He drifted into the ever darker depths, his sight fading, his thought fading, his feeling fading. Molten ice poured down his throat and filled his lungs. He sank deeper and deeper until, finally, the shadows overcame him, and he slipped into nothingness.

∾

At the top of the tower, Samuel heard the smack of his son's landing and watched the glow on the edge of the half wall fade away. He dropped to his knees, then onto his side. His quivering hands managed somehow to keep going. Somehow, the notes continued to flow. But his tune drifted into a somber remorse, its drawn out notes humming out over the sea like a slow-moving fog. The hollow tune sounded like a funeral song. Still as a statue, Samuel played, too stricken to do anything but lay there and let the song go on.

For to cut it short, to play an unfinished trance on so many birds so close to the castle, would cause devastation.

Samuel could felt the storm of birds approach as though he, himself, flew among them. They would arrive almost silently—birds of all kinds, shapes, and sizes. The clouds of death would emerge from the fog and descend on the battleground of the city. When they disappeared into the night minutes later, though the grounds would be strewn with feathers, not a single Marauder would remain.

All the sounds from the city suddenly died. It had been done.

The mass of deadly birds swooped up to the tower, curving toward Samuel. He didn't flinch as they flapped past him and out over the sea, past the Navy, to where the Marauders waited, oblivious to their doom.

The silence that followed was thicker than the fog and filled only with Samuel's ringing, ghostly notes. The wind went stagnant and the waves hushed. Stillness and quiet reigned. The variation of his notes and breaths were Samuel's only evidence that time had even continued. And how could it move past this moment?

But then, ever so softly, the quiet shattered. A sound, shimmering and golden, started quietly. It grew until it rang louder than Samuel's song, echoing out over the sea . . . It was laughter.

୧ଠ୨

Isaac Ganthorn stood at the wheel of *The Wooden Swan*, unable and unwilling to close the cracked lips of his smile or hold back his laughter. His shriveled, shaking hands steered the tiny vessel through the fog, hugging the cliffs. Its hull sliced through the waves' quiet pattern. He had to lean against the wheel to keep his thin legs from collapsing, but at least the pangs of starvation had long since dulled. He remained fixated on the last wisps of smoke curling from the water's surface at the edge of his lantern light.

He nudged the anchor off the rail, felled himself overboard, and splashed into the frigid sea. Biting his tongue against the cold, he dug down into the darkness until he came upon the hazy outlines of a boy and a sheep. He grabbed one in each arm and bent his knees to kick back toward the surface, but he didn't have the strength. A burst of bubbles escaped from his mouth as he struggled against his own lack of energy and managed to pull the two bodies upward. He kicked and kicked and kicked, continually on the verge of a collapse. He couldn't stop. It would not end here.

When they broke water's surface, he gasped in air, but already the weight of the lamb and boy pushed him toward the depths. He didn't have the strength to stay afloat, let alone throw them into the ship.

The shepherd boy's eyes fluttered open for a moment, and Isaac found himself again looking into those eyes that had haunted him for so long. He'd never noticed before how blue they were. Or maybe he'd just forgotten. But enough forgetting and enough running. He would get these two onto the deck or die from the effort. He drew out all of his remaining strength and roared as he hoisted Micah's torso up onto the deck, then pushed another leg up. At the last, he plopped the sheep beside him.

His roar caught in his throat. Death inched its way across his body. He had no strength—nothing left in him. Like the last trickling grains of sand in an hourglass, the life drained out of him. His wasted body sank into the water, and the current whisked him into darkness. A grin transfixed his face. He gazed skyward through the water and past the water-skewed stars as he hit the bottom. He closed his eyes, victorious.

Epilogue

Micah woke to the crackling of a fire and the smell of burning cedar. Then the pain hit him. "Aaaaaaaaaugh!" His hands had surely burned into charcoal dust. What else could cause this much pain? An awareness of other injuries blared through his body. Everywhere.

"You're awake." Kestrel dropped a twig between Micah's teeth. "Clamp down and swallow the juices from the grain. It'll help."

Micah gnashed his teeth into the twig. He tried to unclench his fists, but they wouldn't move. In fact, he couldn't move his arms, or his legs, or his neck. So he tightened his diaphragm and winced, his vision too unfocused to make out his surroundings. A pool of bitter liquid collected in his mouth. He swallowed it.

"I survived," he tried to gasp out, but ended up producing an unintelligible sound.

A tingling wave passed through his brain, and his pain numbed to a bearable degree. He slackened his jaw, then spat the twig out.

"Works well, doesn't it?"

Blearily, Micah surveyed his still dark surroundings. Samuel sat on a stump, staring soberly into the fire. Micah's sheep lay scattered a safe distance from the flame. A thick layer of blankets bundled him, and he lay a few feet from the soothing flame. The flickering light highlighted the broad leaves of the trees and vegetation surrounding them.

"We're off the mainland," Samuel didn't avert his gaze, "on an island, not far from shore. I dropped notes with each of your friends. They should be along shortly with that boat I found you in."

"Ariel?" Micah coughed, his lungs felt tender, as though they'd been packed with cold sand and then emptied.

"She's fine." Samuel nodded in the direction of a sparsely coated lamb snuggled close to her flock, covered in bandages. "She's hurt, but she'll heal. The fire of East Plain Sunshine Sheep isn't as severe as most. If it were you'd both be dead."

It warmed Micah's heart to see her content. In fact, it was a relief to see all of his sheep free and happy once more.

"The entire Kingdom is fine. Thanks to you." Samuel glanced in Micah's direction.

Because the Marauders didn't have a target? Micah hadn't thought about that. "The fall. How did I—"

"Surviving a fall like that is rare, but not unthinkable. You broke a lot of bones, though. It took me awhile to set and splint you up. You won't be able to move for a while. And you'll need to apply balm to your skin for months to treat the burns."

"Where are the Marauders?"

"The Marauders are all dead, their weapons are safely at the bottom of the ocean, and the castle stands as strong as ever."

Micah didn't say anything. This news was both wonderful and terrible at the same time.

"You probably have a lot of questions about . . . me," Samuel said. "I'll start from the beginning—"

"Gretchen told me quite a bit."

"I see." Samuel paused. "Then I'll fill in the parts she didn't know, or at least the parts I suspect she didn't tell you." He blinked and looked up into the sky, then back again. "When the Marauders ransacked my home and I was preparing to leave . . . Gloria," his voice cracked at her name, "told me she had something to tell me but I wouldn't listen."

Micah nodded.

"That's because I already knew." He looked upward again. "I knew that she was pregnant with you, but if I'd let her say it aloud I don't think I would have had the courage to leave." He fidgeted and stared into the fire. "I'm not sure if I did the right thing, but I do know I should have destroyed the flute the day I discovered its true power." Samuel stoked the fire and added wood.

"After I left, I tracked the Marauders down and stowed away on *Lady Midnight*, hoping for the opportunity to steal back the flute and get away unnoticed.

"But they found me, and since they'd been unable to work the flute, they offered me a place among them—at knife point. I should have refused then and there and let them kill me. I could have ended it all. But my greed for the flute was strong . . . Joining them was the worst decision I ever made. My plan was to cooperate only until I could make away with it. But they were careful, and as the months wore by, I climbed the ranks until I was the Marauder Head Captain. Before I knew it, I'd become one of the cursed monsters." He spat the last sentence and looked away in disgust.

"I killed and plundered ruthlessly; I convinced myself it was all necessary, even right." He nodded his head toward the darkness surrounding the fire. "I invented those explosion barrels now at the bottom of the sea. I even hatched the plan to destroy the castle and take over Gable, the same one that went into effect this very night.

"Ultimately, though, it was my selfish desire for the flute that drove me away. It tore me apart to have to share it. So when the opportunity came, I grabbed the flute and escaped. In my flight I happened upon a hidden valley filled with truly remarkable birds, including the Aegre Bird."

Samuel put another log on the fire.

"While I was away in that valley, the Marauders took revenge upon me by killing poor, poor Gloria. I—" Samuel's lip quivered. "Somebody warned me beforehand. I . . . found her minutes after she died, and you were gone."

He leaned back and ran a hand through his hair, never looking in Micah's direction. "I was furious. I mounted the Aegre Bird and flew after the Marauders in a rage . . . killed most of them, but I couldn't catch that weasel . . . Ganthorn." Samuel's face darkened at the name.

"We'd discovered long before that sulfur, in large amounts, was enough to break the trance. So when Ganthorn fled amongst the sulfuric hot springs of the Heather Mountains, I could neither pursue him in flight nor find him on foot.

"I searched for you for weeks. And then—" Samuel bit his lip and leaned in closer to the flame, revealing his wrinkled face in greater detail. "I gave up."

Micah didn't know how to respond. *That's all right* seemed neither appropriate nor true. "I forgive you."

Samuel delved back into his narrative. "I retired to the continued study of birds in that hidden valley. Meanwhile, the whole Marauder clan hid away in the Heather Mountains, where they knew they were safe.

Micah considered asking why the Marauders had taken him into the Heather Mountains, why they hadn't just killed him with his mother. But he decided to let Samuel continue his story.

"Years passed by until I learned that you were alive and that you could be found in the village of Sampter. Immediately, I traveled there and fell right into the Marauder's trap, their whole reason for keeping you alive and transporting you to the Heather Mountains. The village was crawling with disguised Marauders, and quite a few members of the King's Guard happened to be there, as well. Since the sulfur repelled any chance of escape, I was stuck. I waited, with no way out, until I spotted you. At first I thought the Marauders must have been using you to lure me out of hiding, but I instantly recognized you, and since I had no other plan, I took a chance. To this day I don't know why the Marauders weren't following you around, waiting for me to reveal myself. I suspect either a miscommunication of some sort, or they knew I was trapped and simply covered all the exits, letting you roam free inside."

It unsettled Micah to listen as Samuel revealed his fondest memory to be so different than a simple, blissful day.

"You had sheep, and in that moment I hatched a plan for my eventual freedom. Since I'd invented the plan to conquer Gable, I knew exactly what the Marauders would do in seven years. So I broke into a carpenter's shed, hid the flute in a crook and gave it to you as a gift. Then I turned myself in to the King's Guard and spread the lie that I'd buried the flute somewhere in Gable."

So Bart was right; Westock had been exaggerating. "Who caught you? I mean, when you turned yourself in."

"I think you know him. His name is Bartholomew, and at the time he was the lowest ranking member of the King's Guard. I told him I'd let him capture me if I got to choose my cell and if he tried to keep the cell next to mine open. He thought that was reasonable and agreed."

Micah smiled. Knowing Bart, it would have been a humorous conversation.

"He was promoted considerably in reward. But he transferred to dungeon duties in order to keep his bargain with me. Whenever a prisoner filled the cell next to mine, Bart moved them."

"How did you know the Marauders wouldn't use a different plan to take over the castle?"

"I was their mastermind. I knew they wouldn't be able to come up with a different plan, or at least none that would have worked. The Gable Kingdom is well defended, much better defended than we made it appear tonight. Besides, since I was in prison, they had no reason to suspect that I would be able to spoil their plan."

"But—how did you know I would be the shepherd picked?"

Samuel smiled for the first time that Micah had ever seen, perhaps his first smile in years; it certainly didn't look natural on his face. "You should have seen how happy you were to receive your sheep. All these seven long years in prison, and not once did I consider that any other shepherd boy would be the best."

And then it was Micah's turn to experience a first; for the first time, he had some idea what his life would have been—just his father, his mother, and himself—no Caelum Flute to speak of. A nice thought.

"But I still don't understand." Micah shook his head. "Why did you need a shepherd boy to take the sheep down there? Why not have the Marauders take them from the Heather Mountains to the tower, or better yet, bag the wool and take only the sacks to the top of the tower?"

"You have to understand the nature of East Plain Sunshine Sheep. Their wool only gives off light when it's bright—the brighter the wool, the better. If they're unhappy, or if their wool is sheared, it dulls in color and in a short time it's just like any other sort of wool—inflammable, which is why your cloak probably saved you from burning to death. But anyway, separating the sheep from their shepherd would have made them very unhappy. Even the short time you were away from them today dulled there wool almost too much. Transporting them in a ship would have made them miserable. Plus, framing the shepherd for theft from the king was a convenient way of getting something as cumbersome as a flock of sheep inside the castle gate."

Micah nodded. It all made sense.

"See? I'm not as old as I look. I didn't forget anything." Samuel smiled again.

A joke. Micah smiled back. "So then, the Marauders weren't even trying to get you out of the dungeon; they were just trying to destroy the castle city."

"Well, no, actually. When the Marauders attacked I was supposed to be at the gallows waiting to be hanged. And if you hadn't arrived, I would have been."

Micah nodded. "You know, I did find that mark on my sheeps' hips fairly early on, though."

Samuel stroked his chin. "The covering would have lasted all the way to the castle if you hadn't. There, the guards would have known to look for it. But fortunately the king's mark was recently changed and nobody you ran into knew what it was."

"How did you know?"

"I'm guessing." Samuel added two more logs to the fire. "Something's been bothering me."

"What?"

Samuel sucked in breath through his teeth. "Why'd you jump off the tower with that sheep?"

"What do you mean? She was on fire."

"Yes, I know. But you should have died. I don't understand. It's just a regular sheep, right? It's not as if it's grateful for your efforts." He shrugged in Ariel's direction.

Micah smiled, thinking back to his conversation with Sandy. "That's a good question."

"It just seems strange to me, for you to throw away your life for something so . . . undeserving, trivial."

"I don't think I can come up with a reason that makes any sense." Micah tried to shrug, but his splints restricted it. "I love my sheep."

Samuel looked from Micah to his sheep and back again, clearly not content with Micah's response, but he didn't press the subject further. "Another thing I'm wondering," he turned his attention to the blazing fire, "is who pulled you into that boat."

"I think you know him."

"Who was it?"

Micah took a deep breath. "I think . . . it was Isaac Ganthorn."

Samuel nearly fell into the fire. "Ganthorn? But what—why?"

Micah thought about it for several seconds. In his mind's eye he could see Isaac's eyes staring into his, in that brief moment of consciousness. They had looked the same as they always had, still dead-looking and swollen. But something had changed. Maybe it was just the smile.

"We'll never know for sure. But if I had to guess, I'd either say he lost his mind or he's found forgiveness."

"*Found forgiveness!* What? Just like that?" Samuel's breath caught and his face reddened. "I don't think the people he *murdered* would forgive him."

"I believe Someone else took his punishment for him. Endured a tortured death for him."

"What are you talking about? The Story? You don't understand!" Samuel rose to his feet in his excitement, his face contorted with hatred. He threw a finger toward the ocean. "You haven't seen the things he's done! You don't know the lives he's ruined!"

"Gloria—" His pained voice was little more than a whisper. He spoke through clenched teeth, his voice low, and his face filled with flickering shadows. "Isaac Ganthorn doesn't deserve forgiveness any more than I do."

"Or me either. That's the thing about humans." Micah bit his lower lip. "We're undeserving."

Samuel sat back on his stump.

For several minutes, Samuel didn't take his gaze from the fire. Micah closed his eyes and listened to the waves, the owls, and the crackling fire. What a day it had been. He opened one eye, just to peek at Samuel, to make sure he really was sitting next to the fire with his father.

246

Gradually, the air around him grew hotter. He opened his eyes to a fire that looked ready to devour a tree.

"What are you doing?" Micah tried to wriggle away from the heat. The sheep stood and migrated several feet away.

His eyes fixed soberly on the blaze, Samuel reached into his pocket and eased the silvery flute out into the firelight. His fingers found their holes. "This instrument has caused enough strife." Samuel stood. "I already played my last song while you were sleeping. The Aegre Bird has been in a trance nearby since then. In a few moments, I'll ride away . . . my last flight. It's time to get rid of this." Without another word he held the flute out to the furious flame. It trembled on the tip of his gradually declining fingers and then spilled into the heart of the blaze. It fell like liquid mercury, twinkling and glinting before it disappeared from sight, consumed by the fire.

Samuel sat abruptly back down on the stump, breathing deeply. Again, neither of them spoke. The fire dwindled to an ember and Samuel added no more wood.

At last he rose to his feet. "Your friends are almost here. It's time for me to go, Micah." He whistled in a low tone.

The Aegre Bird crept with lumbering footsteps into the glowing light, bobbing its head up and down.

Samuel continued. "I'm sorry for all that I've done to you, but just having this opportunity to see you for one day is more than I deserve. And I can't change the past; there are things I have left to make amends for . . . alone." With a swift kick, he killed the fire, unearthing a glowing, misshapen orb. With his hand wrapped heavily in cloth, he lifted it off the ground.

"Goodbye . . . Father," Micah said to the silhouette. The word felt strange in his mouth; it was the first time he'd directed it at a human. Samuel turned his face away, walked over, and climbed onto the Aegre Bird's back.

The Aegre Bird crouched low and launched into the sky. Each

stroke of the wings sounded like wind filling a sail.

Micah followed them with his gaze, squinted at the hazy outline shrinking and melting into the darkness above until, at last, he lay alone in the silence.

Something cold and wet brushed the side of his neck.

"Bah-ah."

He eased his head to the side, grinning as his sheep bedded down leaning against him. Ariel laid her chin on his stomach. He tightened the muscles in his shoulder, lifted his arm slowly, ignoring the twinges that coursed through it, and laid his bandaged fist gently on her head.

Acknowledgments

I 'll be honest. I had no idea what I was getting myself into. In fourth grade, the year that marked my first attempt to write and publish a novel, my plan was to complete it in a few months, ship it off to a publisher, and then sign the mult-million dollar contract before middle school. (I decided I would sign for a few less million than the publisher would offer, because I'm nice like that.) Bestseller lists were sure to follow. Simple. Straightforward. Nothing like how it really works.

I could write for pages about the hard truths missing from my delusion, such as the gazillions of other people competing for my dream, the gazillions more rejection letters flowing from editors and agents nationwide, and the shear difficulty of writing a novel worth reading.

These hard truths I discovered along the way as I typed out quarter-novels and half-novels that petered out before the heroes reached their goal. In many ways my naivety persisted past my fifteenth birthday, when I embarked on *Kestrel's Midnight Song*, then titled *The Shepherd*. Not until I had entered the fray of the publishing world did I come to appreciate the biggest hole in my vision—the work of everyone who doesn't get their name on the cover.

So thank you God, first and foremost, for allowing me to reach this point. I am blessed. What more can I say?

Thank you, Scott Appleton, for publishing my story, and then developing it to much more than it was when you wrote "I am most intrigued by your work" in a blog post comment sixteen months ago.

Thank you, Jill Williamson. Where would I be without you, Jill? Hopelessly lost, that's where. You are a very special person (and superb author). I could never fully pay you back for all that you've done for me, but I can attempt to pay it forward.

Thank you to every teacher who had a hand in teaching me how to write. I guess that came in handy, huh? But thanks also for your encouragement, such as when you, Mrs. Stolley, enjoyed my story assignment so much that you sought me out at lunch to tell me that if I wrote a book, you would buy it. At that point, the piling up of my failures had pushed me to the verge of giving up. Your comment was a spark. You're holding the flame.

Thank you to my family and friends for all your encouragement and support, and for understanding when I kept the fact that I was writing a book a secret for so long. I thought spreading the word that I was "writing a novel" would be sufficiently head-bloating that I would lose my desire to finish. Little did I know that your frequent inquiries of "How's the book coming?" would have been enough to spur me onward.

To three fellow teens I say thank you as well. Jon Maiocco for the brilliant score on the book trailer, Leighton Hajicek for the equally brilliant CGI, and Christian Miles for the hours of chatting about the best way to fix the problems in the story. If this is the first time you've heard of these three talented fellows, it won't be the last.

Thank you to my critique group and all the pre-readers and editors of *Kestrel's Midnight Song*, for slogging through the book in its unrefined stages, and for your comments and criticisms. Especially your criticisms.

Last but not least, thank you dear Reader, for picking up the result of all of these peoples' work. I hope you enjoyed it.

And now, in many ways, my journey has just begun. I'm told that publishing a book is the easy part. Now I move on to marketing and promotion and book tours. But this time I am armed with the knowledge that if I am to emerge successful, it certainly won't be alone.

LaVergne, TN USA
16 November 2010

205083LV00001B/2/P